MURDER
IN THE MUSEUM

MURDER IN THE MUSEUM

A FETHERING MYSTERY

SIMON BRETT

THORNDIKE
WINDSOR
PARAGON

This Large Print book is published by Thorndike Press®, Waterville, Maine USA and by BBC Audiobooks, Ltd, Bath, England.

Published in 2003 in the U.S. by arrangement with The Berkley Publishing Group, a member of Penguin Group (USA), Inc.

Published in 2003 in the U.K. by arrangement with Pan Macmillan Ltd.

U.S. Hardcover 0-7862-5865-9   (Core)
U.K. Hardcover 0-7540-8691-7   (Windsor Large Print)
U.K. Softcover 0-7540-9358-1   (Paragon Large Print)

The text of this Large Print edition is unabridged.
Other aspects of the book may vary from the original edition.

Set in 16 pt. Plantin.

Printed in the United States on permanent paper.

British Library Cataloguing-in-Publication Data available

**Library of Congress Control Number: 2003108551
ISBN 0-7862-5865-9 (lg. print: hc : alk. paper)**

To
Norman and Hilary

1

Carole Seddon was good at meetings, but only when she was running them. She got restless under the chairmanship of others, particularly those she didn't think were very impressive chairmen.

And Lord Beniston fitted firmly into that category. Carole's years in the Home Office had been, amongst many other things, a consumer guide in the conduct of meetings. While honing her own style of calm efficiency, she had endured the chairmanship of the overanxious, the underprepared, the nit-picking, the lethargic, and the frankly incompetent. But Lord Beniston brought a new shortcoming to the role — a world-weary patrician arrogance which suggested that the afternoon's agenda was a tiresome interruption to his life and that the trustees of Bracketts were extremely privileged to have him present amongst them. They might represent the Great and the Good of West Sussex, but he represented the Great and the Good on a national scale. Their names might look quite good on a charity's letterhead, but Lord Beniston was confident that his name looked a lot better (even though the reforms of New Labour no longer allowed him a seat in the House of Lords).

He was in his sixties, with steel-grey hair whose parallel furrows always looked as if it had just been combed. He had a claret-coloured face, and yellowish teeth that looked permanently clenched, though his manner was too arrogant to be tense. Presumably there were times when he didn't wear a pin-striped suit and a blue and red regimental tie, but none of the Bracketts trustees had ever seen him out of that uniform.

The Bracketts Trust met six times a year, and this was Carole's second appearance. She had accepted the offer of a trusteeship with some misgivings, and the first meeting had strengthened these to the extent that now, only halfway through her second, she was already assessing graceful ways of shedding the responsibility she had taken on.

She didn't get the feeling she'd be much missed. The offer to join the Bracketts board had come from Bracketts' new director, Gina Locke, and seemed to have been issued in the mistaken belief that

8

Carole's background as a civil servant might provide some shortcuts through the tangles of government bureaucracy, and also that she might have wealthy contacts who would prove useful in the eternal business of fund-raising. When, at the first meeting, it had become clear that their new recruit was unlikely to fill either of these needs, the other trustees seemed to lose interest in her.

And Carole Seddon's own interest in the affairs of Bracketts was finite. The house was a literary shrine, and she couldn't really claim to be a literary person. Her reasons for accepting the trusteeship had been surprise at being asked, a sense of being flattered, and a feeling that she ought to make more of an effort to fill her years of retirement. Well-pensioned, comfortably housed in High Tor, a desirably neat property in the West Sussex seaside village of Fethering, Carole Seddon did have time on her hands. A thin woman in her early fifties, with short grey hair and glasses shielding pale blue eyes, she reckoned her brain was as good as it ever had been, and deserved more exercise than the mental aerobics of the *Times* crossword. But she wasn't convinced that listening to the bored pontifications of Lord Beniston was

9

the kind of workout it needed.

The setting was nice, though; hard to fault that. The trustees' meetings always took place in the panelled dining room of Bracketts, and were held on Thursdays at five, after the house and gardens had ceased to admit visitors. This was the last meeting of the season; at the end of the next week, coinciding with the end of October, the site would be closed to the public until the following Easter.

Bracketts, set a little outside the Downland village of South Stapley, was one of those houses which had grown organically. The oldest part was Elizabethan, and additions had been made in Georgian and Victorian times.

Through the diamond-paned leaded windows, Carole Seddon could see over the house's rolling lawns to the gleam of the fast-flowing River Fether, which flowed into the sea some fifteen miles away at Fethering. It was late autumn, when the fragile heat of the day gave way at evening to the cold breath of approaching winter, but perhaps one of the best times of year to appreciate the beauty and seclusion of the estate. Bracketts was an idyllic place to be the home of a writer.

The writer to whom the shrine was dedi-

10

cated was Esmond Chadleigh. His father, Felix, had bought Bracketts during the First World War, getting the property cheap, in a state of considerable dilapidation, and spending a great deal on loving restoration of the house and gardens. When Felix Chadleigh died in 1937, Bracketts was left to his son and, funded by family inheritance and his own writing income, Esmond Chadleigh had lived there in considerable style until his death in 1967.

Esmond Chadleigh was one of those Catholic figures, like Chesterton and Belloc, who, in that unreal, unrealistic world of England between the wars, had made his mark in almost every department of the world of letters. Adult novelist, children's storyteller, light versifier, essayist, critic — it seemed there was no form of writing to which Esmond Chadleigh could not turn his hand. But when the derisory adjective "glib" was about to be applied to him, critics were brought up short by a series of deeply felt poems of suffering, published in 1935 under the title *Vases of Dead Flowers*. Of these, the most famous, a staple of anthologies, school assemblies, memorial services, and Radio Four's *With Great Pleasure*

11

selections, was the poem "Threnody for the Lost."

Written, according to Esmond Chadleigh's Introduction, nearly twenty years before its first publication, this was a lament for his older brother Graham, who at eighteen had set off for the battlefields of Flanders and never returned, even in a coffin. In the room where the trustees were meeting was a glass-topped display case, dedicated to the memory of Graham Chadleigh.

The space was divided down the middle. On one side there were photographs of Graham as a boy, in a house before Bracketts, with his younger brother beside him; both carried tennis rackets. Then Graham appeared as a member of a cricket team in a gravely posed school photograph, dated 1915. Beside this was the faded tasselled cap of his cricket colours. There was a letter he had written from school to his parents, politely requesting them to send him more tuck.

On the other side of the division was the pitifully small collection of memorabilia from Graham Chadleigh's wartime life. There was a letter written to him in the trenches by his father. There were a cap badge and a service revolver. That was all

12

that had been recovered.

It was the totality of his absence that could still shock visitors to Bracketts at the beginning of the twenty-first century. Like many others in the muddy holocaust of Passchendaele, Graham Chadleigh had just vanished off the face of the earth, literally blown to smithereens. That was why his brother's famous poem carried such emotional impact. "Threnody for the Lost" was a powerful evocation of bereavement, particularly the pain of the mourner left with nothing tangible to mourn.

No grave, no lichened tombstone,
*   graven plaque,*
No yew-treed cross beneath its cloak
*   of moss,*
No sense but absence, unforgiving dark,
The stretching void that is eternal loss.

No one of Carole Seddon's generation could have got through school without having learned those lines, and the revival of interest in the Great War towards the end of the twentieth century had ensured that the name of Esmond Chadleigh was not forgotten.

But, as was being made clear at the Board of Trustees meeting that autumn after-

13

noon, though his name was familiar, it was not familiar enough. The teetering finances of Bracketts required the profile of Esmond Chadleigh to be a lot higher than it currently was. Without a substantial injection of cash, closure of the estate as a heritage site was a very real possibility.

Gina Locke spelled out the reality in typically uncompromising style. "Unless something happens, Bracketts might be closing at the end of October for the last time."

Gina was mid-to-late thirties, slight and dark, with undeniable charisma. Carole had met her at a dinner party in the nearby town of Fedborough, and been immediately taken by the enthusiasm with which she talked about her new job as director of Bracketts. It was that enthusiasm which had carried Carole into her current position as a trustee, and which made her feel guilty for her recent thoughts of escaping the role. (But then a suspicion that was hardening into a reality made her feel less guilty. She was increasingly certain that she'd been taken on board — and indeed onto the board at Bracketts — to provide more support for Gina Locke's personal agenda. If the director thought she was going to get subservience from Carole Seddon, she couldn't have been more wrong.)

14

"Aren't you being a little bit alarmist there?" The languid voice that challenged Gina Locke's pessimism belonged to Graham Chadleigh-Bewes, one of the two trustees who were blood relatives of Esmond Chadleigh. He was the great man's grandson. Chubby, in his fifties, with a round body that threatened to spill out of the chair in which it sat, Graham Chadleigh-Bewes had one of those faces whose babyishness is only accentuated by the advance of wrinkles and the retreat of hair. His permanent expression was one of mild pique, as though someone else had just appropriated a treat he had been promising himself. Apparently he had had some minor literary career of his own, but most of his energies were now focused on perpetuating the image of his grandfather.

The other trustee from the Chadleigh family was Belinda Chadleigh, the younger of Esmond's daughters. (Her sister Sonia, Graham's mother, had died of a brain tumour in 1976.) Though not yet seventy, Belinda behaved as though she were a lot older. She never failed to attend the trustees' meetings, but always failed to make much of an impression once she was there. She was a few lines behind the general discussion, and on the rare occasions she

15

spoke, it was usually to clarify something she had misunderstood. Once she had had the point spelled out to her, the unchanging vagueness in her bleached blue eyes suggested that the explanation had left her none the wiser.

"I don't think I'm being alarmist," Gina Locke replied coolly to Graham Chadleigh-Bewes's interruption. "I think I'm being realistic."

Lord Beniston cleared his throat testily, unwilling to have even that amount of conversation not conducted through the chair. "It would be useful, Gina, if you could give the trustees a quick overview of the current state of Bracketts' finances."

"Exactly what I was about to do."

This reply, though not overtly rude, still didn't contain the amount of deference Lord Beniston would have liked. He harrumphed again and said, "Let's hear the worst, then."

"Right." Gina Locke picked up a sheaf of papers in front of her. "You've all been circulated copies of the last six months' accounts, which I think are self-explanatory. If there are any details you'd like to pick up on, I'm more than happy to give you fuller information." She allowed a short pause, but no one filled it with any enquiry.

16

"Basically, as you'll see, there is a worrying shortfall between income and expenditure."

"Couldn't a lot of that be put down to the foot-and-mouth epidemic? Keeping the visitors away?" The new voice was marinated in Cheltenham Ladies College and money. It belonged to Josie Freeman, whose husband, John, had started a very successful car-parts franchising operation in the late 1980s. His shrewdly calculated marriage had been the first step in a gentrification process that had recently been crowned by an O.B.E. "for services to industry." Josie brought to their partnership the class her husband lacked, and by way of gratitude he passed on to her the responsibility of channelling a part of his considerable income into the kind of good causes suitable to the status towards which he aspired.

Her acceptance of a trusteeship at Bracketts was a part of that process. Josie Freeman had access to a group of equally well-groomed and well-blonded wives of the wealthy, just the kind of essential fundraising contacts that Carole Seddon lacked. Because of her status, Josie was constantly approached by the outstretched begging bowls of heritage sites, theatres, hospitals, hospices, animal charities, and a

17

thousand and one other worthy causes. The skill with which she selected those to whom the Freeman endorsement should be granted or withheld, and her masterly control of her calendar of charitable events, would have qualified her for a diplomatic posting in the most volatile of the world's trouble spots.

"Foot-and-mouth had an effect," Gina Locke replied crisply, "as it did all over the heritage industry, but it only exacerbated problems that were already established here at Bracketts. A place like this can never be kept going by the money from visitor ticket sales alone."

"It used to be," said Graham Chadleigh-Bewes with some petulance. "When it was just run as a family concern. Before *management experts* were brought in."

Gina ignored the implied criticism in his emphasis. She was too shrewd an operator to get diverted into minor squabbles. "Bracketts was a much smaller operation then. And staffed almost entirely by volunteers. Now that it's a real business with professional staff, obviously the outgoings are much greater."

"But what about the *atmosphere* of the place?" asked Esmond Chadleigh's grandson, in the mumble of a resentful schoolboy wanting to be heard by his friends but not the teacher.

Again Gina didn't let it get to her. The trustees' meetings every couple of months were just part of the director's job — a boring part, perhaps, but something she had to get through. If she was polite, kept her temper, and made sure that the trustees could never complain that they didn't have enough information, then she could soon get back to running Bracketts the way she wanted.

"So," demanded Lord Beniston with the aristocratic conviction that there must be an answer to everything, "where are we going to get the money from? I've forgotten, what's the state of play with the lottery?"

"Come to the end of the road there, I'm afraid. After all that work we put into the application, the answer came back last month, and it was no."

"What was a no?" asked Belinda Chadleigh, picking up on the word and making a random entrance into the discussion.

"The lottery."

"Ah, I've never won anything on that either," she said, and retired back into her shell.

From long experience, the trustees all ignored the old lady's interpolations. "Any reasons given for the refusal?" asked Lord Beniston.

"They didn't reckon the Bracketts project offered enough 'ethnic diversity and community access.' "

"Of course not," Graham Chadleigh-Bewes agreed bitterly. "And no doubt all their literature budget has been paid out to one-legged, black lesbian storytellers."

Gibes of that sort about British arts funding's predilection for minority groups were so hackneyed that his words, like his aunt's, prompted no reaction at all amongst the trustees.

"Any other grant applications out at the moment?"

Gina shrugged. "Trying a few private trusts, as ever, but I wouldn't give a lot for our chances. That kind of money may be available for big projects — new building and so on — not for the kind of continuing financial support we need here at Bracketts."

This prompted a response from a short man whose curly hair and pepper-and-salt beard were a reminder of those Victorian pictures that still look like a face whichever way up they're held. "Surely our plans for the Esmond Chadleigh Museum qualify as

20

a big project — and as a new building, come to that?"

Carole had been introduced to him at the previous meeting. George Ferris, former assistant county librarian. In his retirement, he had become involved in a variety of literature-related projects, including writing a book with the catchy title *How to Get the Best from the Facilities of the County Records Office*, of which he was inordinately proud. George Ferris had been asked to become a trustee of Bracketts on the assumption that he would bring some literary know-how to the group. On the evidence Carole had seen so far, all he had brought was a nit-picking literalness.

This mention of the Esmond Chadleigh Museum wrought a change in the Board of Trustees. There was a soft rumble of recognition and anticipation. Members shifted in their chairs or straightened agendas. The proposed museum was a thorny issue, and one that the meeting could not avoid discussing. Though architectural plans had been drawn up and work started on clearing the old kitchen garden where the structure was to be built, the project did not yet have the full support of all the trustees.

The museum polarised the differences between two schools of thought on the

21

committee, because it was intended to broaden the appeal of Bracketts beyond Esmond Chadleigh himself. The collection would incorporate exhibitions about other Catholic writers of his period, and there would also be a strong South Stapley local history element. The museum would also have a visitors' centre, incorporating an academic library, a coffee shop, a relocated gift shop, and a performance space for literary events.

Those in favour of the scheme were certain that this development would increase the appeal of Bracketts to tourists and scholars alike. Those who opposed it — led with ineffectual vehemence by Graham Chadleigh-Bewes — saw the very idea as a betrayal of all that Esmond Chadleigh had stood for. The appeal of Bracketts should be its focus on *his* life, not that of his contemporaries. (His grandson's hypersensitivity on the subject was perhaps inherited. During his lifetime, Esmond Chadleigh had always had a chip on his shoulder about what he perceived as neglect by the literary establishment, and the greater interest universally shown in his more illustrious peers. For Esmond Chadleigh, in common with most writers, paranoia was never far below the surface.)

Gina Locke had been prepared for the subject of the museum to be raised, though a slight tug of annoyance at the corner of her mouth suggested she'd wanted to be the one who raised it. But she quickly recovered and began her preemptive strike on the matter.

"Thank you, George. Yes, we had indeed hoped that the Esmond Chadleigh Museum would attract a substantial grant — indeed, that was the basis of our lottery application — but I'm afraid we didn't get it, so we're still looking elsewhere for funding. This is the kind of project for which we need a very big sponsorship. But it's important that we separate the funding needs of the museum from the financial requirements for the day-to-day running of Bracketts. I think we —"

Gina Locke was stopped in her tracks by the clattering opening of the dining room door. An impressive woman of about sixty stood in the doorway. She was nearly six feet tall, with dark blue eyes and well-cut white hair; she wore a black trouser suit. Her wedding finger was clustered with rings. Under one arm she carried a sheaf of cardboard folders; under the other, a black leather briefcase.

"Sorry I'm late, everyone," she announced in a breezy, cultured accent.

"Ah, Sheila," said Lord Beniston, half-rising from his seat in welcome. All the other trustees seemed to know her, too.

But the person on whom the new arrival had the greatest effect was Gina Locke. All colour drained from her face, and through the tight line of her mouth, she hissed, "You have no right to be here. You're no longer a trustee!"

2

Lord Beniston, however, was not going to worry about details of protocol, so far as the new arrival was concerned. "Oh, for heaven's sake, Gina. We don't have to bother about that. Of course you're welcome to the meeting, Sheila. Shuffle up and make room for another chair there. Now do you know everyone?"

As she stepped forward to take her place at the table, the tall woman had an undoubted air of triumph about her. And from the way the director of Bracketts continued to react, Gina Locke was the one being triumphed over.

The newcomer looked around the table, dispensing greetings and little smiles to the trustees. But she stopped when she reached Carole. "We haven't met."

"No, of course not." Lord Beniston gestured bonhomously. "Carole Seddon. This is Sheila Cartwright. Carole's only just joined us as a trustee."

"Oh?" asked the tall woman, requiring more information.

25

"Ex-Home Office. Isn't that right?"

Carole nodded confirmation of Lord Beniston's words, and the tall woman seemed satisfied, accepting the credentials. There was an aura of power about Sheila Cartwright, and the reaction of those present — except for burning resentment from Gina Locke — seemed to be one of deference, though not perhaps affection.

Lord Beniston provided the explanation. "I'm sure you know all about Sheila." Before Carole had time to say she did know a certain amount, he went on, "Without Sheila, this place would just be a private house, and very few people would know that it had any connection with Esmond Chadleigh. Without Sheila, Bracketts in its current form wouldn't exist."

Everything fell into place for Carole. When the issue of her trusteeship first came up, Gina had mentioned a "Sheila" at Bracketts, and her tone of voice had suggested a degree of tension in their relationship. That tension was vividly illustrated now the two women were in the same room. Carole turned to Sheila Cartwright. "So you're the one who actually set up the initial campaign to turn Bracketts into a heritage site? You did all that fundraising in the Seventies?"

26

"Yes." The reply had the complacency of achievement. "Yes, I'm the one."

More details came back to Carole's memory. What Sheila Cartwright, a housewife with no previous business or organisational experience, achieved had become the stuff of legend. Her vision fixed solely on turning Bracketts into a shrine for Esmond Chadleigh, Sheila Cartwright had charmed, cajoled, bullied, and battled to raise the money to buy the estate. She had then enthused hundreds of volunteers to help its transformation into a visitor attraction, and presided over the grand opening on 17 April 1982, fifteen years to the day after Esmond Chadleigh's death. When Lord Beniston had said that without Sheila Cartwright, Bracketts in its current form would not exist, he had spoken no less than the truth.

Her arrival that afternoon changed the mood of the trustees' meeting. All the members — except, of course, Gina Locke — seemed visibly to relax in Sheila Cartwright's presence. With her there, the director's gloomy prognostications became somehow less threatening. Sheila Cartwright had already overcome so many obstacles at Bracketts, she would surely have ways of dealing with the latest challenge.

She knew everyone with any power in West Sussex; she could fix it. The older trustees thought the place had been run better under her amateur administration, and had never really supported the appointment of a full-time professional director.

Lord Beniston beamed as he brought her up to date. "Gina's been spelling out our rather tight current financial outlook . . ." — a private chuckle defused the seriousness of this — ". . . and we were just going through potential sources of funding to rectify the situation. We've already discussed the lottery. . . ."

"Which I'm sure proved as unhelpful as ever."

A more general chuckle greeted this. Sheila Cartwright had so much experience in the affairs of Bracketts. Whatever new solution was suggested for the organisation's predicament, she had been there and tried it. Carole Seddon began to see just how inhibiting Sheila's presence at the meeting must be to Gina Locke. Every suggestion the director made would now be referred for the blessing of Bracketts's originator and moving spirit.

Lord Beniston continued in his condescending chairman's role. "We had actually just got on to the subject of the museum," he said, knowing the word would prompt a response.

All Sheila Cartwright actually said was "Ah," but the monosyllable was a huge archive of previous discussions and arguments about the subject.

"Still, before we move on to that — the museum is actually listed on the agenda as item seven — I thought we should have a little more detail on potential sources of funding." He flashed a professional smile at Gina. "If that's all right with you . . . ?"

It was a question that could have only one answer, and the director dutifully supplied an "Of course" before reordering her papers and beginning. "Well, not a lot has changed on that front since our last meeting. As you know, we have always received a certain amount of legacy income, but as the generation to whom Esmond Chadleigh was important dies off. . . ."

"I don't think you can say that," protested Graham Chadleigh-Bewes. "There is a universality about Esmond's work. Children still respond with enormous pleasure to *Naughty Nursie's Nursery Rhymes*."

"That's good," said Belinda Chadleigh, recognising the title through the miasma of other words.

"I'm sure they do." Gina Locke, like everyone else, ignored the old lady and spoke calmly, repeating a response that she had often had to make before. "But the fact remains that *Naughty Nursie's Nursery Rhymes* are out of print."

"Though I am in discussion with a publisher who's considering reprinting them."

"I know that, Graham. However, since those discussions have already gone on for over a year, and since very few children at the beginning of the twenty-first century actually have 'Nursies,' naughty or otherwise, I would think it unlikely that. . . ."

"You don't know anything about publishing!"

"I admit I'm not an expert, but I do know enough about. . . ."

"What's more, you don't know anything about literature!"

"Listen, Graham. . . ."

Ever diplomatic, Lord Beniston intervened. "Now, please, can we take things in order? There'll be time for everyone to raise any points they wish to. Gina, you were talking about legacy income. . . ."

"Yes." Managing quickly to cover her anger, the director went on. "Basically there's less of it. Esmond Chadleigh's contemporaries have mostly died off, and I don't think we can expect much more from that source. We've only had one legacy of two thousand pounds in the last six months."

"So what else might we hope for?"

"The royalty income from the estate is also going down." Gina gave Sheila Cartwright a gracious nod, which clearly cost her quite a lot. "Of course, we enormously appreciate the work Sheila did in getting the agreement of Esmond Chadleigh's heirs to pay twenty-five percent to Bracketts . . . but *Naughty Nursie's Nursery Rhymes*. . . ."

"That's good," murmured Belinda Chadleigh.

". . . isn't the only book that's out of print. . . ."

"I'm in discussion with publishers about a lot of the others, too," said Graham Chadleigh-Bewes petulantly.

Gina Locke gave no reaction to this, as she went on, "So I can't see the royalty income going up much in the future . . . unless there's a sudden revival of interest in Esmond Chadleigh's works."

"Presumably that will be stimulated in 2004 . . . centenary of Esmond's birth . . . and of course when the biography comes out." As he spoke, Lord Beniston looked across to the writer's grandson.

Graham Chadleigh-Bewes squirmed. "Still

31

a bit behind on that," he confessed. "You know, new material keeps being unearthed . . . and then I'm kept very busy by my discussions with publishers about getting Esmond's books back into print and. . . ." The words trickled away into nothing, rather as, Carole Seddon began to suspect, the much-discussed biography might.

"What about the opposition?" asked George Ferris slyly.

"What opposition?" Lord Beniston sounded testy. He clearly disliked the ex-librarian, though whether this reflected the natural antipathy of the aristocrat to the pen-pusher or had some deeper cause, Carole did not know.

"A letter was read at the last meeting. From an American academic. Don't you remember?"

The chairman resented the implication. "Of course I remember, George."

"Her name was Professor Marla Teischbaum. She wrote asking for the co-operation of the Bracketts trustees with a biography of Esmond Chadleigh that she was proposing to write."

"And we very rightly refused such cooperation!" Graham Chadleigh-Bewes snapped. "We don't want any unauthorised biographies of Esmond. We only want the authorised biography!"

"I agree," said George Ferris drily, "but how long are we going to have to wait for it?"

"I'm working as hard as I can!"

"Just a minute," Josie Freeman interrupted. "Was this Professor Marla Teischbaum from the same American university that wanted to buy the Esmond Chadleigh papers?"

Gina Locke had the facts at her fingertips. "No, that was the University of Texas. Marla Teischbaum's at Berkeley."

"Wasn't there a *Bishop* Berkeley . . . ?" asked Belinda Chadleigh, insubstantial and, as ever, ignored.

"Well, I still think we dismissed that American interest in the papers far too casually." Josie Freeman gave a cool look at her perfectly manicured nails. "The money they were offering would have guaranteed the financial future of Bracketts for the next five years."

"But," Graham Chadleigh-Bewes spluttered, "it would also have removed the reason for Bracketts's existence! Bracketts without the Esmond Chadleigh papers in its library is just another country house."

For once, Gina Locke found herself in full agreement with him. "And if we sold the papers, we'd remove the main exhibit that's going to be put in the Esmond Chadleigh Museum."

"Surely, though . . . ?"

But that was as far as Josie Freeman was allowed to get. With proper deference to her status and money, Lord Beniston silenced her and tried to get the meeting back on track.

"Fellow trustees, we are rather going over old ground here. We discussed the letter from Professor Marla. . . ."

"Teischbaum," Gina supplied.

"Thank you . . . at the last meeting. We put the matter to the vote, and the idea was rejected. So, with respect, Josie, I don't think there was anything casual about our discussion."

"She won't go away, though," said George Ferris with gloomy certainty. There was also a smugness in his manner; he had special knowledge that he intended to share with the other trustees at his own chosen pace.

"What are you talking about?"

"Professor Teischbaum. I've heard through colleagues — former colleagues — at West Sussex Libraries, and in the County Records Office . . . on which, incidentally, I am something of an expert. I have even published a modest tome on the subject.

34

It's called *How to Get the Best from the Facilities of the County Records Office*, in case I haven't mentioned it before." (He had mentioned it before, at every opportunity.) "Marla Teischbaum's been making a lot of enquiries. You see, she's going ahead with her biography, with or without the cooperation of the Bracketts trustees."

"Well, good luck to her. She won't get far," said Graham Chadleigh-Bewes with childish satisfaction. "The best authorities on Esmond are sitting here in this room as we speak. And so long as none of us agree to speak to this dreadful woman, then we'll be fine."

"How do you know she's a dreadful woman?" asked Carole, intrigued.

"With a name like that, she's got to be, hasn't she?" There was a playground snigger in his voice. "So . . . absolute solidarity, all right? None of us must talk to her."

"I'm not so sure about that, Graham." There was an evil twinkle in George Ferris's gnomelike eye. "A bit of competition might be healthy. Might put a rocket up you to get *your* bloody biography finished."

"Now that's not fair. As a literary executor, I'm kept incredibly busy, talking to publishers about new editions of Esmond's work, getting together a selection of the

35

letters, going round doing readings at schools, lobbying literary editors to. . . ."

"Gentlemen, gentlemen!" Once again Lord Beniston felt the meeting was getting too far out of his control. "Could we get back to the agenda, please? We've agreed we are not going to cooperate with Professor Marla Teischbaum's proposed biography. If we have any trouble from her, we will deal with it as the need arises."

"Which may be sooner rather than later," murmured George Ferris.

"What do you mean by that?"

"I happen to know" — the former librarian slowed his words to give his revelation full impact — "that she will soon be in Sussex — if she isn't here already — to continue her researches."

"That's not a problem. So long as none of us trustees tell her anything."

"But we can't stop her coming round Bracketts as a member of the general public, can we?"

"No, of course we can't, but she's hardly going to be able to write a definitive biography on the basis of one guided tour, is she? I really think you're making rather too big a thing of this."

George Ferris looked suitably deflated — and not a little peeved — as the chairman moved the agenda on. Gina Locke, without much optimism, enumerated various possible sources of funding, and Sheila Cartwright compounded the gloom by saying that all the director's suggestions had been tried in the past, without success. Sheila hinted at the existence of potential sponsors, to whom she had exclusive access, who might save the day. But she couldn't provide details at that time. Everything, she said, building mystery around herself, was at a delicate stage of negotiation.

Carole got the feeling Gina was only going through the motions, providing the data Lord Beniston had asked from her, but awaiting the right moment to put forward her real agenda.

The moment came after Josie Freeman had asked Graham Chadleigh-Bewes about "any developments on the film front." At a meeting some two years previously he had announced to the trustees with enormous excitement that a production company had been enquiring about the rights to *The Demesnes of Eregonne*, a children's fantasy novel by Esmond Chadleigh which had had a considerable vogue in the 1930s. The delusion had spread of a blockbusting movie, generating huge book sales, and of the elevation of Esmond Chadleigh to Tolkien-like status. The huge publicity buildup surrounding the film of *The Lord of the Rings* fed this fever. If ever the time was right for a movie version of *The Demesnes of Eregonne*, it was now.

But after the initial spurt of enthusiasm, the project seemed to be going the way of all films. At first the production company was going to commission a draft screenplay; then it was going to take the idea to Hollywood ("where it's just the kind of thing they'd love"); then the name of an A-List international star was attached to the project; then there was talk of Anglo-Australian funding; then an actor about to leave a popular British soap was said to be "looking for a vehicle" and *The Demesnes of Eregonne* "could be the one"; then there was a suggestion of repackaging the idea and pitching the book as the basis for a six-part children's television series. Then everything went quiet.

When Graham Chadleigh-Bewes had last spoken to the production company (which, incidentally, had never come up with any evidence of actually having produced anything), he had been told that "while the enthusiasm for *The Demesnes of Eregonne* within the company remained as strong as ever . . . it wasn't really a good time." The trouble was, they said, the hype and success surrounding *The Lord of the Rings* had really ruined the chances of any other project in the same genre.

It was when Graham came to the end of this predictably depressing saga that Gina Locke moved up a gear and started to put forward what she really believed in. "All of which leads me to the conclusion, Mr. Chairman . . ." (she wasn't going to risk stumbling on meeting protocol now that she was talking about something important) ". . . that Bracketts can no longer go on with its current amateurish attitude to money, crossing our fingers and living on hope. If this organisation is going to have any future at all, it is time we employed the services of a professional fund-raiser."

"That's ridiculous!" snapped Sheila Cartwright, too incensed even to be aware that meeting protocol existed. "That's just creating another job for some Media Studies graduate with no knowledge of the real world!"

Even if she hadn't herself been a Media Studies graduate, Gina Locke would have bridled at that. "No, it is not! It is living in the real world. Bracketts may have been founded on volunteers and goodwill. . . ."

"And what's wrong with volunteers and goodwill?"

"There is nothing wrong with. . . ."

"When I think of the work I put in to build up the network, then opening it out to gap-year students, helpers with learning difficulties, day-release prisoners from Austen Prison, not to mention. . . ."

"No one is diminishing your achievements, Sheila, but the heritage industry is now a highly sophisticated, professional business."

"Are you suggesting my methods weren't sophisticated?" blazed Sheila Cartwright. "Are you calling me an amateur?"

"I am saying," said Gina with great restraint, "that what you did worked wonderfully at the time. But that time was twenty years ago and, in the leisure industry particularly, times have changed."

"Leisure industry!" Sheila Cartwright had considerable supplies of contempt, and she loaded them all onto the two words. "Bracketts is not part of the *leisure industry.* Bracketts is a vision, the vision of Esmond Chadleigh, shared by me and by other lovers of his work. Heaven forbid that this beautiful place should ever be turned into a kind of literary Disney World."

Her adversary knew the power of cheap

rhetoric, but Gina Locke managed to sound calm as she pressed her point. "I agree, Sheila, and there is no danger of that happening. All I am saying is that Bracketts can't continue to lurch from crisis to crisis. There are many more demands on potential sponsors and benefactors than there were twenty years ago, and in that time the business of fund-raising has become a deeply specialised one. Most other heritage organisations of this size employ professional fund-raisers, and I think such a post should be an accepted part of the management structure at. . . ."

"*Management structure!*" Sheila Cartwright dug even deeper into her reserves of contempt to smother these two words. "That I'd ever hear an expression like that used in Bracketts! In the house of the man who wrote these words:

Oh, spare me the fate of the
    pen-pushing man
In the comfortless gloom of his office,
Where there's never a blot and it's all
    spick-and-span.
And he never spills mid-morning coffees.

But grant me instead my own mess of a desk
With my books and my letters and clutter,

41

Where the tea has been spilt and the
    filing's grotesque,
And the drawers may contain bread
    and butter.

And let me thank God that I don't have to be
Like that miserable office-bound blighter.
  I'm disorganised, messy, untidy — and free!
Thank God for the life of a writer!"

Again it was cheap rhetoric. And again it worked. The quotation from one of Esmond Chadleigh's most famous light verses brought an instinctive round of applause from the trustees. They had been won round by someone who was no longer even a trustee.

As the clapping died, Belinda Chadleigh smiled at no one in particular and said, "I like that poem."

3

Carole Seddon decided there was no time like the present. The squabblings and confrontations at the meeting had only strengthened her resolve to resign from her trusteeship. She couldn't pretend the same level of interest in the fate of Bracketts that had been shown by the other committee members. It was time for a dignified withdrawal.

As they left the main building, Carole hurried to catch up with Gina Locke, who was walking determinedly towards the converted stable block that now housed the Administrative Office. The director didn't have the air of a woman who had just suffered a humiliating defeat.

"Gina, I just wanted to say sorry . . . ," Carole began.

"No need to say sorry to me. Nothing that happened in that meeting was your fault. I was glad to have your support."

"No, I didn't mean. . . ."

"Sheila may reckon she's won this round, but she won't win in the long term. She no longer has any power at Bracketts, and soon she's going to have to come to terms with that."

"She seemed to have power over that meeting," said Carole.

"Oh, yes, she won a cheap propaganda victory with the trustees, but she no longer has any influence in the day-to-day running of the place."

"Your tone could almost imply that the trustees aren't very important."

Gina stopped, adjusted her papers, and looked up into Carole's pale blue eyes. She hesitated for a second, then seemed to make the decision that she was on safe ground. "It would be rather offensive for me to say that, wouldn't it? To such a new trustee?"

Carole shrugged, and gave a reassuring grin. "My back is broad."

"All right, then, I'll tell you." Gina grinned. "In the overall scheme of things here at Bracketts, the trustees aren't that important. They have to be there — that's part of the terms of the way the charity was set up — and some of them have very useful contacts, which can make my job a lot easier. But a lot of what they do is just rubber-stamping decisions that have already been made. The Bracketts trustees are a very typically British institution, a system of checks and balances. . . ."

"There to provide the illusion of consultation and democracy . . . ?"

"Exactly." The director smiled at Carole's ready understanding of the situation. "So while in my job it would be very foolish of me to antagonise the Trustees — and while on major issues I must bow to their decisions . . . at least for the time being — most of the time I get on with running Bracketts exactly as I think it should be run. For heaven's sake, the trustees meet only six times a year. There's the occasional exchange of letters and phone calls between meetings, but most of the time I can get on with my own job without any interference."

"The use of that word implies you'd be happier if there was no Board of Trustees."

"No question about that." Gina's response was so instinctive that she felt she should perhaps soften it a bit. "I'm sorry, that's the knee-jerk reaction you'd get from anyone in my position. Professional administrators always resent the presence of amateur advisory boards. That's just one of the rules of business — as true in the heritage industry as it is anywhere else. From my point of view, the trustees are just a pain in the butt."

"Well, thank you for being so frank," said Carole in mock affront. "For telling me that, as a trustee, I am entirely redundant."

"Oh, I didn't mean. . . ."

"Don't worry. I'm not at all offended. In fact, what you've told me makes it rather easier for me to say what I was about to. . . ."

"No, the trustees are a pain in the butt, but they exist, and that's it. I have to work with them — which is why it's so important that I get as many like-minded people on the board as possible. Which is why I persuaded them to ask you to join, Carole. The more support I can get at those meetings from people like you, the easier my job becomes."

"Ah." Suddenly what Carole was about to say had become more difficult again.

They had reached the entrance to the stable block. "But if there's something you want to talk about, come on in."

"Well. . . ."

Carole's indecision was interrupted by the ungainly arrival across the yard of a stocky young man in clean blue overalls. He moved with the suppressed excitement of a child with a secret to tell, and his face was childlike, too. Though probably in his twenties, he had the flat face and thick

46

neck that characterised Down's syndrome. He was ruddy and freckled from outside work. Excitement sparkled in his watery blue eyes.

"Gina. Gina."

"Yes, Jonny. Look, you can see I'm talking to someone," she reprimanded with surprising gentleness. "You shouldn't interrupt."

"I know, but sorry, I. . . . There's something. . . ."

"This is Carole Seddon. Jonny Tyson."

The young man held out his hand very correctly, then thought better of the idea, and wiped it on his overalls. "Bit dirty. Been digging."

"Jonny's one of the volunteers. They're working in the kitchen garden, preparing the space where the museum will be built." Gina smiled, again with great compassion. "We couldn't manage without Jonny."

His beam of gratitude for the compliment nearly split his face in half, but he was still agitated, bouncing uneasily on the balls of his feet, as if trying to contain the power of his muscular body. "Please, Gina. There's something . . . where we've been digging. Could you come and have a look?"

"Yes, all right, Jonny." The director moved towards the stable block door. "I'm just going to have a word with Carole, and then I'll. . . ."

"Please, it'd be better if you could come straightaway."

There was no panic in his voice, but the urgency communicated itself from the trembling intensity of his body.

"All right. Carole, we can talk as we go along . . . if that's all right with you?"

"Fine."

"No, I don't think. . . ." But the two women had already moved on before Jonny Tyson could articulate his objection.

The kitchen garden of Bracketts was between the main house and the field that had been tarmacked over into a car park, so it had the ideal position for a Visitors' Centre. Every new arrival would have to pass by at the start of the tour, and as they left, they would hopefully visit the gift shop to load up with Esmond Chadleigh mugs and tea towels, as well as copies of those of his books which remained in print.

Though the building of the new museum would be done by professional contractors, the basic clearing and digging over of the space had been delegated to the Bracketts volunteer force. The kitchen garden had long ago given up its original function and been used increasingly as a convenient tipping ground. (The wall that surrounded it left tourists blissfully unaware of the accumulated mess.) Old farm machinery and garden implements had ended their life there; so had generations of superseded visitor signs. There were collapsed chairs and tables from the old tearooms, broken glass display cabinets, and rejected souvenirs.

When Carole had arrived earlier that afternoon, the clearing process was well advanced. Through the open gates to the kitchen garden, she had seen the estate manager organising some half-dozen workers of various ages. All wore faded blue overalls palely emblazoned with the words "Bracketts Volunteer" and the logo of some long-defunct or merged insurance company. They appeared to be enjoying their work. Piles of rubbish were being enthusiastically dragged to a large bonfire outside the walls. The acrid smell of burning plastic tainted the autumn air.

As Carole and Gina approached, almost all the debris had been removed, and the fire had subsided to glowing embers. Within the kitchen garden walls, freshly turned earth showed that a start had been made on digging over the surface soil.

But the work had stopped. The Bracketts

volunteers in their faded blue overalls were clustered round a corner near the gate, and turned uneasily at the approach of Jonny Tyson and the two women.

"I found it," said Jonny, with a mixture of pride and trepidation. Then, treating the words as if they were too big for his mouth, he confirmed, "Yes, I found it."

The volunteers moved back, and Gina and Carole looked down at the "it" they revealed.

Though only partially uncovered by Jonny's spade, "it" was undoubtedly a human skull.

4

"Right, can we just deal with this calmly, please?"

Carole turned to see the tall figure of Sheila Cartwright approaching through the kitchen garden gates.

"Of course, we'll deal with it calmly," said Gina Locke, determined not to allow another usurpation of her authority. "Has anyone notified the police yet?"

The volunteers shook their heads, and instinctively looked to Sheila Cartwright for their next instruction. At Bracketts old habits died hard.

"And does the estate manager know?"

More shaking of heads. "Jonny only just found it," said one of the girl volunteers.

"Well, could you go and tell him?" The girl set off obediently towards the stable block.

While Sheila Cartwright issued further instructions, Carole looked down at the skull and tried to analyse her reactions. The way it lay suggested that further digging would show the skull to be attached

51

to an entire skeleton. And the jagged hole in the back of the cranial dome raised the possibility that its owner had met an untimely end. But to her surprise, Carole realised she felt only the mildest shock at the sight. The predominant emotion she felt was curiosity, a need for explanations.

Another incipient conflict between Sheila Cartwright and Gina Locke brought her back to the present. The fuse was lit by Sheila's assertion that she would notify the police of what had happened.

Gina instantly dug her toes in. "I don't think that's your job."

"Why?" The older woman withered the younger one with her stare. "I rather doubt whether you know the chief constable as well as I do."

"This is hardly a matter to go up to chief constable level."

"If I may say so, Gina, that shows how little you know. The finding of a dead body somewhere like Bracketts is the kind of thing that must be kept from the press for as long as possible. If it can be kept quiet till the house closes for the end of the season, that will save a lot of disruption. Paul — the chief constable — will know exactly how to control the publicity. I'll go and make the call."

Then she turned her dominant eye on the little group that stood around the skull. "I need hardly say that this is something you keep entirely to yourselves. No information must be allowed to leak out before I release an authorised press statement."

"It isn't *you* who will be issuing a press statement."

"Oh, for heaven's sake, Gina! This is important. And dangerous. This is no time for petty demarcation disputes."

The director's mouth was open for her response to that, but she didn't manage to get it out before Sheila Cartwright turned the beam of her disapproval onto one of the volunteers. "Mervyn, how is it you always seem to be on the scene when there's trouble?"

He was a thin man in his thirties with a shaven head, and the effect of her words was unexpected. Suddenly he started to sob; his whole body shook with the strength of his emotions. Jonny Tyson moved to the man, and enfolded him in an instinctive hug, the comfort given by one child to another who had just fallen on the school playground.

"Oh, for heaven's sake!" snapped Sheila Cartwright. "This is a serious situation. We've got enough on our plates without you having hysterics!"

"I'm sorry, it's just. . . ." Mervyn's thin, Northern voice trembled. "Seeing a dead body . . . I've never been able to stand that. . . ."

"Must make life difficult for you," said Sheila Cartwright unsympathetically, "given your past history."

5

"I've been sworn to secrecy. . . ."

"Carole, I just love openings like that." Jude rubbed her hands together with glee. "The ones that mean the exact opposite of what's being said. 'I'd be the last one to criticise,' but that's exactly what I'm about to do. 'To be perfectly honest . . .' always sets the alarm bells ringing for me. And, of course, 'I've been sworn to secrecy. . . .' But that's not going to stop me telling you every gory detail."

"Well, perhaps I shouldn't."

"Oh, come on. You know you're going to tell me eventually. Just get on and do it."

It was two days after the discovery of the skull. They were sitting in the bar of the Crown and Anchor, which was full of Saturday seaside visitors, bulbous parents bursting out of sweatshirts, children with sand in their plastic sandals. The tables outside were even busier. The day was hot for late October, the kind of weather that made local residents talk darkly of "global warming."

Fethering's only pub had about it the feeling of a well-used armchair, and the same could be said for its landlord. Ted Crisp's shaggy hair and beard were the same all the year round, but now he was in his summer uniform of grubby T-shirt rather than his grubby winter sweatshirt. Carole had an uncomfortable feeling that he might be wearing shorts, too, but since Jude had been the one to buy their glasses of Chilean chardonnay and Ted hadn't emerged from behind the bar yet, she had no proof of this.

There was an air of ease about Jude, too, a lightness that was unusual in a woman of her ample dimensions and fifty-five years. The sun had generously toasted her broad face and bare arms; the blonde hair, secured by an insufficiency of pins, made a gravity-defying structure on top of her head. As ever, she breathed serenity, a quality that Carole recognised her own more uptight personality could never hope to attain.

The two women could not have been more different, and yet, ever since Jude had moved into Woodside Cottage next door to Carole, their friendship had flourished.

"So tell me," said Jude.

"There's not much to tell. Just the finding of a skeleton."

56

"That doesn't happen every day."

"Not to most people. I think you and I are bringing up the national average, though."

Jude chuckled. "But we are talking about a murder, aren't we? Please say yes."

"I've no idea."

"You haven't heard anything from the police?"

"No. They were around Bracketts, of course. Still are around, I imagine. They interviewed all of us, told us not to tell anyone anything. . . ."

This prompted a grin. "An instruction that, I'm glad to say, you, Carole, have ignored completely."

"Look, this goes no further. O.K.?"

"Of *course* not." Jude grinned innocently. "What do you take me for?"

Carole didn't bother to answer.

"I'm sure it's a murder," Jude persisted. "You said that there was a hole in the skull."

"You can get a hole in your skull from something falling on it. Doesn't have to be foul play."

"But if someone dies accidentally, you don't hide their body in a kitchen garden, do you?" Jude's face took on an expression of childlike insistence. "Go on, say it was a murder."

"I can't say that," Carole responded primly. "The person who owned the skull is dead; beyond that, I haven't got anything definite to go on. Everyone at Bracketts has clammed up. Certainly no information coming out of there."

"Not even to a trustee?"

"*Particularly* not to a trustee. Or particularly not to this trustee. The director was acutely embarrassed that I even saw as much as I did."

"Who is the director? Sheila somebody?"

"No, you're thinking of Sheila Cartwright, the one who got the place going as a literary shrine."

"Yes, that's the name."

"So do you know Bracketts?"

"I did the guided tour soon after I moved down here. I had a friend staying who's interested in that period of literary history."

"Oh, did I meet her?"

"Him. No." Carole would have liked more information about the friend, but Jude had already moved on. "We saw Sheila Cartwright then. She was pointed out to us by the guide, almost as if she was one of the remarkable exhibits. Very much lady of the manor, I thought."

"Well, she's no longer in charge of the

place . . . though you'd never know it from the way she goes on." Jude raised interrogative eyebrows, but Carole shook her head. "Complex management politics that I'm not going to go into at the moment. I'll fill you in soon enough."

"Then what *are* you going to go into at the moment?"

"Just the discovery of the skull."

"You used the word 'skeleton' earlier."

"Yes, there were other bones around. Certainly part of a spinal column. Only the top bit had been unearthed, but it was lying as if it was still with the rest of the skeleton."

There was a silence. Jude prompted, "There was something you thought odd, though, wasn't there?"

"I told you. There was a hole in the skull."

"Yes. Must be murder. Did it look like a bullet hole?"

"Jude, I've no idea."

"Hole made by surgery? Or by an ice pick, as in the case of Trotsky?"

"I just don't know." Carole looked thoughtful and took a long sip of her chardonnay. "It wasn't the skull itself so much . . . it was the people's reaction to it."

"Like . . . ?"

"Well, Sheila Cartwright was desperate that no publicity should leak out about the find."

"Fair enough. She didn't want the status quo at Bracketts disrupted."

"Her reaction seemed more than that. She said it was dangerous. She actually used the word 'dangerous.'"

Jude shrugged. "Just meant that bad publicity could be dangerous."

"Possibly." But there was something else nagging at Carole. "Then there was this man who broke down in tears."

"At the sight of the skull?"

"That's right. He said that he couldn't stand seeing dead bodies, but his reaction was very violent."

"Some people are spooked by that kind of stuff. It's a nasty shock for anyone."

"Yes." Carole sighed and nodded. "Yes, I suppose so."

"Do you know who this man was?"

"One of the day-release prisoners from Austen. Do you know Austen, the open prison?"

"I know it," replied Jude, with a new seriousness in her manner. "Did you get the man's name?"

"Sheila Cartwright called him Mervyn. And — this was the strange thing — she

60

implied that this man was used to seeing dead bodies."

"Was that explained at all?"

"No. That's all I got, before I was summarily whisked off the premises."

Jude looked thoughtful.

"Why, do you know an Austen prisoner called Mervyn?"

"No. I don't." Introspection was swept away with a toss of the blonde hair. "Come on, we're going to have lunch here, aren't we?"

"Well, I've got a cottage cheese salad in the fridge."

"In that case, we are *definitely* going to have lunch here. Cottage cheese is an abomination in the sight of God and man. Ted!" Jude called across to the bar, "What do you recommend today?"

Instantly ignoring the queues of the thirsty in front of him, the landlord turned to his favoured customers and replied, "Well, putting my good self on one side, I don't think you'd go far wrong with the fillet of fresh cod. Tell you, this morning that fish was still in the sea at Littlehampton, worrying about paying the mortgage on its special piece of seaweed."

"Right, I'll go for it." On a nod from Carole, "Make that two."

"Two fillet of fresh cod it is, ladies." Ted Crisp called the order through to some unknown person in the kitchen. Then he turned back to the two women and emerged from behind the bar.

He was wearing shorts. They might once have been blue and didn't, it had to be said, do a lot for him. His stomach sat on the ledge of their belt like a jelly on a plate.

"You two haven't been finding any more dead bodies, have you?" he asked.

"No," Carole replied primly.

"Oh, well, there you go," said Ted, and returned to serve the holiday hordes.

"So that's it," said Carole flatly. "I was present at the unearthing of a skull. Full stop."

"In that case, maybe you'd better go through the boring stuff now."

"Boring stuff?"

" 'Complex management politics' was the phrase you used."

"Oh. All right."

And so Carole outlined to her friend the conflict between the former and current directors of Bracketts, thinking — wrongly, as it turned out — she'd never hear any more about the skeleton that had been found there.

6

Jude didn't have strong feelings about lying, when it was necessary. She felt no guilt for having lied to Carole about not knowing anyone named Mervyn. Even given the detail that the Mervyn she knew was currently serving time in H.M.P. Austen.

Nor did she feel any guilt for keeping her own connection with the prison a secret from her neighbour.

Jude's work at Austen was voluntary and semiofficial. The prison had a very imaginative education officer named Sandy Fairbarns, who was always doing her best to extend the definition of the word "education" and to introduce new activities to alleviate the boredom of the prisoners. Since her budget was small and getting smaller, this meant that she was constantly looking out for opportunities, homing in on people who might have a skill they could share, and pursuing them with relentless charm until they agreed to do a session or series of sessions at the jail. She had built up a good relationship with the governor, who, recognising that the more the prisoners had to do, the less trouble they were likely to cause, encouraged Sandy's alternative programme.

As a result, Austen Prison became the destination for a disparate group of writers, musicians, artists, and local historians. Some found the working conditions impossible; prisoners would wander in and out at will, and it was difficult to impose any structure on the sessions. For others the experience was very positive, and they pressed Sandy Fairbarns to organise further courses for them.

The continuity of the programme was always under threat. Only one disciplinary problem was required, one whiff of adverse publicity, and the governor would put a stop to it. But the education officer walked her tightrope with skill, and the project prospered.

Jude had met Sandy at a Mind, Body, and Spirit Fair in Brighton, and Sandy had immediately responded to Jude's aura of equanimity. Within minutes she had suggested involving her new acquaintance in the Austen courses, and over a drink that evening, Jude had agreed to do an exploratory session on "new approaches."

The vagueness of the subject had suited

her well, and she'd launched into the first visit to Austen with an open mind, prepared to go where the participants led her. Seven prisoners had been there at the beginning of the session, three left during it, and two more wandered in. Sandy said that was par for the course, and pressed Jude to do another session a few weeks later. The sequence had now continued, more or less on a monthly basis, for nearly nine months.

Though there were one or two faces that reappeared, Jude got used to being confronted at each occasion by a roomful of strangers. The shifting nature of the prison population made her realise how acute the problem of continuity was in Sandy Fairbarns's job. Individuals might be encouraged and nurtured towards individual goals — exams and qualifications — but a lot of the educational effort was regarded by the prisoners as an optional entertainment, to be assessed against the rival attractions of the television, the gym, or a kickaround with a football.

The subject matter of Jude's sessions usually started with her talking about some alternative therapy — be it yoga or acupuncture — but very soon the conversation moved away from the medical to the more general. There was usually resistance to be overcome. Jude was an attractive woman, so she had to survive an initial onslaught of sexist banter from men starved for female company. There was a lot of swearing, and frequently aggression between the prisoners, reviving old quarrels.

But each time her good sense, good humour, and serenity would gradually allow discussion to flow. Amongst the shifting group of multi-ethnic, multi-faith prisoners, discussion quickly homed in on human psychology and belief systems. Because Austen was an open prison, there were a good few highly educated prisoners — mostly solicitors, as it happened — who were skilled in reasoned argument, but Jude was usually more impressed by the articulacy of the less privileged. Many of them, unused to discussion of abstract concepts, quickly caught on to the idea, and more than held their own with the more highly trained debaters.

Each session creaked for the first twenty minutes, then gained fluency. There was a lot of laughter, too, and the arrival of the warder to announce the two hours were up always came as a surprise. "New Approaches" frequently ended up as philosophy, and always as a form of therapy.

And each time Jude was escorted by Sandy back across the compound to the Austen main gate, where she would hand in her visitor badge, Jude felt a sadness. She was going back out into the real world. The men whose ideas had flowed, whose identities had been so alive for the previous two hours, were going back to the stultifying, imagination-cramping repetitions of prison routine.

The reason Jude kept her activities at Austen secret was not the false modesty of philanthropy. It was the respect that she had for what Sandy Fairbarns was trying to achieve, and an unwillingness for knowledge of it to get to the wrong people. She could imagine the mileage in newsprint that a hang-'em-and-flog-'em right-wing politician could get out of the news that prisoners were being given instruction in healing and alternative therapies.

She also felt that talking about her work would be a betrayal of the confidences which some of the prisoners had shared with her. They had their integrity, and she had hers.

It was serendipity that Jude's next visit to Austen was scheduled for the Monday after she had had lunch with Carole at the Crown and Anchor. As she got off the train from Fethering, she made a private prayer to one of her gods that Mervyn Hunter would once again be part of her group.

The walk from the station to the prison was pleasant in the autumn sunshine. H.M.P. Austen was set on the flat coastal plain only about a mile from the sea. Behind her Jude could see the blue-grey humps of the Downs, receding ever paler into the distance. The town of Fedborough nestled in the crevice where their undulations began. If you had to be in prison, there were worse venues.

And yet Austen was still bleak. The path she trod, past the redbrick houses of prison officers, made Jude think of the other people she had seen walking along the same route on other afternoons. Harassed wives, snapping at trailing, whining children, going to snatch an hour's visit with their errant husbands.

She remembered some words of Sandy's. "You see them coming in, wiped-out, totally exhausted, worried about money, worried about how the kids are behaving, forced into single parenthood. Then you see the men — a lot of them down here have been putting in time in the gym, and they're brown from all that working outside, positively glowing with health. And you ask yourself: Who's actually being punished here?"

And yet Austen Prison was a place of punishment. Undeniably so. Though the dark redbrick entrance Jude approached could have belonged to a College of Further Education, the fact remained that there were walls all around the compound and the blocks in which the men slept were locked at night.

Compared to other prisons, of course, the security at Austen was light. Anyone sufficiently determined to get out wouldn't need to form an escape committee. It would be easy enough to hop over the wall, or become detached from an outside working party and slip away. Indeed, round Christmas that did happen a lot, as home-loving prisoners decided they needed a few hours with their families. But such events were rare. Most of the prisoners with experience of Category B and C prisons knew just how easy they had it in Austen. They knew how many fewer locked doors there were between them and the outside world. They knew how much more time they were allowed to spend outside their cells. It wasn't the perimeter walls that kept the men inside Austen Prison; it was the knowledge that if they escaped and were —

as they almost inevitably would be —
recaught, their next sojourn would be back
in a Cat B or C nick. And that would not
be funny.

Apart from the white-collar criminals —
the aforementioned solicitors, bent finan-
ciers, and careless accountants — most of
the Austen population consisted of young
men banged up for minor offences that
didn't involve violence. There were also
quite a few lifers, serving out their last few
years of punishment in an environment that
had a little more in common with the world
outside than the grim compounds where
they had spent the bulk of their sentences.

Sandy Fairbarns was in the entrance hall
to greet her, and vouch for the incomer.
Jude was issued her pass by a cheery
prison officer who recognised her from a
previous visit. They went through into the
prison grounds and walked across towards
the Education block.

Austen Prison was laid out with generous allowances of space between the
blocks. These were one-storey brick rectangles with pitched roofs, and the walls
were painted a pale institutional yellow.
The gardens between were beautifully
kept. Some of the gardeners were crouched
over beds, shirts removed to build up their

tans even in the weak October sunshine. Men in blue overalls or denims wandered around with a kind of purposeful aimlessness. In spite of the space and the sunlight, there was a hangdog air about the place.

When she did her first session, Jude had refused the offer of a prison officer actually in the room, but she was instructed to leave the door open and issued an alarm whistle to summon the officer on the landing if there was trouble. But there had never been trouble, and she didn't anticipate any. The men in her group might have been threatening to each other, but never to her.

Even the lifers. In fact, particularly the lifers. Jude knew, because Sandy Fairbarns had told her, that, defined by their sentence, they were almost all murderers; and yet never had she met a less dangerous, less frightening group of men. She longed to ask each the circumstances of his crime, who he'd actually killed and why, but she knew that was beyond the limit of her position in the prison. She also knew that she was seeing a specific minority of murderers. The truly vicious would not be given the relatively soft option of Austen at the end of their sentences. But it was still strange to encounter them. They were a quiet bunch, tainted by sadness and inadequacy. If all murderers were as gentle as these men, she decided, there could be no more crime fiction.

Mervyn Hunter appeared the most vulnerable of the lot. He had the haunted look of a man rarely untroubled by his own internal demons. At the first of Jude's sessions he had turned up, febrile with shifty paranoia, and had not opened his mouth once. She hadn't expected to see him again, but to her surprise he was there on her next visit, and became one of her most regular participants. Gradually he relaxed and began to make his own contributions to the discussion. They were never ribald or trivial; Mervyn took the issues seriously, and was particularly intrigued by the definition of personal morality. Though he never referred to the crime that had brought him to Austen, he seemed constantly to be judging himself, finding personal applications in the abstracts of their discussion. He remained hypersensitive and twitchy, but Jude liked to think that she had begun to get through to him.

As they entered the Education block that afternoon, it struck her that she knew nothing about Sandy Fairbarns's life outside her work. They got on, Jude responded to Sandy's tenacity and enthusiasm, and yet all that energy was job-related. Of the woman's life outside Austen Prison, Jude knew nothing. There was no wedding ring, but at the beginning of the twenty-first century that could have any number of meanings.

The realisation increased Jude's admiration for Sandy. Knowing that people found her easy to talk to, Jude had got used to hearing more of their lives than she volunteered of her own. The situation suited her very well. Her life had many strands; different friends matched up with different strands, and there was rarely cause for them to intertwine. Without being deliberately secretive, Jude retained her privacy. She had never felt the need, which seemed to be such a common one, to tell everything about herself.

In Sandy Fairbarns, she recognised a practitioner of the same method, and she respected what she saw.

"Good luck," said Sandy. Through the open door at the end of the first-floor landing, Jude could see her group assembled. A couple sat neatly in chairs like schoolchildren. Others lounged against the walls in attitudes of insouciant independence. The smell of stale masculine sweat, which permeates all prisons, was stronger.

"What are you going to start with today, Jude?"

"Thought I'd start with psychosomatic symptoms — how the body provides its own reactions to stress. And see where we go from there. And who knows in which direction that will be . . . ?"

She took another look through the door, and waved at a face she recognised. "Can't see Mervyn in there. He's usually one of the first, sitting upright waiting for teacher."

"Mervyn won't be there today," said Sandy.

"Why not?"

"He's with the police."

"Police? What, is this something to do with his release, the terms of his parole or . . . ?"

"No. A dead body was found up at Bracketts. It's a place on the tourist map, house and museum. . . ."

"I know it." Jude reacted as if the discovery of the body was news to her.

"Anyway, Mervyn's been working up there . . . you know, day-release stuff. Bracketts've taken quite a few people from Austen over the years. Mervyn's a keen gardener, and it all seemed to be working very well for him . . . until this. That's what the police are talking to him about."

"Oh, for heaven's sake! A dead body's found somewhere, and so the police instantly turn on the one person present with a criminal record. I thought they were supposed to be getting more sensitive and imaginative these days. Why can't they . . . ?"

"Jude, the police had no option."

"What do you mean?"

"Mervyn's confessed to the murder."

7

"Is this Carole Seddon?"

"Yes." She was slightly mystified, trying to think whom she knew with an American accent.

"Oh, hi. My name is Marla Teischbaum."

Carole was caught on the hop. She should have been prepared for a phone call like this. As it was, she couldn't think of anything to say.

"From the University of California. Berkeley." But the voice wasn't Californian; it carried the nasal twang of New York. "You probably know my name."

"No, I don't think I've. . . ."

"Then you're the only Bracketts trustee who doesn't."

Carole felt like a naughty schoolchild, caught out in her instinctive lie. She was normally better in control of herself, but the American's forceful directness flustered her.

"Oh, yes," she said feebly. "Professor Teischbaum. Now you've put yourself in context, I know exactly who you are."

"I'm writing a biography of Esmond Chadleigh. . . ."

"I know that too."

". . . and I'd like for us to meet."

Again Carole was uncharacteristically tentative in her reaction. "Well, I'm not sure. . . ."

"Listen, I know the official line on this. All you trustees have been told about this crass American vampire who's out to suck the lifeblood out of Esmond Chadleigh's reputation. . . ."

"It wasn't quite put like that."

"No, but basically you've been told you mustn't talk to me. And I thought — because, if you like, I'm American and pushy — why should I just accept that? Why don't I talk to the trustees individually, and maybe explain what my agenda is on Esmond Chadleigh, and who knows . . . some of you might realise I'm not the monster I've been painted."

"I really don't think I should talk," Carole floundered on. "Apart from anything else, I'm a very new trustee. I don't know much about the Bracketts setup. And I'm certainly not a literary person, so I'm afraid my knowledge of Esmond Chadleigh is. . . ."

"All I'm asking is, could we meet, have a chat? I'm still going to do my biography if I get no cooperation at all from the Chadleigh family or the trustees, but establishing a dialogue would seem to me to be a more civilised approach to the situation. I object to being branded as a muckraking mischief maker by people who've never met me."

"Well, I can see you have a point, but. . . ."

"Listen, Carole, I'd like to talk to you. Think about it for twenty-four hours. I'll call you tomorrow. Tuesday. Good-bye."

And the connection was broken. Carole thought of all the more assertive things she should have said during the conversation.

Immediately she rang the number of the Bracketts Administrative Office. "Gina, I've just had this Professor Teischbaum on the phone."

"You, too?"

"She's working through trustees, then, is she?"

"Oh, yes. Started at the top with Lord Beniston."

"Presumably no one's told her anything?"

"No."

"And presumably you want me to clam up, too?"

"Well, actually," said Gina, to Carole's considerable surprise, "I'm not sure."

"Really?"

"She won't go away. I had her on the phone for an hour yesterday. Marla Teischbaum's a tenacious woman. I think maybe we should chuck her something."

"In the same way you chuck a bit of meat to a circling shark?"

"In exactly that way, yes." The director made a decision. "Fix to see her, Carole."

"But I know virtually nothing about Esmond Chadleigh. Of all the trustees, I'm the newest and the most ignorant." There was a silence, which Carole filled in. "Which is exactly why you want me to talk to her, isn't it?"

"Spot on."

"I'm not sure I like the idea of. . . ."

"I'll get a pack of stuff together for you. Some biographical articles and what-have-you, photocopies of some of Esmond Chadleigh's correspondence. . . ."

"Though none of the important stuff?"

"Of course not. If Bracketts and its trustees are positively antagonistic to Professor Teischbaum, we'll make an enemy of her. This way we maintain cordial relations. . . ."

"And really give her no help at all?"

"That's it, Carole. Excellent. The trustees have appointed you to liaise with her."

"No, they haven't. You have."

"Professor Teischbaum doesn't know that. All requests for information about Esmond Chadleigh and Bracketts must be channelled through you. And we solve our immediate problem very neatly."

Carole was getting a bit sick of being steamrollered by dominant women. Her own character was strong, too, and it was about time she asserted it.

"I think that's a bad idea, Gina. I'm sorry, I'm not going to do it."

"Oh, please." There was genuine entreaty in the young woman's voice. "Please, you must."

"Why?"

"Because if you don't. . . ." Gina Locke sounded young and distinctly vulnerable.

"What'll happen?"

"Sheila Cartwright will do it. She said if the trustees didn't appoint a spokesman today, she'd talk to Professor Teischbaum herself."

And Carole realised she wasn't the only one being steamrollered by a dominant woman.

"So what about the dead body?" she asked, effectively conceding that she would take the role appointed for her. "What's the trustees' official line on that?"

"I don't think you'll need an official line on that. It's all still under wraps. Nobody except the people who witnessed the discovery and the police know anything about it."

"But it can't stay that way for long. The press is going to get hold of the story soon."

"Hasn't happened yet. Sheila's influence with the chief constable really seems to be working." Even a sworn enemy like Gina couldn't completely exclude admiration from her tone.

"You haven't even told the other trustees about the body?"

"I told Lord Beniston. Couldn't avoid that. But he, with his military background, said the information should be spread on a strictly 'need-to-know' basis. At the moment, in his view, none of the other trustees 'need to know.' Which, I must say, is a great relief for me."

"Oh?" Carole picked up the potential lapse of professionalism in Gina's words. Was the director about to say something else diminishing about her esteemed trustees?

She was, but she couched it in relatively diplomatic terms. "It's Graham Chadleigh-

Bewes. He'd be on the phone instantly if he knew about it."

"For a long conversation?"

"There is no such thing as a short conversation with Graham. In fact, there's hardly such a thing as a conversation. His favoured method of communication is the long monologue."

"So at least you've escaped that."

"On the subject of the skeleton, yes. Don't worry, though, he'll be on about something else before the day is out. Phone calls from Graham Chadleigh-Bewes are one of the drawbacks of my position here. Unfortunately," Gina said ruefully, "they weren't mentioned in the job description."

"Or you might not have applied?"

"Oh, no, I'd still have applied." There was a new grit in the director's voice. "I'm going to make Bracketts work . . . in spite of any obstacles that may currently be in my way."

"Right. So, going back to my position on the skeleton, you're pretty sure Professor Teischbaum won't know anything about it?"

"Positive. And, for heaven's sake, don't tell her."

"I'm not entirely stupid," said Carole with some asperity.

"Sorry. I'm just so concerned that it's kept quiet."

"There won't be any lapse of security through me."

"No, of course not," said Gina, humbled by the continuing sharpness in Carole's voice. Carole felt a twinge of guilt for the lapse of security she'd already committed by telling Jude.

"So," she asked more gently, "you haven't had any information from the police? About the identity of the body, for instance?"

"Nothing at all. As they always say — unhelpfully — 'Investigations are proceeding.' I think the skeleton's undergoing forensic examination and tests, but we haven't been told anything definite."

"So there have been no developments at all on the case?"

"None," said the director.

The inaccuracy of Gina Locke's words was made clear as soon as Carole saw Jude that Monday evening. But whether the director had been deliberately lying or merely ignorant was impossible to know.

"The police have actually had a confession to murder?" They were in the sitting room of High Tor and, as she spoke, Carole was pouring white wine.

"Yes."

"I'd call that a development in the case. Wouldn't you?"

"Oh, yes." But Jude sounded distracted. She toyed with a tendril of blonde hair that had escaped the pile on top of her head, and looked around the room. Carole had had the place redecorated the previous autumn by an interior designer named Debbie Carlton, but already the owner's intrinsic neatness had taken the softness out of the décor. The relaxed pale apricot and dreamy blue of the paintwork were at odds with the disciplined ranking of the books on the shelves, even the exact alignment of *The Times* on the coffee table. No make-over could ever fully blunt the spikiness of Carole Seddon's personality.

"You don't sound certain, Jude. . . ."

"Oh, no, I know it's happened, but. . . . The confession was from Mervyn Hunter."

"The one I saw break down when the body was discovered?"

Jude nodded.

"But you said you didn't know anyone named Mervyn."

"I lied."

It was said with disarming honesty, but Carole wasn't disarmed. "For heaven's sake! What is this, Jude? I thought the whole point of our discussions about cases like this was that we shared information. I don't hold stuff back from you, and I'm pretty angry to hear that you've been holding stuff back from me!"

Carole's skin was very thin. Only the smallest friction was required to lay bare her subcutaneous insecurity. She was quick to imagine slights, but in this case did not need recourse to her imagination. Her supposed friend had deliberately withheld material information from her.

Jude tried to ease the situation. "Look, I'm sorry. I felt there was an issue of confidentiality between me and Mervyn . . .

because I've met him through the prison."

"Through the prison? What are you talking about?"

"I've met Mervyn Hunter at Austen Prison. He's a lifer finishing off his sentence there."

"Jude, how on earth do you come to make the acquaintance of lifers at Austen Prison?"

Jude sighed. Her reticence on the subject had a perfect logic for her, but she knew Carole wouldn't see it so simply. The last thing Jude wanted to do was antagonise her friend, and yet, given the personality involved, it was all too easily done.

She started on the laborious process of fence-mending. "The last few months I've been doing some sessions at Austen Prison."

"Sessions? On what?"

"Alternative stuff. Alternative therapies, alternative ways of looking at life."

"Oh." The frost in the voice said everything about Carole's views on such matters. She reckoned trying to lead a straightforward normal life was quite difficult enough, without complicating the issue by offering alternatives.

"Anyway," Jude hurried on, "in the course of these sessions I have met Mervyn Hunter."

"And does he seem like a murderer to you?" asked Carole, thinking of the skeleton at Bracketts.

"Well, I know he *is* a murderer, so what he seems like is a bit irrelevant. But no, in the accepted sense, he doesn't *seem* like a murderer. And, indeed, I'd be very surprised if he were ever to commit a second murder."

"The first one being the one he's in Austen for?"

"Yes."

"So who was that? Who did he kill before?"

"I've no idea."

"But surely that was the first question you asked?"

"I can assure you, Carole, as an outsider inside a prison, that's the last question you ask. If a prisoner wants to volunteer information to you about his crime, fair enough. If he doesn't, don't go there."

"Oh." The response remained frosty. The fence was still by no means mended.

"Anyway, I've talked to Mervyn a bit, mainly in group sessions, but occasionally had the odd word with him on his own."

"You knew he'd been working up at Bracketts?"

"Yes. He mentioned it."

"Apparently there's been quite a history of that, with men from Austen. Set up by Sheila Cartwright. For the right sort of prisoner, who's interested in gardening, or even in the heritage side of the place, it's worked very well."

"And from what Mervyn told me, it was working well for him, too. He's a very wound-up kind of character, really needs the right sort of opening when he gets out of Austen. Somewhere like Bracketts is ideal for him."

"I'm sure it would be," said Carole huffily, "if he didn't go on murdering people."

"Oh, for heaven's sake," protested Jude, uncharacteristically testy. "You don't think he did it, do you?"

"Well, he's told the police he did. If Mervyn himself doesn't know what he's done, then who does?"

"I'm absolutely certain he didn't do it. I think he confessed only because he thought he ought to."

"What!" But further expansion of Carole's disbelief was stopped by her phone ringing.

"Hello, is that Carole Seddon?" The voice was vaguely familiar, slightly effete, and, at that moment, deeply anxious.

"Yes, it is."

"This is Graham."

"Oh?"

"Graham Chadleigh-Bewes," he said peevishly. "I gather from that Gina at Bracketts that you're going to be meeting the Great American Predator."

"Well, there was some talk of. . . ."

"It's very important that you come and see me before any such meeting."

"I'm not sure that it'll be possible for me. . . ."

"You have to. I have some papers that you must give to Professor Teischbaum. You must come."

Carole was getting a bit sick of the way everyone connected with Bracketts ordered her around.

"What papers are these?"

"Some material about Esmond."

"Do you mean you *are* going to cooperate with her, after all?"

"No." He chortled. "I'm going to fob her off with some unimportant stuff."

"Oh. Well, I'm not sure that I want to be a party to any kind of. . . ."

"The importance of your doing what I say cannot be overestimated," Graham went on in his prissy academic's voice. "Particularly in the circumstances."

"What circumstances?"

"The circumstances of a skeleton having been found in the kitchen garden at Bracketts."

So much for Lord Beniston's need-to-know policy amongst the trustees, thought Carole.

9

By the time Jude returned from High Tor to Woodside Cottage that evening, a second bottle of white wine had been consumed and the fence had been, if not fully mended, at least temporarily repaired. She felt sorry for Carole, whose reticent personality was always going to require much bridge-building and fence-mending. There was no element of superiority in her pity. Jude just felt blessed to have been born with a more direct approach to life; the differences between them had never, from her point of view, offered any threat to their friendship.

Amidst the draped and cluttered chaos of her sitting-room the red light of the answering machine blinked. There were two messages.

"Hello. Voice from the past. It's Laurence. Love to talk to you. Love to meet, come to that. I've actually come sufficiently into the twenty-first century to get myself a mobile. Let me give you the number."

She felt a remembered warmth as she wrote it down. A few of Jude's affairs had ended in "I never want to see you again!" acrimony, but she was still in occasional touch with most of her lovers, and her recollections of Laurence Hawker were almost entirely benign. She wondered if he was still an academic, still researching in the English Department at the university in Prague, still as irresistibly attracted to all those stunning-beautiful Czech female students. But for that predilection of his, and the way it encroached on their time together, Jude's relationship with Laurence would have been near perfect. Be good to see him again.

The second message was from Sandy Fairbarns. "Need to talk to you urgently, Jude. If you can get back to me tonight before twelve, be great. If not, at Austen in the morning, as soon after nine as possible."

It was two minutes before midnight. Jude keyed in the mobile number. Sandy sounded as bright and enthusiastic as ever. Loud music sounded in the background, but it wasn't referred to. Sandy's private life remained private.

"Jude, thank you so much for getting back to me. It's about Mervyn."

"Anything wrong with him?"

"I don't know. He never did talk to me."

"He's back at Austen?"

"Yes."

"Any charges?"

"I don't know. Basically, Jude, I want you to see him."

"But I'm not scheduled to do another session till. . . ."

"I know. I'm suggesting you come and visit him. If I get it to the governor first thing in the morning, I can get a V.O. for you for tomorrow afternoon."

"Sorry? V.O.?"

"Visiting order. Can you do tomorrow?"

"Sure."

"Good. Because Mervyn seemed to respond in your sessions. I think he might open up to you."

"I'll do my best. But what's his problem?"

"I don't know, Jude. But I'm worried about him."

10

Graham Chadleigh-Bewes's house was symbolic of his life. From childhood it had been dominated by his famous grandfather, so there was a logic that his home should be almost in the shadow of Bracketts. The cottage had once housed an estate worker, and though firmly separated by its own fence, still gave the impression that it was part of the grounds. A rather tart notice by the front gate read: THIS HOUSE IS PRIVATE PROPERTY. VISITORS TO BRACKETTS SHOULD ENTER THROUGH THE CAR PARK 100 YARDS DOWN THE LANE. An arrow showed the way.

Searchers after symbols might have seen that, too, as an expression of Graham Chadleigh-Bewes's semidetached relationship with Bracketts, half-loving and half resenting the connection.

They could have seen symbolism in his surname as well. The anonymous Mr. Bewes, whom Sonia Chadleigh had married in 1945, had been half-erased by a hyphen, so that his son would retain the famous literary name.

As she approached the cottage door on Tuesday morning, Carole again reflected on how bossy everyone involved with the place seemed to be. And how meekly she continued to submit to their bossiness. Graham had quickly rejected her suggestion that they should meet on neutral ground, a café or pub somewhere midway between Fethering and South Stapley. "No, no, I've got all the papers here. You'll have to come to me." But Carole sensed that it was not simply a matter of convenience. Graham Chadleigh-Bewes felt insecure off his own territory. He gained strength from his home environment, so close to the splendour of Bracketts.

It was raining heavily. The brightness of the last few days had been suddenly eclipsed, and the water sheeted off Carole's precious Burberry.

To her surprise, the cottage door was opened by Belinda Chadleigh, who had only just come in herself. She was swamped in a huge, dripping blue waterproof coat that bore the same "Bracketts Volunteer" labelling and logo that had been on the overalls Carole had seen in the kitchen garden.

At first Carole's name seemed to mean nothing to the old lady. The trustees meeting, during which they had sat at the same table only a few days previously, might as well not have happened.

But when Carole said she'd come to see Graham, a kind of recollection entered the faded eyes. "Oh, yes, of course. He said someone was coming. He's very busy, as ever. You know, with the biography. And it's not just that. You wouldn't believe all the demands there are on Graham's time, just the day-to-day dealing with the estate."

"I'm sure I wouldn't," said Carole politely, but she was beginning to wonder how much work was actually involved. Belinda Chadleigh's manner confirmed her previous impression of Graham Chadleigh-Bewes: that he was basically rather lazy, but kept going on about his workload and surrounded himself with people who endorsed his self-image as the impossibly stressed keeper of Esmond Chadleigh's flame.

His aunt was evidently a willing partner in this conspiracy. The way she behaved suggested that she lived in the cottage, even acted as a kind of housekeeper to the tortured genius who was her nephew. Her offer of tea or coffee, when she ushered Carole into the great man's presence, was both automatic and practised. Carole said she'd like a coffee, and Graham conceded that he could probably manage another one, too. With the subservience of a house-maid from another generation, his aunt went off to make the necessary arrangements.

There was a chaos about Graham Chadleigh-Bewes's study that might once have been organised, but had long since got completely out of control. He sat on an old wooden swivel chair in a recess backed by small cottage windows, against which that morning the rain rattled relentlessly. In front of him was a structure that logic dictated must be a desk, but the surface was so crowded with papers and the sides so buttressed by books and files that no part of it was visible. All available wall space was shelved, and books were crammed in double ranks, some hanging precariously off the edges, others stuffed in horizontally over ranks of the unevenly vertical.

Hanging slightly askew from a nail on one shelf end was a small crucifix with an ivory Christ. Atop one of the peaks of the desk's topography perched an old black telephone with a white dial and nubbly brown fabric-covered wire. There was no sign of fax, photocopier, or computer —

indeed, of no technology invented in the last fifty years.

Graham himself, poring importantly over some papers, did not rise to greet Carole. Having rather grandly given his coffee order to his aunt, he waved his guest to a chair from which she had to remove a pile of flimsy carbon copies. "Be careful with that lot," he admonished, without looking up. "Mustn't get them out of sequence."

Sequence? As Carole sat down and looked around the room, she couldn't see much evidence of sequence anywhere.

After dutifully watching Graham read for a couple of minutes, she decided she'd had enough. He was the one who had summoned her, after all.

"Could we get on, please?" she said. "I don't have all day."

He looked up from his letters with some hurt, as at a philistine interruption of the creative process. His expression was calculated to make her feel like the visitor from Porlock, breaking Coleridge's flow on "Kubla Khan," but if he thought it'd have that effect on Carole, he'd got the wrong woman.

"I gather you want to give me some kind of briefing before I speak to Professor Teischbaum."

"In a way." Reluctantly, he added the letters he was reading to the refuse tip on his desk. "I have to say, I'm not in favour of your meeting this frightful Yank."

"I'm not that keen on it myself, but Gina is very insistent that I should. When I agreed to be a trustee, I took on certain responsibilities, and this is just one of them. If we clam up completely and refuse to let anyone talk to Professor Teischbaum, she'll just think we've got something to hide."

"Yes. I suppose I see the logic of that." He didn't sound convinced. He still reckoned that if the Bracketts hierarchy completely ignored his rival biographer, then she'd go away. "But I don't think Gina should be the one to decide who talks to the woman."

"Gina is director of this organisation. I would have thought this was exactly the sort of decision that she should make."

"Yes, I know she's *director*" — he dismissed the title as an irrelevance — "but she doesn't really *know* Bracketts. She hadn't even read any Esmond before she mugged him up for the job interview. And though she's absolutely fine as a kind of office manager, she shouldn't be making decisions about important things like this."

"So far as I can gather, her thinking

in suggesting that I talk to Professor Teischbaum is that I know relatively little about Bracketts, and therefore won't be able to give much away."

Graham Chadleigh-Bewes pulled at his fat lower lip disconsolately. "It still should be someone aware of the issues at stake."

"You're not suggesting *you* should talk to the professor, are you? Rival biographers meeting at dawn? Who'd have the choice of weapons?"

"No," he replied testily. "The obvious person to do it is Sheila."

"Why?"

"Because she *knows* Bracketts. She knows everything about the place, everything about Esmond. She would see this woman off with no problem at all."

"But, as I understand it, Graham, Sheila no longer has any official role at Bracketts. She certainly isn't the director. I gather she isn't even a trustee."

"Oh, that's just office politics."

"What, do you mean she was voted off by the other trustees?"

"No, no, no. She went entirely of her own accord. Sheila had been wanting to reduce her commitment to Bracketts for some time. She's put so much into the place, she wanted to have a bit of time to herself. Who can blame her?"

"Nobody."

"Of course not. So eighteen months ago, she resigned as director — for which, incidentally, she was never paid — and she became a trustee. Then after six months, she resigned as a trustee."

"Why?"

"She didn't want to affect the freedom of the trustees to take new initiatives. Sheila knew the management of Bracketts had to change. She was the one who suggested advertising for a professional director, for heaven's sake. She said she didn't want to outstay her welcome, like Margaret Thatcher. She wanted to give whoever took over from her a completely free hand and, as for herself, just withdraw gracefully."

If Sheila Cartwright's behaviour at the recent trustees meeting had been an example of her graceful withdrawal, Carole had even more sympathy for the impossible position into which Gina Locke had been placed. The new director's power was only theoretical. Every decision she made was going to be scrutinised — and quite possibly countermanded — by her predecessor.

The Board of Trustees, the regulatory body with the mandate to control such behaviour, seemed to be so awed by — or possibly in love with — Sheila Cartwright, that they gave Gina Locke no support at all. And since the discovery of the skeleton in the kitchen garden, no one even attempted to maintain the illusion that Sheila had taken a back seat.

"Well," said Carole firmly. "It is going to be me who talks to Professor Teischbaum, so what do you want me to say to her?"

Whether Graham might have argued his point further was impossible to know, because they were interrupted by the arrival of his aunt with the coffee. And not just coffee, either. As well as the silver pot and bone china cups on the tray — with a tray cloth! — there was an untouched circular sponge cake whose midriff revealed a jam and cream filling. Side plates and silver cake forks completed the layout.

In the speed with which this apparition distracted Graham Chadleigh-Bewes from their conversation lay the explanation for his spreading girth. His Aunt Belinda not only pampered his ego and kept house for him; she also saw it as her duty to fatten him up. And the gleam in Graham's eye showed that he loved being fattened up. The arrival of the sponge cake crystallised a vague feeling that Carole had formed about the man — that he was asexual, driven by pique rather than passion, that even his enthusiasm for the works of Esmond Chadleigh was in some way automatic. But there was nothing halfhearted or unspontaneous about his love of food.

Carole refused the offer of a slice. She had had breakfast only a couple of hours before and, anyway, didn't ever eat between meals. Having resisted the biscuit-nibbling culture of the Civil Service all her working life, she wasn't going to relax her standards in retirement.

Her host had no such scruples. His aging face looked ever more babyish as he watched his Aunt Belinda make one incision in the powdered surface of the sponge and remove the knife. Then she went through a little pantomime of moving the knife round the arc to find exactly the size of slice he favoured. An angle of twenty-five degrees was condemned as "Too mean," and her overreaction of moving the knife round to forty-five degrees prompted a squeal of "Don't be ridiculous, Auntie — I'll explode!" But the slice he ended up with was still a pretty substantial one.

Carole found the display a little unwholesome, because it was clearly such a well-established routine. The two of them did this every day — possibly at every meal

— the elderly woman playing mothering games with the middle-aged man-child. Carole found herself wondering what had happened to Graham's real mother, and how long Belinda had been looking after her nephew.

As soon as he'd got his slice of cake, Graham Chadleigh-Bewes said, with some brusqueness, "Now you must go, Auntie. Carole and I have got important things to discuss."

The old lady, unoffended, reached for the tray. "Shall I take this with me?"

"No," her nephew replied hastily. "I . . . or my guest . . . might want some more . . . coffee."

The coy exchange of looks between them made Carole realise that this was an extension of their game. Aunt Belinda threatened to take Graham's cake away every morning. Every morning he stopped her — and no doubt later helped himself to a second slice. Carole felt increasingly uncomfortable as, with a little chortle, Belinda Chadleigh left the room.

"Now where were we?" asked Graham, as though he were a serious executive in a serious business meeting.

"We had just agreed," replied Carole, removing the possibility of further argument, "that since I'm going to see Professor Teischbaum, you were going to give me some stuff for her."

He looked puzzled. His recollection had not got their conversation to quite the same point. But Carole didn't give him time to respond — and his mouth was too full of sponge cake for him to make a very effective remonstrance.

"That's what you mentioned on the phone, Graham. That's why I'm here. You said you wanted to give me some papers for Professor Teischbaum."

"Oh, yes."

"In fact, to use your precise words, you said you wanted to 'fob her off with some unimportant stuff.' "

Graham Chadleigh-Bewes chuckled at his own cunning. "Exactly. I've got it all ready here." Clearly he'd given up on plan A, persuading Carole to cede her meeting with Marla Teischbaum to Sheila Cartwright, and he was moving on to plan B.

Given the chaos on his desk, it was surprising how quickly he found the documents he was looking for. And how neatly they were ordered in a cardboard file.

He flicked through the contents. Carole could see holograph and typewritten letters. "These are only copies," he said. "Obviously we wouldn't let her have the originals. Original Esmond Chadleigh material is like gold dust. My mother and Aunt Belinda wouldn't let a single scrap of paper be destroyed when he died."

"Not even stuff that wasn't to his credit?"

Graham Chadleigh-Bewes looked at her sharply, piqued like the baby whose rattle has been taken away. "I don't know what you're talking about. There were no secrets in Esmond Chadleigh's life."

Oh no, thought Carole. *Then that makes him unique in the history of the human race.* But she didn't pursue the point. "So all this material I'm passing on to Professor Teischbaum is completely useless, is it?"

"By no means. And they're documents I know she won't have seen, because they're from our archive here at Bracketts."

"Very generous of you all of a sudden," she observed.

Once again he glowed at his own cleverness. "Oh, yes," he agreed, "very generous." He tapped the file. "Useful stuff. No biographer could write anything about Esmond without access to this."

"But equally, I assume, all pretty uncontroversial."

"Hm?"

"Material that reinforces the accepted image of Esmond Chadleigh, just a further illustration of information that could be obtained from other sources."

Graham nodded complacently. "That is exactly right. Sheila and I worked out a strategy on this, you see. If we give the Teischbaum woman — I might almost call her 'the Teischbaum Claimant'. . . ." He chuckled at his own verbal dexterity. The play on words about a famous Victorian fraudster, "the Tichborne Claimant," was exactly the sort of joke to tickle Graham Chadleigh-Bewes's fancy — obscure, academic, and completely pointless.

"If we give her this lot, there's no way she can accuse the Esmond Chadleigh estate of being uncooperative. And when we refuse to give her anything else, we won't appear to be unreasonable."

Carole took the file. "From the way she sounded on the phone, I don't think she'll be satisfied with this."

"That is her problem, not ours. That is all the documentation that will be granted to . . . the Teischbaum Claimant." He was rather pleased with the nickname that he had coined, and would undoubtedly be using it on many other occasions.

"And what about the family?" asked Carole.

"What do you mean?"

"I would think it quite likely that Professor Teischbaum would ask to talk to you . . . to your Aunt Belinda, I imagine . . . and I don't know whether there are other living descendants of Esmond Chadleigh. . . ."

"There are a few, yes."

"Well, what will you say when the request comes in?"

"I'll tell the bloody woman to get lost and. . . ." But his instinctive anger dried up. A little smile irradiated his baby features. "No, maybe there, too, I'll follow Sheila's route of conciliation."

"So fobbing Marla Teischbaum off with the stuff in this file was Sheila's idea, was it?"

"Oh, yes." Graham spoke as if the question had not been worth asking. He was more excited by the new thought Carole had planted in his mind, and he spoke slowly as he worked it out. "Yes . . . I will agree to meet the Teischbaum Claimant . . . and I will be terribly nice to her . . . and I will endeavour to answer all of her questions . . . in my inimitably helpful and charming manner. . . ." He grinned with childish glee. "And I will tell her absolutely nothing at all."

"Well, good luck," said Carole. "I hope she plays ball."

"It is not a matter of her 'playing ball,' " snapped Graham Chadleigh-Bewes, suddenly angry. Perhaps, after all, there was something other than food that could rouse his passion. "It is a matter of the truth. And of the truth being told to the public. Esmond Chadleigh was a wonderful man, a good Catholic, and a writer of extraordinary genius! It is important that the public knows that about him."

"And that is what they will know when they read your biography?"

"Yes. And what they won't know if the muckrakers are allowed to defile his memory!"

"Your use of the word . . . suggests that there might be muck to rake. . . ."

"No! There is none!" With an effort, he calmed himself. There was a silence, filled only by the persistent rain outside. "God, it's a comment on the modern world, isn't it, that everyone is assumed to have a 'dark side'? Literary biography these days doesn't look at a man's *writings;* it starts its researches in the divorce courts and the VD clinics. Unless there's some sleazy scandal, nobody's interested. Why can't people still believe in the concept of goodness? Esmond had no 'dark side.' He was a genuinely good man. And that's how he'll be remembered . . . in spite of the worst excesses of the Teischbaum Claimant."

His tirade seemed to have both satisfied and exhausted him. The eyes in his chubby face gleamed as they moved towards the tray.

"Now, are you going to have another slice of cake . . . ," he asked as his hand moved forward to the knife, ". . . or is it just me?"

11

They heard the rattle of the front door opening, a loud female voice saying, "It's all right, Belinda, I'll see myself in," and Sheila Cartwright's height suddenly filled the room. She, too, was wearing one of the long Bracketts Volunteer waterproofs, and she shook the rain off as she lowered its hood.

Graham Chadleigh-Bewes was instantly on his feet. Though he'd shown no such deference to Carole, there were clearly some guests for whom he had respect — or possibly fear.

"I'm glad you're still here, Carole," said Sheila without preamble of greeting. "I wanted to make sure you'd got the message right about what I want you to do, and I know Graham's hopeless at that kind of thing."

The grandson shrugged ineffectually. "Sheila, would you care for a bit of cake or . . . ?"

"No, thank you. Unlike you, I don't spend my entire day stuffing my face. Carole, has he made it clear to you what you have to do?"

"Yes, thank you." She indicated the file on her lap. "I have my olive branch at the ready."

"Mm. My first thought was that I should do it, but it makes sense to use someone more ignorant." Unaware that she'd said anything mildly offensive, Sheila Cartwright swept on. "The important thing is that you are very pleasant to *this dreadful woman*." She infused the words with the same level of contempt that Graham had. "You say the trustees are happy to cooperate with her in her researches, but you also make it clear that those documents are the beginning and end of that cooperation."

"I somehow doubt if she's going to take that very well."

"I don't care how she takes it! That is all she's getting. Which is why it's a good idea for you to act as my ambassador." (*Interesting choice of possessive pronoun,* thought Carole. Not even the pretence that she was being sent as the representative of the trustees. It said a lot about how Sheila Cartwright viewed her own relationship with Bracketts.) "Because I know so much about Esmond Chadleigh, the Teischbaum woman might try to winkle more out of me."

"It'd be the same if I talked to her,"

112

asserted Graham Chadleigh-Bewes, who thought he'd been out of the conversation too long.

Sheila Cartwright turned a withering look on him. "There was never any question of you meeting Professor Teischbaum. You'd have messed it up, like you mess up everything."

Carole saw a momentary blaze of anger in his eye, but it was quickly extinguished. Graham was used to being diminished by Sheila Cartwright; what angered him was the knowledge that her assessment of him was accurate.

She hadn't finished, either. "If you'd done what you'd promised, and delivered your biography of Esmond last year, we wouldn't have any of these problems."

He looked sulky. "I thought we'd agreed that it'd be better for the book to come out for the centenary of his birth in 2004."

"We agreed to that only when we saw there wasn't a chance in hell of it coming out any earlier."

Wounded, Graham shrank back into his chair. "It's a massive undertaking. You wouldn't understand, Sheila, because you've never been a writer. New material keeps being discovered."

His whingeing defence prompted no

more response than a dismissive "Huh." Sheila turned her attention to Carole. "When are you going to meet the woman?"

"Actually," Graham interrupted, "I've got a rather good name for her. . . ."

"What?" asked Sheila testily. "Good name for who?"

"La Teischbaum. I call her 'the Teischbaum Claimant.' "

His esoteric pun didn't even get an acknowledgement. "So when are you going to see her, Carole?"

"We haven't fixed a time. She was going to ring me back today."

"Make it as soon as possible. We need that woman safely back in America. We've got quite enough on our plates here without distractions of that kind."

"Are you referring to the body in the kitchen garden?"

Carole was favoured by the kind of look she might have given her dog Gulliver if he'd made a mess on the carpet. "That is one of the issues concerning us here at Bracketts," said Sheila Cartwright loftily. "And, incidentally, whatever you do, don't mention anything about that to Professor Teischbaum."

"Of course I won't." Carole was getting sick of being treated like an unreliable schoolgirl. "So it hasn't become public yet?"

"What do you mean?"

"The police haven't made an announcement to the press yet?"

"No. Mercifully, the whole business is still under wraps."

"It can't stay that way forever."

"I am well aware of that, thank you."

Carole was enjoying being more combative, and she could see that Sheila Cartwright disliked the taste of her own medicine. "Have the police arrested the Austen prisoner who made the confession?"

The shock on Graham Chadleigh-Bewes's face showed that he knew nothing of this, but Sheila Cartwright's reaction was even more extreme. "How on earth did you hear about that?" she hissed.

Carole thought it was time to show that she could do "lofty," too. "From a contact in the Prison Service."

"Well, you keep it to yourself. Don't breathe a word about it to another soul."

"Of course I won't. I do understand the responsibility of being a trustee, I won't mention it to anyone." Except Jude, of course. "Anyway, what's happened? Have they arrested him?"

"The police are continuing their enquiries." Sheila Cartwright sounded like an official spokesman at a press conference. "The remains found in the kitchen garden are currently undergoing forensic analysis."

"Oh? Well, do let me know when you hear anything, won't you?"

This question was not even thought worthy of an answer.

"I must go," Sheila announced abruptly. "There's always so much to do round this place."

Even when you no longer have any official function here, thought Carole.

Graham quailed when the beam of Sheila's eye was turned on him. "Forget you ever heard anything about the confession — right?"

"Right," he echoed feebly.

"I know what a blabbermouth you are. For once, just keep that mouth of yours zipped, Graham. Not a word to a soul. Not even to Belinda — all right?"

His reaction to her last words suggested she had anticipated an intention to spill the beans to his aunt at the first opportunity. "No. No, of course not, Sheila."

Then, straightening her tall frame, raising the hood of her waterproof against the weather, and with the most perfunctory of good-byes, Sheila left the cottage. Carole had seen plenty of the energy that had created the Esmond Chadleigh shrine. But she had yet to see evidence of the charm, which must also have been there, to enlist the army of volunteers and wheedle large sums of money out of people to set up the project.

Still, at the end of the encounter, Carole felt pleased with the advance that she'd made in her relationship with Sheila Cartwright. There had been no rapprochement between them — and Carole thought such an event remained extremely unlikely ever to happen — but she had found a level at which to deal with the other woman. By exactly matching the abruptness and aggression, Carole could neutralise her power.

At the sounds of departure, Belinda Chadleigh appeared in the doorway (prompting speculation about how much else she had heard of the conversation). As Sheila bustled past her, the old woman caught her nephew's eye. They watched the former director leave the house, and Carole was surprised to see on both their faces an expression of pure loathing.

12

The first thing that hit Jude when Sandy Fairbarns ushered her into the hall was the noise. Then the smoke. Children screamed and shrieked above the low rumble of conversation. There was a crèche area cordoned off in the corner, manned by a couple of inmate orderlies with red armbands, but few of the children were in there playing with the plastic toys. The very tiny ones sat on their mothers' knees, but all the rest seemed to be rushing round the room, making as much noise as they possibly could, while their parents tried to make meaningful contacts between their fragmented lives.

The prisoners and their visitors sat in low easy chairs around low tables (low so that nothing could be passed unseen beneath them). Everyone seemed to have a cigarette in his or her mouth — in the case of the prisoners, usually a roll-up. Individual plumes of smoke rose up to join the fug that blurred the metal girders of the pitched roof above. The smell of smoke was more powerful than that of male sweat.

Jude knew she'd have to change all her clothes when she got home, hang them out in the garden for a long time, and have a bath to get rid of the tang of tobacco.

The weather outside made the space feel even stuffier. As a bass motif under the high-pitched chatter and shrieking, rain drummed on the building's metal roof.

But the atmosphere inside was quite relaxed. A prison officer by the door was checking visiting orders and handbags in a desultory way. Recognising Sandy, he waved the two of them through.

They looked around. Jude remembered Sandy's words about the exhausted-looking wives and their finely toned men-folk, and she did see a few examples of that, but the overall impression was not as depressing as she had expected. Beneath the layer of children's noise, there was quite a lot of laughter. People wandered back and forth to the canteen in the corner, returning with cups of tea, biscuits, and chocolate bars. No doubt there were many personal crises being played out in the conversations in the room, but there was very little sign of them on the surface.

Intuitively, Sandy read Jude's reaction. "Like a Sunday afternoon picnic, isn't it?"

she said. "You'd notice a big difference in a closed prison."

"Yes, I've been in a few."

Sandy did not follow this up with any enquiry, as most people — certainly Carole — would have done. Again Jude felt the relaxation of being with someone who truly respected her privacy.

"There he is."

Jude's eyes followed the pointing finger. Mervyn Hunter sat alone, uneasily upright on an easy chair, away from the noisy clusters, as near to the wall as he could possibly be.

He sprang up nervously as soon as he saw the two women approaching him. He didn't look much less nervous when he recognised who they were.

"Have you really come to see me?" he asked. His Northern voice was thin and tight, permanently stretched by emotion.

"Yes," said Sandy. "Didn't they tell you?"

"Well, obviously they told me, because I'm here. But they didn't tell who was coming."

Sandy sighed with exasperation. "The communications in this place are absolutely appalling."

"At least there is someone," said Mervyn.

"Blokes in my hut thought I was doing a 'moody visit.' "

This prompted a chuckle from Sandy, and Jude looked at her for elucidation.

"A 'moody visit' is a well-known prison scam. Men pretend they've got a visitor, so they don't go off on their afternoon's work duty, but are sent back to their huts to smarten up. Then they stay there all afternoon. Just another way of skiving."

"Ah. Thank you."

"Look, Jude, I've got some stuff to sort out, so I'll be off."

"You're not leaving me alone with her?" Mervyn Hunter's reaction was instinctive, panicked, surprisingly fearful.

Sandy turned back. "Yes, I've got things to get on with. Jude has come to visit you."

He slumped back into his chair, and leant his cheek against the wall, as if he wanted to burrow inside it, to disappear. Jude drew up another easy chair to sit in front of him, close enough to be heard, but no closer.

Amidst the raging noise of the hall, there was a long silence between them. Then, slowly, Mervyn moved his head round to take a quick look at her. When he saw she was looking at him, his gaze flickered away.

"You don't mind being alone with me, then?"

Jude shook her head and looked around the room. "Hardly alone, are we?"

"No. You're never alone in the nick. That's part of the punishment."

Again, in the general cacophony, they were a little pool of silence.

"You don't get a lot of visitors?" asked Jude finally.

A twitch of a head shake. He wouldn't let his eyes meet hers. "No. My family didn't want to keep in touch after. . . . And then of course her family. . . . Well, they wouldn't have come to see me, anyway. . . . And other people . . . no. But I manage," he concluded with an unsuccessful attempt at bravado.

Jude nodded, and let the stillness around them grow. She didn't make the mistake of pursuing anything, picking up the hints from his words. If he wanted to tell her anything about his crime, he would do so in his own good time.

"Reason I'm here," she said, "is because Sandy asked me to come."

"Why's that?"

"She thought you were down."

"I'm in the nick, aren't I? Hardly going to be dancing round the room celebrating."

"No. Sandy was thinking you seemed able to talk to me in our sessions."

"Other blokes there then, aren't there? Not just two of us." Once again he turned his cropped head to the wall, and closed his eyes as though in pain.

"Mervyn, are you afraid of being alone with a woman?"

A long time elapsed before he replied. Rain drummed relentlessly on the roof. Then, without moving his head or opening his eyes, he said, "Wouldn't be that surprising if I was, would it? Given my history?"

"I don't know your history," said Jude evenly.

"You want me to tell you?" he challenged.

"That's entirely up to you."

He hesitated for a moment, then shook his head. "It's in the papers, if you want to find out. Mervyn Hunter. Wetherby. 1991. You can find it if you're interested."

"I might do that."

He flashed her a quick look, checking whether he was being sent up, and seemed to relax a bit when he realised he wasn't.

"How're things going up at Bracketts? I heard that was working out quite well for you."

"Yes, it was. Thought that might be a way forward. That kind of work. I like the house. I've got quite interested in history,

123

read a lot since I've been in the nick. And up at Bracketts it's like . . . well, history's right there. They've got some books about the house in the library there, and sometimes on my lunch break they'd let me go in there and read the stuff. I liked that, learnt a lot."

"But the actual work you were doing . . . ?"

"Liked that, too. Gardening. I like the gardens up at Bracketts. I used to be. . . ." His mood changed. "Wouldn't imagine they'd want me back there now."

"After your confession?"

"So you know about that. Bet the whole bloody world knows about that now."

"But of course you had nothing to do with the crime?"

"No. As the police made clear to me . . . when they tore me off a strip for wasting their time. . . ." Strong emotion gripped him. "I'm sorry, it's just when I saw the body . . . I feel all this guilt, and I thought maybe there was something else I could be guilty for, and. . . ." He ran out of words.

"Why did the police let you go so quickly?"

"Because what I said didn't stand up. Even the most basic forensic examination had shown that the body was dead long before I was born. They said it was probably buried ninety years ago. Besides. . . ." His voice went very soft, hard to hear in the prevailing clangour ". . . I couldn't have been the murderer, because it was a man's body."

"And you reckon you're only a threat to women?"

He nodded, too overcome to speak.

"That's why you're afraid to be alone with a woman?"

Another nod. Then he said bitterly, "Perfectly reasonable fear . . . considering what happened last time I was alone with a woman. . . ."

"You don't seem to be frightened of me, Mervyn."

"No," he conceded. "But you haven't bossed me around. You haven't told me what to do . . . yet."

"Perhaps I never would."

"Oh, no." His voice was heavy with irony.

"Not all women are the same," said Jude gently.

"No, they don't *seem* to be the same. They may start out all nice and relaxed. But there comes a point, with all of them, when they start demanding things of you. Expecting things of you. Wanting you to do things." He closed his eyes, as if in reactive pain to the strong tremor of emotion that ran through his body.

"Have you seen a psychologist since you've been here at Austen?" asked Jude.

"Any number of them."

"And do they think you're a danger to women?"

"No. But what do they know? Every week you read another case. Some guy's let out of the nick, every psychologist in the world says he's no longer a public danger . . . first weekend out, he tops someone."

"And you're afraid you might do the same?"

Another silent, frightened nod, then, after a time, he went on. "That's why I was quite glad when they put me inside. Won't be a danger anymore, I thought. That's one thing at least I won't have to worry about. So I haven't minded being inside. The violence, the bullying, I don't like that, but at least I'm safe in here . . . and women are safe. . . ."

It seemed incongruous to imagine this thin neurotic as a danger to an entire gender, but Jude said nothing and let him ramble on.

"Most men in here — and in the other nicks before — they can't wait to get out. All they think about, all they dream about.

Me . . . that's when the pressure'll really start. When I get out. I won't trust myself then. It's less than a year now." He emitted a pained little laugh. "And I've behaved myself. If I'd been a bad prisoner, I'd have to serve my full sentence — might even get it extended. But I've been so good, I'll be out after the minimum tariff. Twelve years, that's all."

"Unless you start misbehaving now," Jude suggested lightheartedly, trying to ease the atmosphere.

"Don't think I haven't thought of it! Thought of getting reconvicted for something else." He shot her a sharp look, then relaxed a little. "I'm here at Austen to 'get used to the real world.' I don't think I'm ever going to fit in the 'real world.' It's too dangerous."

"The real world's too dangerous?"

"The real world with me in it's too dangerous."

"So you're afraid that in the real world, when you come out of here, you'll kill another woman?"

He nodded slowly. "Seems logical. That's why I'm in here, after all. I'll try not to, I won't go looking for it. I'll try never to be alone with a woman, but one day it's going to happen, isn't it? By accident.

There'll be me and some woman in a room, and. . . ." Savagely he choked back a sob. "It'll be just like the last time."

"Not necessarily." Jude used her most healing voice, which had soothed many more troubled than Mervyn Hunter. "You're still full of guilt, and you're still full of fear. That doesn't mean. . . ."

But she'd lost him. Abruptly, he rose to his feet. "Thank you for coming. It's very kind of you. But I'm afraid it won't work. This is my problem. No one else can help me with it."

And the thin figure in blue denim moved swiftly across the hall to the exit. Jude watched him go, all the way, out into the rain. She saw how carefully, how gently, he stepped around the hurtling children in his way.

And her imagination could not accommodate the idea that Mervyn Hunter would ever be a danger to anyone other than himself.

13

There was nothing on her answering machine when Carole got back from her visit to Graham Chadleigh-Bewes. Professor Marla Teischbaum would be ringing her later in the day.

The fridge offered little of excitement for lunch and, in a spirit of righteous abstinence, Carole made herself a cottage cheese salad (even though Jude would think she was eating "an abomination to God and Man"). Graham's greed had left her with a reaction of distaste, and she felt the need to be cleansed, detoxified of the memory.

After lunch, once she had tidied everything up, Carole sat back at her dining room table, and took out the file she had been given by Graham Chadleigh-Bewes. Although literature had never excited her that much — except as a point of reference for *The Times* crossword — recent events had made her hungry to find out more about Esmond Chadleigh.

There were twenty or thirty papers, some single sheets, others untidily stapled together. Only one dated from later than 1935, and she soon decided that it had been put in the file by mistake. Sent only the week before and addressed to Graham Chadleigh-Bewes, the letter was from a publisher, asking permission to reprint "Threnody for the Lost" in an anthology of war poetry for schools.

She rang through to Graham immediately, describing the letter and asking if it was meant to be handed over to Professor Teischbaum. Her surmise proved correct. He reckoned he must have picked it up with the other papers. (Having seen the state of his desk, she didn't find this hard to believe.) With no apology, he asked if she was going to be back at Bracketts soon, could she drop it in? Carole said that was unlikely, and he instructed her to post it back to him as soon as possible. The petulant tone in which he said this suggested that the misappropriation of the letter was her fault rather than his.

After this rudeness, she had no qualms about reading the contents of the file. (Nor did she feel guilty when, later in the afternoon, she went down to Fethering Stationers and made photocopies of all the documents.) If she was going to be used as a mere messenger by the Bracketts trustees,

130

then at least she had a right to know the message she was carrying. Besides, the schoolboy glee in Graham's manner had suggested Professor Teischbaum was going to be offered little that was controversial or confidential.

So it proved. The photocopies were mostly scraps of drafts from articles and verses written by Esmond Chadleigh, or correspondence written to him. His distinctive, untidily small handwriting, which veered slowly upwards to the right-hand side of unlined pages in his creative writing, was in evidence on none of the letters. Somewhere, presumably, was a collection of the letters that he had actually sent, rather than received. As she had the thought, Carole remembered Graham at the trustees meeting talking about "getting together a selection of the letters." If he was making as much progress on that task as he was with the biography, it might be a while before the published edition saw the light of day.

Thinking back to the trustees meeting, Carole also recalled the vehemence with which Graham had insisted that no contact should be made with "that dreadful woman." He'd had quite a change of heart since then; now he was actually volunteering material — albeit of minor importance — to Professor Teischbaum. Carole felt pretty sure it hadn't been Graham's own idea. His assertiveness was simply the bluster of a weak man; he'd be easily swayed by a stronger personality. The diplomatic rapprochement towards Professor Teischbaum was a sensible idea that could have come equally from Gina Locke or Sheila Cartwright. The latter must have been responsible, Carole felt pretty sure, given the total eclipse of Graham Chadleigh-Bewes's personality when in Sheila's presence.

There were only a few of the photocopied documents to which Carole gave more than a cursory glance. The first attracted her attention because it looked like a pastiche of a schoolboy's letter home. There were crossings-out and misspellings, and occasional sputterings of ink, where the writer's pen could not keep pace with his thoughts.

17 Leinster Terrace,
London W.
29 December 1917

Dear Chadders
  It was topping to see you over Christmas.

Back here in London under the beedy eye of Aunt P., I realise what an absolute collosal bore it would have been had I had to stay with her right through the festive season. I don't think she likes anyone — certainly not me or Mr. Lloyd George, so she's in an even sourer mood than usual. You're a real brick to have arranged my visit to Bracketts, and, as a small expression of my gratitude, my tuck box is open to you any time you feel a bit peckish next term. You never know. I might some day soon get some scoff through from the Aged Ps. When he started the war, the Kaeser should have been a bit more considerate, and thought about the effect it was going to have on communications between people in Calcutta and their poor starving sons incarserated in British public schools.

Talking of Aged Ps, I have, needless to say, done the proper thing by yours. The Bread and Butter Letter went off by yesterday's first post, so I hope it's arrived by now. They were real sports to take on another ravening inkey thirteen-year-old, and I really apreciated their generousity. I thought they seemed in frightfully good spirits, given the beastly circumstances.

I was also glad to meet Lieutenant Strider — what a brave chap. Seeing someone like him makes me feel really cheesed off yet again that we aren't old enough to go out and have a pot at Fritz ourselves. I'd like to get a bit of revenge for all those chaps Strider lost on the Somme. He seemed raring to go back, didn't he, champing at the bit to finish the job? Now our boys have got those new-fangled tanks out there, it shouldn't take long. You can see why Lieutenant Strider wants to be in at the kill, can't you? Be a real frost to miss the end, wouldn't it — like being run out on 99 and not making your century? Did you hear, incidentally, that old "Rattles" Rattenborough, School Captain of a couple of years back, has died of wounds he sustained during that Somme fixture? Bit of a damper when you hear about chaps you know, but it seems to be happening all too often these days.

On a more chearful note, your new house is an absolute pip. I just hope, when the Aged Ps finally come back from India, they get somewhere half as nice for us to kick our heels in. I know the place is a bit run down, but gosh, it's going to be topping when the builders and gardners have been let loose on it. I enjoyed the shooting we had on Boxing Day and, when the woods have been properly tidyed up, it'll be even better. Lieutenant Strider's a pretty handy shot, isn't he? I wonder if there's anything that fellow can't do? From what he was saying — though of course he didn't brag — he's a very useful batsman too. (I'm really determined to get into the nets early next season and consentrate on my batting.) You've got plenty of space in the grounds at Bracketts too, haven't you? I hope you do manage to persuade your Old Man to have a tennis court laid. That would be corking fun in the summer, and I hope I'm invited to have a game with you. Maybe I'll get my revenge for the trouncing your lot gave us in the House Cricket Competition!

So thank you, my dear old chum, for a topping Christmas. I was delighted to be part of your first one at Bracketts, and wish you and your family many more happy Christmasses in that jolly house. And you and I will meet up all too soon, won't we? Assuming the Kaeser doesn't suddenly invade, or we haven't starved because of the price of bread, within a week the prison gates will once again close behind us, and we'll face another term sentenced to the inhuman cruelty of Father Grey's pep-talks about "Unhealthy Thoughts" — not to mention "Blotter" Parsons' Irreg-

*ular Verbs. "Moritui te saluant," or what-
ever that wretched tag is he keeps quoting.
It's a monumental bore to have three more
years of school to face, when I for one
would much rather be out there for King
and Country giving Fritz a bloody nose!*

*On the train, make for the second car-
riage from the back, last compartement, as
usual. If there are any little Remove Worms
in their before I arrive, I know I can rely
on you to send them packing with flees in
their ears.*

Your chum,
Pickles

1917. So it was in that year that the
Chadleigh family had moved to Bracketts.
The year their elder son, Graham, was lost
at Passchendaele. "Given the beastly circumstances," it must have been hard for
Mr. and Mrs. Chadleigh to appear to be
"in frightfully good spirits" that Christmas.
She flicked through the papers and
found confirmation of their moving date in
a photocopy of what appeared to be a page
from a diary. The original must have been
blotched and foxed by damp, which made
it difficult to read. The handwriting was
much better than Esmond's, a spidery but
regular copperplate, and the contents sug-

gested it must have been written by his father. There was a splotch over the year, but the writer had firmly written in "1917" over it.

12 November 1917
The Lord and all the Holy Saints be praised! After all the exhausting uncertainty of the last few months, we did finally today take possession of Bracketts. There is an infinite amount still to be done, but I insisted that Mrs. Heggarty make up the beds in Sonia and my rooms, so that we can spend the first night of what I pray will be many happy ones in this blessed spot. When the rest of the servants arrive tomorrow, we will set about making the place habitable. I'm sure that over the next few months when the builders start their works, we will have to spend many nights in The Crown Inn at South Stapley, but at least for today, Bracketts is ours. It is a source of great pleasure to me that there is a cunningly hidden and complex Priest's Hole here, a sign that for many years this has been a home to good Catholics. I have asked Father Ternan to come over tomorrow to bless the house. Here we will put our griefs behind us, and look forward to however much more life God in His

wisdom sees fit to grant us. Thanks be to Him for this day!

So Graham Chadleigh had never lived at Bracketts. His young life had been cut short in the Flanders mud before his family took possession of the house.

This seemed to be confirmed by the photocopy of an undated letter written in an uneducated hand.

Dear Mr. Chadleigh,

I'm writing to you at the request of my commanding officer who had a request from Lieutenant Strider for anyone who witnessed what happened to his men on 26th October 1917 at Passchendaele. I was there on stretcher duty that day and bringing a wounded man back from the front over near Houthulst Forest when I saw Lieutenant Strider. I recognised him because I'd stretchered off a couple of his men during the big push on 12th October. On the 26th he was advancing at the head of maybe twenty men. It was hard to tell, what with the rain and fog, but they went past us on the duckboards what had been laid over the mud.

They'd only just gone past us and we wasn't no more than a hundred yards be-

hind them when a German shell landed and blew us off our feet. It put paid to the poor blighter on our stretcher and my mate got a big lump of shrapnel in his back. I was pretty shook up but thank the Lord not more than a bit brused.

When I managed to get up and look back towards the German lines, it was like the whole landscape had changed. When the smoke cleared, I could see this huge crater, which was already filling up with water and mud. Where the duckboards had been, there was nothing. Where Lieutenant Strider's men had been, there was nothing. They must have took a direct hit. I heard later that Lieutenant Strider himself survived, though badly wounded. I reckon that must've been because he was far enough ahead of his men, leading by example, to miss the full force of the blast.

But the others in that mud, I don't think they'll ever be found. And if, as I hear, your son was one of them, I'm very sorry. No one could have survived that.

I wish I didn't have to write what I'm writing, but I've been told you want to know the truth, and that's what I'm writing. I'm sorry I didn't know your son and can't give no personal memories of him, but I hope it will be a comfort to you *to know that he died bravely, facing the Boche. And now the War's going our way and victory's in sight, you can be sure that your son did his bit for King and Country.*

With condolences,
Yours truly,
J. T. Hodges (Private)

The fourth document Carole read seemed to be a draft for an essay, or a piece of journalism. Even if the upwards-slanting handwriting had not given it away, she had still heard enough about Esmond Chadleigh since she had become a trustee to recognise the tub-thumping, populist style.

Heroism

In these diminished days, what need do we have for heroes? Does the wage-slave travelling in the clockwork regularity of his train from dusty office to leafy suburb still have need for anyone to look up to? Do young working men, their minds full of the newest craze — wondering which greyhound chasing a mechanical hare can make their fortunes — ever dream of aspiring to heroism? Do young women, the brains inside their bobbed heads full only of the cacophony which goes by the name of "jazz," look for more solid qualities in a potential suitor than his pecuniary ability to buy a solitaire engagement ring? Do the deeds of Drake or Marlborough, Nelson or Wellington no longer strike any resonating chord in the tone-deaf ears of today's Britain?

I devoutly hope they still do. It is hardly yet ten years since the end of the greatest conflict ever witnessed on this poor benighted planet, hardly ten years since David Lloyd George, positing the question: "What is our task?," came up with the resounding answer: "To make Britain a fit country for heroes to live in." And has the great Welsh Wizard's task been accomplished? Or have we forgotten? Have we let our minds fill up to the brim with the newer wonders of the age — motor cars and telephones for every man jack of us, trains impelled along their rails by electricity rather than steam, and cinemas in which the actors can be heard to speak aloud, murmuring endearments that will be thought by each shopgirl to be meant for her ears alone?

By George, I hope we haven't! Heroes are no less important to a society than are gods. As the Almighty provides us with a pattern to which we can aspire but never attain, heroes are closer to our capabilities,

141

they are gods with human faces. Nelson was a mere mortal — and a sickly one at that — yet in the boiling seas of Trafalgar he triumphed over the might of Napoleon. Only a man, but what a man! Oh, yes, we need heroes.

I had the good fortune to know a hero, to know him well when I was a boy, and in him I found the qualities of manliness and good judgment on which I have tried to model my subsequent life.

The hero I know was a man called Lieutenant Hugo Strider. He was a friend of my father, and before 1914 shared with him those pursuits of fur and feather and fish with which the gentlemen of that long-gone age were wont to fill their leisure hours. But come the clarion call to arms, Hugo Strider, without a backward glance, gave up the pampered indolence of his former life, and turned all his mighty energies to the business of soldiering.

He was a fine officer, fierce in the face of the enemy, firm but compassionate amongst his own. Hugo Strider was loved by his men, who knew that he would never send them on a mission he was not prepared to face himself.

I had many reasons to know of his kindness, not least because he cut through the niceties of army regulations to ensure that my brother Graham could join his own regiment. I myself, then a bellicose stripling of some thirteen summers, tried to cajole him into making the same arrangements for me, but Lieutenant Strider wisely dissuaded me from such ambition. Not only would I be breaking the law, but a brat like me would also, as he told me with gentle firmness, be a perishing nuisance in the heat of battle!

My brother Graham did not survive the war. He gave his life to sustain the freedoms that we now enjoy — even if some of the denizens of this fine country use that hard-won precious freedom only to listen to jazz music! I am confident that my brother showed a degree of heroism, but I know for a fact of the heroism that was shown by Lieutenant Strider. He was the only survivor of the push at Passchendaele in which my brother died. At the head of his men, while behind him lives ended in the savage suddenness of shellfire, Lieutenant Strider was as good as his name and, oblivious to the fatal bullets and shellfire which filled the air, strode on towards the enemy lines.

And of that whole company he alone survived, though regrettably I cannot add to that verb "survived" the common ac-

companying adjective "unscathed." No, the Great War left its marks on Lieutenant Hugo Strider. After the doctors had done their makeshift repair work on his shattered body, at my father's invitation he came to stay at our family home Bracketts, there to convalesce and to contemplate the mighty actions in which

The piece stopped, suddenly, leaving two-thirds of the page blank. Whether Esmond Chadleigh had lost interest in what he was writing, decided the article wasn't up to standard, or had been interrupted, was impossible to know.

Carole was intrigued, not so much by the piece's content, as by why Graham Chadleigh-Bewes had thought it a suitable inclusion in the package of papers that she was due to hand over.

There were two more short letters she glanced at, both written in the same hand as the diary entry, that of Gerard Chadleigh, the boys' father. The first was a copy of the letter in the dining room display case at Bracketts, a rousing directive to stiffen the lip of his son in France, full of references to "King and Country," "doing the job that has to be done," "knowing instinctively and never questioning how a trueborn English man should behave." There was also some rather heavy-handed humour: *"After your exploits on the rugger pitch, where you were always wallowing in the stuff, I shouldn't think a bit of mud's going to put you off."*

Given the fact that the date was 24 August 1917, it was doubtful whether the letter had ever reached its intended recipient. Indeed, Gerard Chadleigh may never have posted it, the news of his son's death having rendered such an action tragically irrelevant.

The other letter, written by his father to Esmond at school, was dated 5 June 1919. The paragraph that caught Carole's eye concerned the heroic Lieutenant Strider.

Hugo is still with us, and I think could stay at Bracketts for a long time. He's still horribly crocked up by the beastly things that happened to him in the war, and the quacks don't think he'll ever recover the power of speech. But he never makes a fuss — against his nature to do anything like that — and I must say I'm extremely grateful for his companionship. He's still not keen on shooting, says he heard more than enough guns in Flanders to last him a lifetime, but we've had some very good days fishing on the Fether and caught some good size pike. I enjoy Hugo's company because we share so much — not just our religion, but a kind of bond forged by Graham's death. So I'm sure Hugo will still be here when you come home for the summer hols and. . . .

At that moment Carole's reading was interrupted by the ringing of the telephone. She gave her number.

"Good afternoon. This is Marla Teischbaum."

14

Laurence Hawker was a lot thinner than when Jude had last seen him, but still very good-looking. Though the face had fined down, making his nose more prominent, the lips retained their fleshiness; and his hair, though now grey, was still abundant. He wore his uniform black — leather jacket, shirt, jeans, and clumping lace-up shoes. He carried his laptop in a soft leather bag that somehow looked Italian. Laurence was too much the archetypal intellectual to be accepted without irony in England. His style went down much better abroad, which was presumably why he had spent most of his working life out of the country.

In spite of the coughs that intermittently rattled his body, at the corner of his mouth a permanent cigarette still hung. The smell brought back to Jude the atmosphere of the Austen Prison visiting hall, which she had only just managed to rid from her clothes.

But it was good to see Laurence, as she had rather suspected it would be.

It was Wednesday lunchtime, and they were in the Crown and Anchor. He had been quite happy to come down to Fethering. By train. Moving from university city to university city, he had never felt the need to learn how to drive. And the time involved in taking a trip out of London didn't seem to be a problem for him.

"I'm virtually retired now," he had said on the phone.

"Virtually? What does that mean?"

"Completely," he had replied.

Jude had her customary large Chilean chardonnay. Laurence drank whisky. No water, no ice. It was the only alcohol he drank, and he had at times drunk quite a lot of it.

"Funny," he drawled. "I'd never envisaged you ending up in a seaside town in West Sussex. You of all people."

"Who said anything about 'ending up'? I'm here at the moment. That's all. I've got a long way ahead of me, a lot of time to go to other places."

"Maybe," he said thoughtfully.

"And you? Are you 'ending up' in England?"

He nodded. "Oh, yes. Here for the duration."

His cigarette had reached a point where

he instinctively knew it needed stubbing out. The hand movements that killed it in the ashtray, found the packet in his pocket, shook out and lit the next one, were entirely automatic. He sucked on the new cigarette as though it were providing him with sustenance.

It certainly interested him more than the food on the plate in front of him. Laurence had never been much of an eater, though he loved restaurants. So long as he had his whisky and his cigarette, he was quite happy to — no, he positively enjoyed — watching his female companion of the moment tucking into the biggest platefuls that the chefs could provide. At that moment he drew pleasure from the sight of Jude working her way through the Crown and Anchor's crispy fish pie, while he broke the occasional morsel off his ham roll.

Jude would have put money on the fact that he still didn't sleep much. Still liked staying up late, talking the circular talk of academics, then snatching a few jumpy hours in bed before rising early to light up the first cigarette of a new day.

Laurence Hawker had cultivated self-neglect almost into an art form.

Jude often wondered why she was so drawn to him. Had she ever attempted to describe him, she knew she would project the image of a total poseur. The black clothes, the languid voice, the total unconcern for the practicalities of life, the cigarettes, the whisky, the promiscuity . . . they all made him sound like a refugee from the Seventies, the redbrick academic who could spout for hours on the minutiae of the latest vogue in critical theory.

But what no description could put across was Laurence Hawker's in-built irony. There was always a twinkle in his eyes, and awareness of his potential absurdity that removed the risk of his ever being thought absurd. He had always been postmodernist, even before the expression was coined.

"What about you?" he asked. "Are you working?"

"Not a full-time job. But I do some of the healing, counselling stuff, you know. . . ."

He nodded. That was another thing about Laurence. Though he could be excoriatingly funny at the expense of other academics, he never sent up his friends. If there was something they took seriously, he respected that. He had never uttered a word of criticism or scepticism about Jude's alternative therapies.

Mischievously, she thought she'd test the limits of his tolerance. "And I have got involved in solving the occasional murder."

This, too, he took at face value. "You'd be good at that. Good understanding of human nature, suitably lateral mind. Yes, would suit you."

"Ever appealed to you, Laurence?"

He chuckled languidly. "Well, I certainly know about back-stabbing in academia. Trouble is, there are always too many suspects."

"There's something around at the moment on which you might be quite helpful."

"Oh?"

"Well, I say there is. Not much to go on yet. A body's been found, that's all. A skeleton. No news yet whether it's even a murder."

"Let's assume it is. Always makes for more fun."

"Mm."

"But why might I be helpful?"

"There is a literary connection, Laurence. The body was found in the grounds of a house called Bracketts."

"Ah." He was there instantly. "Esmond Chadleigh."

"You know his work?"

"Hard to avoid knowing 'Threnody for the Lost.' Or, if you had parents like mine, *Naughty Nursie's Nursery Rhymes*. I even read the impossibly twee *Demesnes of Eregonne*. Yes, he was an interesting figure. Minor figure, of course. I think he knew that, and I think the fact made him very miserable. Versatility can be a curse for a writer, you know. The curse of being 'almost good at everything.' "

"Have you studied Esmond Chadleigh, then?"

"No, not studied seriously. Read a lot of stuff around him. I'm quite interested in that between the wars period, when it was still possible to make a living as a 'man of letters.' " There was a wistfulness in his voice, and Jude wondered whether that was what Laurence himself would really like to have been.

"Do you think Chadleigh was more interesting as a man than he was as a writer?"

"Sadly, no. Settled comfortably at Bracketts at a relatively early age, cushioned by a bit of family money. Stayed married to the same woman till he died. No great emotional upheavals in his life, I'm afraid. Not the stuff of biographies."

"At least two are being written of him."

"Are they? I'm afraid I won't be rushing out to buy either. Esmond Chadleigh was too like too many other literary figures to be that interesting in his own right. There was the Catholicism, of course, but there are plenty of other, more interestingly neurotic Catholics in English literature."

"Had he got a strong faith?"

"Like many others Catholics, Esmond had a crust of the Catholic complacency over a thin layer of doubt, which spanned a deep morass of sheer terror."

"Right. Well, nice to know an expert." Jude grinned at him. "When I need further information, I'll come and pick your brains mercilessly."

"Sounds fun." Laurence Hawker looked at her plate, now empty of crispy fish pie, then at his equally empty whisky glass. "Could I offer you another drink, perhaps?"

"I have both whisky and wine back at home."

"Ah."

"Would you maybe like to see the delights of Woodside Cottage?"

"Yes. Thank you, Jude. I'd like that very much."

"Hello?"

"Carole, it's Jude."

"Where are you calling from?"

"Home." That was odd. Jude would never use the phone when just dropping in was an option. "Just a couple of things I found out from Mervyn Hunter."

"I didn't know you were going to see him." Once again pique was not far from Carole's voice.

"No. Well, I told you, I don't talk a lot about that prison stuff."

"Right." But it didn't sound as though everything was quite right, so far as Carole was concerned.

"Anyway, I found out two important details about the body."

"The Bracketts body?"

"Yes. These were the reasons why the police didn't take Mervyn's confession seriously. For a start, the skeleton is a man's. And second, it had been buried in the kitchen garden for a very long time."

"How long?"

"Before Mervyn was even born. Possibly as much as ninety years ago."

Carole quickly did the calculation. Second decade of the twentieth century. "That's very interesting. Thank you for telling me."

Carole was about to ask why Jude hadn't come round to give the information in person, but missed the opportunity, as her friend went on, "You didn't find out anything more at Bracketts?"

"About the body? No."

"I'm amazed there still hasn't been anything in the press. It's not the sort of thing you can keep quiet for long."

"Sheila Cartwright claimed to have a direct line to the chief constable. Maybe that's it. She's persuaded him to sit on it."

"Can't do that forever."

"No. By the way, I've fixed up my meeting with Professor Teischbaum."

"Ah." Jude sounded intrigued, as if she wanted to know more. But then there was a sound on the line, and she seemed to change her mind. "Tell me all the details when the deed is done."

"Yes. Of course," said Carole.

"Must dash. 'Bye."

It was with a familiar frustration that Carole put down the phone. Jude could sometimes be so infuriating. She didn't deliberately withhold information, just rarely volunteered it. There remained vast areas of her life about which her neighbour knew nothing at all.

And was Carole being fanciful to imagine she'd heard the distant rumble of a man's voice on the line just before Jude rang off? Not, of course, that it was her business. Jude had a perfect right to live her life exactly as she chose, giving away only as much information about it as she chose to. And, thought Carole with a return of frustration, that was a right of which Jude took full advantage.

Still, no time to brood. She was meeting Marla Teischbaum in Fedborough at four. The professor had offered to come to High Tor, but Carole thought she'd feel safer on neutral ground, so they'd agreed to meet at Marla's hotel, The Pelling Arms.

Which meant that if her Labrador, Gulliver, was going to get his walk on Fethering Beach, Carole would have to get her skates on. Even though he found the hot weather oppressive, Gulliver was panting, pathetically grateful to her for being taken out.

She didn't exactly look at Woodside Cottage as they walked past, but Carole couldn't help noticing that the curtains of Jude's bedroom were drawn. Maybe she wasn't well? Maybe Carole should go round with some neighbourly grapes? No, probably not.

She wondered what was going on, and again her sense of frustration returned.

It wasn't that Carole didn't like mysteries. But she liked mysteries that were capable of rational solution. And those which surrounded her friend Jude very rarely were.

Carole wasn't quite sure what she'd been expecting from Professor Marla Teischbaum. The voice on the phone had suggested that though she worked there, she wasn't a native of California. She certainly wasn't expecting the extremely tall, elegant woman who uncoiled from a chintzy armchair to greet her in the residents' lounge of The Pelling Arms.

"You must be Mrs. Seddon."

"Please, call me Carole."

"And I'm Marla." They sat down. "Can I get you coffee or something?"

"Coffee would be nice, thank you."

"Well, I'll do my best. The secret in this place seems to be to get your order in quickly. Then, after the second or third time you order it, something may arrive. Excuse me, I'll go to the bar. Passing waiters in this lounge are rarer than passenger pigeons. Regular coffee, is it?"

"Please."

Carole watched the tall figure leave the room. Marla wore trousers in the subtlest of green, and a loosely hanging oatmeal top that, in spite of its price, was probably still designated a T-shirt. Her neatly sculpted hair was a rich chestnut, almost copper beech in tone. Her makeup was expertly applied, highlighting the dark eyes and full lips. She didn't match any of the scruffy stereotypes of academics; someone passing her in the street might mark her down as an actress or a model.

When she returned, Marla Teischbaum sank with a graceful mock ennui into her armchair. "They appeared to get the message," she said dubiously.

"Do I detect you're not overimpressed with The Pelling Arms?"

"Gard, where do I start? Goodwill, friendliness of staff, I give them one hundred percent. Efficiency . . . I'm afraid a bit lower down the scale." She enumerated on her long, beautifully manicured fingers: "No elevators, no air-conditioning, no ice machines, no. . . ." She stopped and smiled, setting off a ripple of fine lines around her mocha-coloured eyes. "Sorry, I'm sounding terribly American."

"Don't worry. You're not treading on any toes. The local reputation of this place isn't that great."

"Right. Anyway, it's somewhere to stay. Right area. Location is what counts, after all. Convenient for the County Records Office in Chichester." She paused significantly. "And, of course, for Bracketts. . . ."

"Yes."

"By the way, Carole, I do know why you're here."

"Well, yes, of course." Carole found herself unaccountably flustered. "I'm here because you wanted to meet me."

Marla Teischbaum raised a single long finger of objection. "Not entirely correct. With no offence to you at all, I hope, Carole, I did not initially ask for a meeting with you. I approached the Bracketts trustees requesting cooperation for my researches into Esmond Chadleigh."

"Yes. And the trustees are prepared to cooperate." Carole tapped the folder on her lap. "This is an expression of their willingness to share with you. . . ."

But the slow shaking of Marla's head dried up her words. "No," said the American

159

calmly. "You know and I know that that is just a gesture, throwing a bone to the slavering dog in the hope that it will get distracted and forget to attack you." The assessment was so accurate that Carole could only hang her head in embarrassment. "And I wouldn't be surprised if such expressions have been used about me in your trustees meetings."

Again it was too close to the truth for any sensible argument to be offered. All Carole could say was "I'm sorry. I'm not really an expert on Esmond Chadleigh."

"I am well aware of that. Also well aware of the fact that that is why you have been sent to see me."

Marla Teischbaum's understanding of the situation was so total that Carole started to wonder whether the professor actually had a spy in the Bracketts camp. Was one of the trustees feeding her information? If that were the case, Carole didn't have to look far for her chief suspect. She remembered the glee with which George Ferris had brought up Professor Marla Teischbaum's name at the last meeting. And he'd been the one who knew she was about to visit West Sussex. Yes, Carole could see George Ferris relishing the glamour a woman like Marla might bring into the tedium of his retirement.

"You're the perfect emissary," the American went on, one hand unconsciously smoothing the contours of her chestnut hair. "Since you know virtually nothing about my chosen subject, you can't let slip anything about Esmond Chadleigh that you shouldn't."

"What kind of thing did you have in mind?" asked Carole, suddenly assertive. The trustees had cast her in a subservient role, but that didn't mean she had to play it their way. "Some dirt? That's what the trustees think you're after. You won't be surprised to hear that when your name came up for discussion, the word 'muckraker' was used."

"I'm not surprised at all. It is, as it happens, an inaccurate description, but there's no reason why you should believe that. What I am after, in fact, is not dirt but truth."

Carole did not disbelieve her. Increasingly she was feeling a tension between the part she was meant to be playing and her instinctive trust in the other woman. But all she could say was "I'm sorry. I'm afraid I can't help you."

"What do you mean, Carole? That you don't deal in truth?"

"In my current situation," came the curt reply, "I deal only with what the trustees have given me to deal with. A very limited role, with which — you will not be surprised to hear — I am far from happy."

Marla smiled. "I was beginning to detect that, yes."

Carole gathered up her handbag from the floor. "So I think I may as well leave, really." She waved the folder. "Shall I take this back with me? If you think it's going to be completely useless to you."

"No, no, I'll take it. Thank you. Could be something there I haven't seen before. I don't think even Graham Chadleigh-Bewes would be quite so crass as to give me all rubbish."

"I had a glance through the stuff. Some of it did look interesting. But, as we have established, I am not an expert."

"No. But you're clearly shrewd. So, if you thought some of the material was interesting, I will accept it with gracious thanks for your recommendation."

As Marla Teischbaum took the folder, she looked again towards the bar. "Sorry. As you see, The Pelling Arms is not really geared to this encounter. There's no chance of the coffee arriving for a short meeting."

"Well, there you go," said Carole, rising awkwardly to her feet. Marla's poise made her feel clumsy.

"So what do you report back to your trustees?"

"Sorry?"

"Presumably they will want to hear what happened at this meeting."

"I suppose they will, but a formal report wasn't discussed."

"It was thought that handing this file over to me would be the end of the matter? That I would gracefully touch my forelock, and return to the wilds of California?"

"Well . . . maybe. Yes, perhaps that was what they hoped."

The professor shook her head in wry disbelief. "Gard, they sure don't know me, do they?" She tapped the file. "This was Graham's idea, I take it . . . ?"

"I, er . . . I'm not sure that he came up with it completely on his own."

"No. Unlikely, I agree. I don't think Graham's ever come up with anything completely on his own. So who was it? Gina Locke, the new director? I'd be surprised. From the correspondence I've had with her, she sounds too bright to think something like this'd work."

"I'm not sure. . . ."

But as Carole floundered, a light of knowledge came into Marla's dark eyes. "No, of course. Oh, Gard, yes, I've got it. Her predecessor. The One Who Will Not Go Away. Yes, this little scheme has Sheila Cartwright written all over it."

There seemed no point in denying this conclusion. "Now I really had better be going."

"Sure." But Marla Teischbaum held Carole there by the force of her personality, as she said, "Even if you haven't got a formal arrangement to report back to the trustees, I do have a message for them. I am going to write my biography of Esmond Chadleigh."

"Can I ask why?"

"What do you mean — *why?*"

"Why Esmond Chadleigh? There are so many other literary figures you could write about. Why did you choose him?"

Marla Teischbaum's head shook slowly, in a mixture of exasperation and disbelief. "You don't get it, do you, Carole? You don't get what being an academic is about."

"Perhaps not," said Carole, trying desperately not to sound humble.

"It's not random, you know. In my line of work, you don't suddenly say to yourself, 'Hey, I feel a biography coming on. Who's it going to be? Whom shall I pick? Maybe I should stick a pin in some list of authors and see who I come up with. . . .' "

Carole felt uncomfortable, as though she was being treated like a child, as the professor continued, "I like Esmond Chadleigh's work. What I know about his life intrigues me. I want to find out more. That is why I'm writing his biography."

The conviction in Marla Teischbaum's voice did not diminish Carole's discomfort. She was silent.

"And I am going to make that biography as accurate as I possibly can. If I discover that Graham Chadleigh-Bewes's assessment of his grandfather is correct, that Esmond really was a saint walking on earth, then fine, that is what my biography will say, too. But if I find information that does not fit in with that rosy picture, I will use it. If this folder is the extent of the trustees' cooperation with me, I'm grateful, but I think they're being very foolish. Continued cooperation with me offers them a much better chance of influencing what I write than they will get by making an enemy of me.

"I don't blame the other trustees for the way they're reacting. I certainly don't blame

Graham. He's just weak, and worried that I'm going to publish my biography before he gets round to finishing his. But I know where the power lies at Bracketts. Still. It's Sheila Cartwright. She's the one behind this deliberate blocking of my researches. She has already made an enemy of me." The lipsticked mouth framed a bittersweet smile. "You have my permission to tell her that, Carole, if you wish."

At that moment a spotty youth in a blue waiter's jacket appeared with a tray of coffee. There was a silence while he put it down on the table between the two women.

"Are you sure you won't have some, Carole? Now it's actually arrived?"

"No. I think I'd better be on my way."

"Fine. Your choice. Just one thing. . . ."

"What?" Carole turned to look back at the elegant creature in the armchair. Again an unconscious hand was caressing the neat contours of her shining hair.

"I do know about the body that was found in the kitchen garden," said Marla Teischbaum.

16

Jude emerged slowly from a deep sleep, and took a moment or two to orient herself. It wasn't that she didn't know where she was. She knew exactly where she was. She was in her own bedroom, but it took a moment or two for her to realise what was different about that bedroom.

A late afternoon breeze had risen and it lifted the curtains, admitting the occasional streak of sunlight across the tousled bed. But the air still felt warm on Jude's ample nakedness.

It was Laurence's presence that made the room different. That, and the smell of smoke he brought with him. The permanent cigarette was back in place now; he had removed it only while they made love. He had his back to her, sitting totally naked on the stool in front of her dressing table while he keyed something into his laptop. The nobbles of his spine stood out like a line of knuckles down his back.

Her slight movement on the bed attracted his attention. He turned and flashed her a little smile of complicity.

"You've lost a lot of weight."

"Uh-huh," he said, and coughed.

"Which is more than can be said for me."

"One of your attractions, Jude. With you, I always got my money's worth."

"What are you doing, Laurence?"

"Just checking my E-mails."

"From other women?" asked Jude languorously.

"I bloody hope so."

She chuckled. Other women had no power to hurt her now. She found, as she got older, she preferred relationships outside the white heat of exclusive, jealous love. Old friends with whom she might not even make love. Or she might. And it was usually good when she did. Certainly Laurence retained his old skills. And their bodies remembered each other.

"Hope you don't mind," said Laurence. "I've plugged into your phone line."

"No problem." She traced a hand idly over her full breasts. "Maybe I should come into the twenty-first century and get E-mail."

"You won't regret it, I promise you. And there's the whole Internet out there, too. Brilliant for my sort of work. Researching articles, going through newspapers for references. The amount you can just download. University libraries hardly get used these days."

"Must spoil your fun rather, Laurence. Seem to remember, you always had a taste for librarians."

"True," he agreed. He had never been secretive about his conquests. That at the time Jude had been obsessively in love with him, had made things worse. She'd even sometimes found herself yearning for a bit of the dishonest duplicity you got from most men. But no. Laurence always told her.

"Hey." She had a thought. "Does this mean you can access any newspaper story?"

"Within certain parameters. I've got subscriptions to a good few of the newspapers. *The Times* and *The Sunday Times*, for example. You can get anything back to about 1985 without too much problem."

Jude swung her legs round to the floor. "Great. See if you can find me something about a man — well, a boy — named Mervyn Hunter. Twelve years back — no, about eleven years back."

"I'll have a go. Can you give me any clue as to what I'm looking for?"

"He was convicted of murder. Murdering a woman."

"Ah. Back to your new hobby, are we?"

"Any objections?"

"No. Murder's quite interesting. Better than the alternatives. Just think," he added with distaste, "it could have been golf."

It was too warm to bother to put anything on. As she passed, Jude ran her hand lightly across his shoulders. "What do you want? Tea? Coffee?"

"Whisky," he said.

When she came back upstairs with his whisky and a herb tea for herself, he had already found what he was looking for. "I'd get you a hard copy, but I don't have a printer with me. I can easily run one off as soon as I get back to civilisation."

"Don't worry. All I need are the facts."

Jude's naked body pressed against Laurence's back as she read what was on the laptop screen.

The facts the report from *The Times* revealed were straightforward. Mervyn Hunter, a jobbing gardener aged just eighteen, had gone out one evening to a club near his parents' home in Wetherby. According to witnesses, he had drunk a lot and been seen dancing with a local girl named Lee-Anne Rogers. She was twenty-three, and worked in a betting shop in Wetherby. They were seen to leave the club together and to get into her car. The vehicle was discovered the next morning in a lay-by, on the road to Sicklinghall, that was popular after dark with couples in cars. Lee-Anne Rogers's body was in the back seat. She had been strangled. When confronted by the police the same morning, Mervyn Hunter had confessed to killing her. At his trial, the judge, saying that he was "a menace to law-abiding society and particularly to innocent young women," had sentenced Mervyn to life imprisonment.

"I'm sure I can do some follow-ups and get more information if you want it," said Laurence.

"No, that's fine for the time being. I just need the basics. Thank you." And joining her arms around his neck, she gave him a big hug.

"I'd forgotten how nice that was," he murmured. "All that warm flesh against me."

He rose from his stool and turned in her arms until he was facing her. Then he put his arms around her in a crushing embrace. They tottered unsteadily, and fell back onto the bed.

In the stillness that followed, Jude held Laurence's bony body in her capacious arms. One hand slid its way along the corrugations of his spine.

"You're ill, aren't you?" she said.

17

There were two messages on Carole's answering machine when she got back to High Tor. One from Sheila Cartwright, one from Gina Locke. Both asking the same thing. How had her meeting gone with Marla Teischbaum?

Sheila's number was engaged, so Carole spoke to Gina first. She gave the director a quick résumé of her encounter at The Pelling Arms, finishing with the news that the American knew about the body in the kitchen garden.

"Oh," Gina responded. "Sheila won't be happy about that." And she couldn't keep the satisfaction out of her voice.

For a moment Carole wondered. Gina's animus against her rival was so strong, was it possible that she might have leaked the information to Marla Teischbaum? An attempt to put Sheila Cartwright in her place? To demonstrate the frailty of her influence over Paul, the chief constable? It was an intriguing possibility.

But when Sheila herself heard that

Marla knew about the body, the reaction was surprisingly muted. "It was bound to get out at some point. Only a matter of time. Did she say what she planned to do with the information, Carole?"

"No."

"Oh, well, wait and see. If we can keep it quiet till the house closes at the end of the week, well and good. If not, *tant pis.* We'll just see to it that all press enquiries are handled through the police."

In spite of her bullying and blackmailing tactics, at times, Carole realised, Sheila Cartwright could be extremely pragmatic and sensible.

"But it can't be kept secret much longer, Jude," said Carole. "I mean, they've managed to keep it quiet for nearly a week, but if Professor Teischbaum has heard about the skeleton, then it's only a matter of time before lots of other people do, and then it's only a matter of time before the press gets hold of the story."

"And you say you think it may have been leaked to the professor by one of the trustees?"

"I don't have any proof of that, Jude. . . ." She wondered whether to confide her recent misgiving about Gina Locke, but it seemed too unsubstantial. "I'm very suspicious, though, of George Ferris. Ex-librarian. Looks like he's escaped from one of the lesser works of Tolkien. He knew Marla Teischbaum was going to be over here. I wouldn't be surprised if he's got a hotline to her."

"And did she imply that she was going to use her knowledge of the body as a bargaining counter or something of that kind?"

Carole screwed up her face. "Not really. I mean, how could she use it? Threaten to break the news to the press? It's got to come out soon, anyway."

"Why do you think the police are sitting on the story?"

"If Sheila Cartwright's to be believed, it's because of pressure she's putting on the chief constable. Her friend Paul." Something of Sheila's autocratic manner coloured the name as Carole spoke it. "I know she's well-connected, but I doubt if she could do that. On the other hand, if they can keep the story quiet just till the end of this week, when the house is closed to the public for the winter, that would make sense. Save a lot of gawpers and ghouls coming round to inspect the scene of the crime."

"If there is a crime."

"Hm."

Carole was feeling resentful. Jude had done it to her again. Just breezed round to High Tor with no explanation for why her bedroom curtains had been drawn earlier in the afternoon. And, as ever, before Carole had had time to ascertain basic facts, the conversation had moved on. Still, too late to do anything about it now.

She went on, "Mind you, there is a logic to holding the story till Bracketts becomes a private house again for the winter. I can see that would appeal to the people who run the place."

"But Sheila Cartwright no longer has anything to do with running the place."

"You try telling her that."

"I had a thought, Carole. . . ."

"Hm?"

"I'd quite fancy doing another guided tour of Bracketts. . . ."

"Good idea."

"If there *is* a mystery to solve, I'd like to get a feeling of the place."

"Yes. Well, it'll have to be within the next week."

"I know. Would it bore you to come too?"

"No, Jude. I'd like that very much." She remembered that she hadn't yet got round to posting the letter Graham had mistakenly left in the file for Marla Teischbaum. "As a matter of fact, there's something I've got to drop in there, anyway."

"How about going tomorrow? That all right for you?"

"Fine."

"And I've got a friend staying with me. He might want to come, too."

"Oh," was all Carole said, but she felt a little pang of disappointment. Was this the explanation of the closed curtains? She hadn't had many friends throughout her life, and she knew she was overpossessive of those she had. But with Jude, she'd been fine, known that her neighbour had a life of many strands, and usually managed not to feel slighted when her friend was off in another part of her life. But never before had Jude suggested involving someone else in one of their mystery investigations.

The weather was much better than the last time Carole had been to Bracketts, but summer was just a memory. Though direct sunlight remained hot, in the shadows she could feel the chill breath of autumn.

Nor had she warmed, on the drive from Fethering, to Laurence Hawker. For one thing, as soon as they all got into her neat white Renault, without asking for permission, he had immediately lit up a cigarette. Even though he had trailed the hand which held it out of the open window, Carole still regarded this as a serious breach of good manners. Nor was she taken by the black leather jacket and matching uniform, or his general air of amused ennui. She saw only the exterior of a languid poseur and, having never been in love with him, could not see any of the better, interior qualities that Jude appreciated.

But he certainly knew his stuff about Esmond Chadleigh and, rather grudgingly, Carole recognised she had to be grateful for that. If Jude had enrolled him on this one particular mission because of his special knowledge of Bracketts's literary background, no problem. He could be a consultant, but not a participant. Jude suggesting any other role for Laurence would sound warning bells.

Carole couldn't work out what the relationship between the two of them was, and that annoyed her. She liked to have things cut and dried in her mind. Jude and Laurence evidently knew one another well, and had done so for quite a while. But whether they ever had been lovers or — an even more incongruous idea — still were lovers, Carole had no idea. She had never possessed those antennae built into many women, which could instantly identify and analyse the sexual content of any relationship. The instinct was not one she actively wished for, though the lack of it did sometimes cause her aggravation.

Because she couldn't define their level of closeness, Carole was awkward in Jude and Laurence's company. Though there was no overt manifestation of affection like handholding or an arm around a shoulder, she still didn't want to crowd them. Going from room to room through the narrow corridors of Bracketts, Carole felt obliged to walk ahead or behind, leaving them the option of walking side by side, should they so wish.

Her discomfort was increased by the fact that she knew she was being stupid, allowing yet another of the infuriating traits of her character to hobble her behaviour. Being Carole Seddon was sometimes a very tiresome business, overreacting to imagined slights and tightening social Gordian knots that cried out to be sliced through quickly.

On this visit to Bracketts they didn't bother with the gardens. Though very beautiful and punctiliously maintained by teams of volunteers, there was nothing in them of literary relevance. The only part of the grounds that Carole and Jude might have wished to inspect, the kitchen garden, was firmly locked off by its substantial gates. Whether behind those gates police forensic teams still beavered away, sifting the ground for clues about a long-dead body, they had no means of knowing.

The interior of the house, however, still breathed the personality of Esmond Chadleigh. His image was hard to escape. The walls were covered with paintings, photographs, and cartoons of the writer at various stages of his life. From his twenties on, he had affected one of those big moustaches with pointed ends that were quite acceptable until Stalin gave them a bad name. Esmond Chadleigh's short, compact figure thickened out considerably as he got older; the floppy hair and moustache turned white, but there was always a look of ease. There was nothing of the tortured artist about him. He was photographed with his wife, with his two daughters, Sonia and Belinda, enjoying the idyllic surrounding of Bracketts, and they looked like a genuinely happy family. If there had been any disappointments in Esmond Chadleigh's professional or personal life, they were not evident in the mood of the pictures selected for display.

In spite of her resentment of Laurence Hawker, Carole could not deny that he was an extremely valuable person to have around on such a trip. The official tour was conducted by one of the Bracketts volunteers. The team who worked inside the house were all of a type, doughty white-haired women in their sixties, unwavering in their devotion to Catholicism and to the blessed memory of Esmond Chadleigh. They didn't have an official uniform, but since they all dressed in white blouses, navy jackets, and dark-coloured kilts, they might as well have done. They knew their set routine very well, and were up to answering basic supplementary questions about Esmond Chadleigh's life and work, but they couldn't provide the kind of detailed glosses that Laurence Hawker could.

Without Laurence, Carole and Jude wouldn't have heard about the rift with Chesterton and Belloc during the early Thirties. Though soon patched up, it was something that in later life Esmond Chadleigh blamed for his relative lack of recognition compared to the other two; they, he said — though with no justification — had poisoned the literary establishment against him. Laurence also told them of the loss of faith that temporarily affected the writer in 1939, in disbelief that any God could allow the repeat atrocity of another world war. And it was from Laurence that Carole and Jude heard of the rumour that in the 1950s, Esmond Chadleigh had a mistress in London who worked for one of his publishers.

None of this — or anything like it — was mentioned by the white-haired lady who led them round the house. Bracketts was a shrine to the extent that its acolytes spoke only words of hagiography. And Carole got the feeling that their version of events would be very similar to the one which would appear in Graham's book . . . if it was ever completed.

There was one exhibit that she had been looking forward to pointing out to Laurence Hawker, perhaps to gain a moment of one-upmanship from her prior knowledge of the building. But when they reached the dining room, she was disappointed. The glass-topped display case, the mini-shrine to the tragic Graham Chadleigh, was empty. In the space, a handwritten note read: "Contents removed for cleaning and restoration."

"I'm sorry," Carole murmured. "I was

hoping to be able to show you the inspiration for 'Threnody for the Lost.' "

"Never mind," drawled Laurence Hawker. "Never my favourite work. Rather too overt and simplistic a plucking of the heartstrings for my taste."

Carole, for whom it was a favourite poem, said nothing.

Laurence looked around with hopeless irritation. "Do you think anyone'd notice if I lit up in here?"

Jude giggled. "You'll find out only if you try."

Which annoyed Carole further. It was, apart from anything else, a very irresponsible thing to say. A smoking ban in a house like Bracketts wasn't just authoritarianism; it was to avoid a genuine fire risk. As a trustee, it would be her duty to make that point very firmly if Laurence Hawker started to take out his cigarettes and lighter.

But he didn't. Instead, he gave in to another of his deep coughs, which rattled through his body, and which Carole was beginning to find extremely irritating.

One of the highlights of the Bracketts guided tour was the priest's hole. The lady conducting them around stopped in front of the section of panelling with practised awe. She was dauntingly well-spoken, but

182

contrived to impart to her commentary no dramatic impact at all.

"And here we have one of the most unusual features of the house. It was incorporated into the original design by the Doughtscombe family, because by the time the building was completed in 1589, the celebration of Catholic Mass had been made illegal, in the wake of the Ridolfo Plot, the Babington Plot, and the execution of Mary Queen of Scots in 1587. Since they couldn't go to Mass in a church, wealthy and devout Catholic families would invite priests to celebrate the rite in their homes. And the very real danger of raids by the Protestant authorities led to the construction of hideouts for those Catholic priests. The one here at Bracketts is one of the best-preserved in the country. Also one of the best-concealed, and there is anecdotal evidence that some of the owners of the house after the Doughtscombe family died out in the early eighteenth century were completely unaware of the priest's hole's existence.

"From the outside of the house no windows are visible, but comparisons of the exterior dimensions and the measurements of this landing demonstrate that there is a space within the walls unaccounted for.

And this is what has always been inside that space."

She drew back a segment of the wall panelling, with all the impact of a wet paper bag bursting. But even her flat delivery could not prevent a gasp from the assembled tour party. Revealed by the sliding panel was a room some twelve feet by eight. It was on a higher level than the landing, and anyone entering would have needed to step up about a foot. Cunningly concealed lighting in the carved ceiling and the lack of windows gave the space an eerie, cell-like quality, which was accentuated by a low table covered with a white cloth. On this stood two lighted candles in tall brass candlesticks, and a large, open leather-bound book. The impression of an altar was for the benefit of the tourists — Mass would never actually have been celebrated in this room — but the image was undeniably impressive.

"Kind of place you'd keep an electricity meter," Laurence Hawker murmured. "Wasn't there a *Monty Python* sketch in which someone came to read the priest?"

"I think they came to read the poet," Jude replied, with a suppressed giggle.

Laurence, too, let out a laugh, which quickly transformed into another of his racking coughs.

It was Carole's view that the revelation of the priest's hole should have been greeted by rather more reverence.

Arrival at the gift shop signalled the end of the tour, and Laurence Hawker reckoned this also gave him permission to smoke. So, while the two women inspected Esmond Chadleigh postcards, mugs, and other wares, he lit up a cigarette. Two new white-haired, kilted ladies immediately materialised and offered him the option of stubbing out the cigarette or leaving the building. With an amiable shrug, he went outside. Jude grinned. Carole couldn't see anything funny about it.

Jude lingered over a white plate with the whole text of "Threnody for the Lost" printed on it in black gothic lettering. "It's so kitsch, I almost feel I should buy it."

"Well, don't," said Carole severely. "You've got quite enough rubbish in your house already."

Jude raised an amused eyebrow at this, but said nothing. She knew the cause of Carole's scratchiness. It had rarely in the past proved a good idea to mix friends from different areas of her life. But Jude wasn't really troubled by the atmosphere. Either Carole and Laurence would find a way of getting on with one another, or she'd arrange things so that they didn't have to meet much. Because, at least for the time being, Jude reckoned Laurence Hawker was going to be a fixture at Woodside Cottage.

They found him near the closed-off kitchen garden, loitering on the path that led from the gift shop to the car park. He had already finished one cigarette, and unthinkingly trodden the butt into the flagstone beneath him; another was already alight and dangling from the corner of his mouth. As they approached, he was looking up at Bracketts.

"I do like literary houses," he observed. "It sounds sentimental and simplistic . . ." (*That seems to be one of his favourite words,* thought Carole sourly.) ". . . and yet there is a sense of place, a feeling of the forces that shaped the thoughts written there. I mean, obviously, the dourness of Haworth for the Brontës . . . the tweeness of Wordworth's Grasmere . . . and then for Jane Austen at Chawton a kind of neat elegance. . . ."

Jude looked along the neatly tiled roofs of Bracketts, admiring the skill with which the architectural styles of difference periods had been homogenised into a kind of inoffensive primness. "So what do you get from this house, Laurence?"

"Ooh, it's bland, really bland. All the rough edges have been smoothed off, to produce a building that, in spite of its antiquity, is quintessentially middle-class."

He seemed to make a point of looking at Carole as he said this, so she asked, "And what does 'middle-class' mean to you?"

He smiled knowingly. "Devious. Secretive. The middle classes are always trying to hide something. Some failed aspiration, some thwarted ambition, someone presenting themselves to the world slightly differently from the way they really are."

Carole couldn't continue to meet the sardonic gaze of his sharp brown eyes. "So how does that apply to a writer like Esmond Chadleigh?"

"I look at that house, and I see pressure to conform. Repression. Secrets."

Jude chuckled softly at this, though Carole couldn't see anything funny about it. "Look," she said brusquely, "I've just got to drop a letter in to Graham Chadleigh-Bewes. Won't be a moment. Do you want to take the car keys, Jude?"

"No, far too nice to sit in the car. We'll just enjoy the final reminder of summer, in this beautiful spot."

"And I'll light up another cigarette," said Laurence.

Carole turned, partly to set off to the cottage and partly to hide the growing resentment that the man triggered in her.

"Oh." Jude's voice stopped her, and dropped to a whisper. "Could you just point out where . . . the thing . . . was found? Just so's we know."

Carole pointed to the locked gates of the kitchen garden. "I'm pretty sure you won't be able to get inside or see anything interesting."

"No. But it'll help to be able to picture the place."

"Couldn't agree more," said Laurence, prompting anxiety in Carole as to how much Jude had confided in him about their case.

There was a solid gate that led from the main gardens of Bracketts to Graham Chadleigh-Bewes's cottage. A notice on it read Private, but Carole had seen other trustees using it, so she went through.

Outside the cottage's front gate, a taxi was driving off just as Carole arrived. She couldn't be absolutely certain, but the height of the woman in the back seat and the flash of sunlight on chestnut hair suggested that the departing visitor was Marla Teischbaum.

Carole had planned just to pop the publisher's letter through the letter slot and be on her way, but she hadn't expected to find the front door of the cottage open.

She tapped on it. There was no response. She called out a gentle "Hello?" Nothing.

Carole stepped into the hall. A coatrack supported a selection of volunteers' waterproofs. Gum boots and walking shoes, some with the previous spring's mud on them, were scattered higgledy-piggledy on the floor.

She tried another "Hello?," but no one responded.

Carole moved on into the cottage. The door to Graham's study was ajar. She pushed it open, and walked in.

Graham Chadleigh-Bewes was sitting behind his desk.

In his hand was an old service revolver.

He was unaware of Carole's presence as he announced, "I can't escape the Chadleigh bad blood. It's always there. This time I'm really going to do it."

Then he placed the barrel of the revolver, pointing upwards, in his mouth.

18

Graham Chadleigh-Bewes caught sight of Carole standing in the doorway, and embarrassment coloured his ageing baby face. He removed the revolver barrel from his mouth and let out an inadequate "Ah."

Clearly it wasn't her he'd been expecting. Carole didn't have any difficulty working that out. Nor was it too wild a conjecture to conclude that the person he had been expecting was his aunt. She lived in the cottage, after all, and there had been a note of familiarity in Graham's words. Were his suicide threats, Carole wondered, another of the rituals that he and Belinda enacted on a regular basis, a darker counterpoint to their cake-eating pantomime?

He put the revolver down amidst the chaos of his desk. "I don't know what you must be thinking," he said, with an incongruous attempt at joviality. "Just a little game I play."

"Russian roulette?"

He chuckled, assuming her to be sharing the lightheartedness he was trying to impose on the situation. But she wasn't. Carole's emotions were more complex. There was an element of shock at seeing the man in that situation, but, more powerfully, a sense of embarrassment, as if she had disturbed some shameful ritual. Graham's reaction to her arrival compounded the impression.

"No, not Russian roulette," he replied tartly.

"You mean there aren't bullets in any of the chambers?"

"Oh, no. In fact, every one is loaded." He let out a manufactured chuckle. "So the odds for any Russian playing games of chance with that gun wouldn't be very good. I don't think even Dostoyevsky would have taken that bet."

"The gun works, then?"

"Oh, yes. Been looked after with great care. The estate manager is a great gun enthusiast. Checks that one out at least once a year. Even indulges in a little target practice in the kitchen garden."

"Is that legal?"

"I'm sure it isn't. But who's to know? When the revolver was originally put on display, it was spiked, so that it couldn't be used. The estate manager thought that was a pity, so he restored it to its original splendour."

Carole moved into the room and sat down. "I assume it's the one that belongs in the glass case in the Bracketts dining room?"

"Yes. Graham Chadleigh's revolver."

" 'Contents removed for cleaning and restoration.' "

"Exactly. It's been to a specialist gunsmith, to be properly cleaned. Has to be done every few years. Only came back from there yesterday."

"And when did it go? When was it sent off to be cleaned?"

"Oh . . . what? Three weeks ago."

"Before the last trustees meeting?"

"Definitely before that, yes."

Carole didn't contest this, but she knew it wasn't true. She remembered seeing the revolver in its display case at the meeting. Either Graham's memory was playing him false, or he was lying. She favoured the second explanation, though she could not guess at the reasons for his duplicity.

"You talked of 'Chadleigh bad blood,' " she said suddenly.

"Sorry?"

"When I came in. When you were playing your . . . game with the revolver. Is 'Chadleigh bad blood' part of the game?"

He looked flustered, and went on the attack. "I don't see why you're bombarding me with questions. There's one very basic one I haven't asked you yet. What do you think you're doing walking uninvited into my house?"

Carole held out the envelope with the publisher's permissions request in it. "I brought you this. Remember? You asked me to."

"Oh, yes." He retreated.

"Your front door was open. I knocked and called out, but got no reply."

"I thought Auntie was here," he said rather peevishly, maybe confirming Carole's guess that the suicide routine had been for Belinda Chadleigh's benefit.

She decided to push forward while he was on the back foot. "I thought I saw Professor Teischbaum leaving as I arrived."

"What?" He considered denial, but thought better of it. "Yes, she was here."

"Offering to cooperate with you? A jointly written biography?"

There a bark of derisive laughter. "Hardly. No, she was trying to blackmail me."

"Oh?"

"Somehow she knows about the body that was found in the kitchen garden." Carole reacted as if this were fresh news.

"She's threatening to tell the press."

"So what did you say to her?"

"I told her to bloody tell them!" he snapped petulantly. Then a comforting thought came to him. "If she does, I think we can guarantee that she'll alienate every single one of the Bracketts trustees. Nobody'll contemplate taking her side after that kind of betrayal."

"I didn't think anyone contemplated taking her side now."

"There are a few waverers." He looked piercingly at her, so that his words became an accusation.

Carole ignored the challenge. "You don't think Marla Teischbaum's going to the press will cause any harm?"

"So long as I warn Sheila what's going to happen, it'll be all right."

"Sheila won't be surprised."

"Oh?"

"I told her Marla Teischbaum knew about the body."

"But how on earth did you —"

Carole didn't let him get any further. "Anyway, what's this about Sheila? Isn't Gina the one you should be telling?"

"Who?" At first, he appeared genuinely to have forgotten the director's existence. "Oh, yes. Yes, of course. Sheila'll tell her."

He smiled with satisfaction. "Actually, we've done very well. Sheila's contacts are brilliant. She's kept the story quiet all this time. Only two more days till Bracketts closes for the winter. And if there is any threat of overinquisitive press or ghoulish members of the public creeping round, we can just close a little early."

"So what was Marla Teischbaum trying to blackmail you for?"

"Sorry?"

"She threatened to spill the beans to the press, unless you did . . . what?"

He coloured, and pushed the revolver around in its nest of papers. "She wanted more information about Esmond, more documentation. Huh. If she thinks I'm going to give up my hard-won research that easily . . . well, she's taken on the wrong person."

Coming from those flabby lips, the attempt to sound macho didn't work.

"Going back to the 'Chadleigh bad blood,' could we . . . ?"

She was interrupted by a panicked voice from behind her. "Graham, what on earth are you doing with that?"

Carole hadn't heard Belinda Chadleigh enter the room. But when she turned and saw the old woman's faded eyes staring

195

with horror at the revolver on Graham's desk, she began to wonder how much of a game his suicide threat had been.

And, also, whether the "Chadleigh bad blood" perhaps referred to a depressive tendency in the family's genetic makeup.

19

There were three butts on the ground by the Renault when Carole returned, and the fourth cigarette was already drooping from Laurence Hawker's mouth. Neither he nor Jude noticed her approach. He was lounging against the car, gazing out over the green downland, while Jude looked at him with unusual intensity, as if trying to impress his image on her mind.

Carole, with some annoyance, interpreted this as a look of love, and in fact she wasn't far wrong. Jude was having increasing difficulty in maintaining her "no love" agreement with Laurence. Insidiously, over the past few weeks, he had become part of her life, and the prospect of losing him was more and more painful to contemplate.

Hearing Carole's approach, she shook herself out of introspection, and observed, "Took a long time to pop an envelope through a letter slot."

"Yes. I talked to Graham."

"And?"

But Carole didn't want to discuss the case with a third person present. Particularly with Laurence Hawker present. Mumbling that Graham hadn't said anything of great interest, she got into the car. Jude knew exactly what was going on, but said nothing.

On the way back, Laurence again trailed his smoking hand out of the window, but Carole was still very aware of the smell.

Graham Chadleigh-Bewes had moved quickly in contacting Sheila Cartwright. There was a message from her on the answering machine when Carole got back from Bracketts. While Gulliver fussed around her legs, as though she'd been away for six months, she listened to the playback.

"This is Sheila Cartwright. The police are about to make a statement to the press about the discovery in the kitchen garden. It is very important that we all sing from the same hymn sheet on this one. So I'm calling an emergency trustees meeting to discuss the situation and the appropriate responses to it. The only time Lord Beniston can make is tomorrow evening, Friday, at seven. Seven o'clock in the dining room at Bracketts tomorrow evening. Do attend if it's humanly possible.

This is very important. Message ends."

Carole smiled wryly. Sheila had realised that the secret could not be kept much longer, and made a preemptive strike. Regardless of whether it was her job to do it or not, she'd summoned the trustees. How would Gina react to this latest usurpation of her authority? The meeting the following night held the promise of a considerable fireworks display. It would not be an occasion to be missed, under any circumstances — least of all by someone who suspected some kind of skulduggery was going on at Bracketts.

There was a brief mention of the body on the local news at six-thirty. A presenter who was going to have her teeth fixed before she made it on to national television announced, "At Bracketts House, near South Stapley, the former home of writer Edmund Chadleigh, there has been a grisly discovery. Human remains buried in a shallow grave were discovered during digging the foundations for a proposed museum at the tourist site. A Sussex Police spokesman said that the body belonged to a man, and he is thought to have died at least fifty years ago. There is no information yet as to his identity or the cause of death."

The report was accompanied by library footage of Bracketts looking at its best in summer sunshine. Then the presenter moved on to the story of a seven-year-old girl in West Durrington who had enlisted her primary school classmates into a team of majorettes.

So much for the profile of Esmond Chadleigh in the wider world outside Bracketts — even a professional news service got his name wrong. Carole wanted to share her reaction to the bulletin with Jude. In fact, she would rather have been watching the news with Jude. But the presence of Laurence Hawker in Woodside Cottage inhibited her from going round or picking up the phone.

Jude had said she and Laurence were going to have supper at the Crown and Anchor, and had, with her customary openness, invited her neighbour to join them. Characteristically, Carole had invented a reason why she couldn't.

But she was desperate to talk to Jude. On her own.

Jude and Laurence had had quite a lot to drink, and he poured himself another large whisky when they got back to Woodside Cottage. She wasn't so worried about the drinking, but in the course of the evening she had managed to tackle him about his smoking.

To no effect, of course. "It's what I do," he said. "It's part of me. Like English literature. Take it away, and there's nothing of me left."

Jude had put her plump arm around his thin waist and pulled him to her. "There's not much of you left, as it is."

"True," he agreed. "Not much." And he had planted a small kiss on her nose. "I'm glad to see you again, Jude. You mean a lot to me."

She cherished the rareness of the moment. Though physically affectionate, Laurence Hawker had never committed himself much verbally. Supremely articulate though he was, he was wary of voicing feelings of attraction. (Cynically, Jude had often wondered whether this was the caution of a man who spent time with so many different women that he didn't want to risk the danger, in a moment of intimacy, of getting a name wrong.) And, though someone with his knowledge of English Romantic poetry must have realised the relative feebleness of "You mean a lot to me," Jude recognised, from that particular source, the sentiment's true value.

As if in punishment for this lapse in his customary reticence, Laurence had been immediately attacked by a ferocious fit of coughing. During which he lit up another cigarette.

Jude had had her mobile off in the Crown and Anchor, but found there was a message when she switched it back on in her sitting room. "I'll just check this," she said.

"Right. See you in bed." Taking the whisky bottle by its neck, Laurence left the room. She heard his cough receding up the stairs.

"Jude. It's Sandy. Ring me as soon as you can, please."

The voice of Austen's education officer was tight with anxiety. Jude rang back straight away. There was the sound of a car's engine in the background, though of where she was going, and with whom, as ever Sandy Fairbarns made no mention.

She told the news as soon as Jude got through.

"It's Mervyn. He's gone over the wall. He's escaped."

20

There were small paragraphs in the national broadsheets the following morning about the body found at Bracketts, but no detail was given. The papers didn't have enough information to voice suspicions or make insinuations.

The local press, however, was not so restrained, as Carole found out at about a quarter to ten. She had just come back from an extended sunny walk with Gulliver on Fethering Beach, and was wiping the sand off his feet with an old towel, when the telephone rang.

"Hello." She was so surprised by the brusqueness of his tone that she didn't take in the name. "I'm from the *Fethering Observer.*"

"Oh, yes?"

"Is that Mrs. Seddon?"

"Yes."

"Mrs. Carole Seddon?"

"That's right."

"And I believe you're a trustee of Bracketts . . . ?"

"I am."

As the voice continued, it sounded increasingly boyish. Cub reporter on one of his first assignments, Carole reckoned. Seen too many movies about hard-bitten journalists.

"Could you give me a statement about the discovery of a body buried in the house's kitchen garden?"

"I'm not sure I'm the right person to ask," said Carole, wishing she'd had a briefing on how much the press should be told, now the story was public property. "I would have thought it would make sense for you to ring the Administrative Office at Bracketts."

"Don't think I haven't tried," came the bitter reply. "All I get there is a recorded message, saying the house and gardens are closed until further notice."

Carole noted the information. They hadn't managed to keep Bracketts open right through to the end of the season. But they'd fallen short by only two days. Whatever Sheila Cartwright's delaying tactics had been, they had worked pretty well.

"I wish I could tell you something," said Carole, "but I'm afraid I don't have any information."

"Oh, come on. I've asked everyone else,"

complained the boy, giving away his inexperience, "and none of the other trustees'll talk to me."

She grabbed the lifeline. "Then I'm afraid I can't talk to you either. I'm sure a press statement will be issued by the Board of Trustees at the appropriate time," she concluded primly.

"For heavens' sake! This is the appropriate time. The story's only just broken. It could be really big."

"The *Fethering Observer*," said Carole, now fully in control of the situation, "is published on a Thursday. I really can't believe that the deadline for your copy is today, nearly a week ahead."

"That's not the point." The cub reporter's callowness was revealed again. "The nationals'd be really interested in a story as juicy as this."

I see the way his mind's working, thought Carole. *JUNIOR REPORTER ON FIRST ASSIGNMENT GETS SCOOP OF A LIFETIME!*

She could have just rung off, but didn't. "What makes you think it's a juicy story?"

"Because of the secrecy. The body was actually found over a week ago, and the news has only now been released."

"I would have thought it was up to the

police when they informed the press about this kind of thing."

"No, it's definitely a cover-up," the boy insisted. "And it's often the case that the cover-up is worse than the original crime. Look at Watergate."

Oh dear. One of the movies that he watched too many times had evidently been *All the President's Men*.

"You use the word 'crime,' " said Carole. "There's no evidence that any crime has been committed."

"There was a bullet hole in the back of the skull."

She wondered where he'd got that from. If it was information released by the official investigators, then it was very significant, the first confirmation that the body in the kitchen garden had been the victim of a shooting. "Did you hear that from the police?"

The boy was evasive. "No. But I heard that there was a hole in the skull."

"And you made the deduction that it must have been made by a bullet?"

"Yes," he replied, with a degree of pride in his detective skills. "What else is going to make a hole in a skull?"

"Quite a lot of things," said Carole severely. "I go back to my point that there is no evidence of any crime having been committed."

"The woman who phoned the office talked about a 'crime.' She even used the word 'murder.' Well, actually, she said 'moider.' "

The cub reporter's attempt at an American accent gave her the information she needed, but Carole still asked, "Which woman was this?"

"I'm sorry," the boy said staunchly, remembering another movie he'd seen. "I can't reveal my sources."

There was no sign of life from Woodside Cottage all day. Jude hadn't phoned, and Carole was damned if she was going to be the one to make contact. Let Jude get on with her love affair, or whatever it was. Carole was quite capable of conducting the investigation on her own.

The weather changed as she drove the Renault sedately towards Bracketts. The spine of the South Downs frequently broke the climatic pattern. The coastal plain down to Fethering and the sea could be bathed in sunshine, while north of the ridge was drowned in rain. The demarcation wasn't quite so pronounced that afternoon, but the air did grow darker the further north the Renault went, and heavy leaden clouds hung truculently in the sky. Autumn was killing off the last stragglers of the retreating summer.

Carole looked at her watch as she stopped the Renault in the almost empty car park. Not even half-past six. Her habit of being extraordinarily early for everything did annoy her. The only thing that would annoy her more was being late. She had always wished she could be one of those people who ambled up to appointments at just the right time. For Carole, any prospective encounter with another human being involved a certain amount of trepidation and realignment.

Still, she wouldn't waste the time. She'd go and have a word with Gina before the trustees meeting started. In doing this she had a double motive. For a start, she could find out what the official line should be for the trustees when approached by the press. And she could also perhaps do something for the director's self-confidence, demonstrating that some of the trustees still thought she was the one in charge at Bracketts.

As Carole approached the former stable block, however, she heard the voice of Gina's rival, raised in anger. Carole stopped awkwardly. Out of sight round the corner, there was clearly a major row going on, and, in a very British way, she didn't relish walking into the middle of that. She looked back towards the car, but what she heard stopped her from retracing her steps.

"I can assure you," Sheila Cartwright was almost shouting, "that Bracketts is bigger than you are! Esmond Chadleigh is bigger than you are! And your attempts to sully his reputation will soon be shown up for the kind of gutter journalism they really are!"

"We'll see about that." The other voice was Marla Teischbaum's, no less angry, but more controlled. "And I don't take kindly to having my writing referred to as 'gutter journalism.' I am a serious academic writer, and all I am seeking is the truth. I'm not setting out to find muck or filth or sleaze or whatever you want to call it in the life of Esmond Chadleigh. I am trying to find out the truth about that tortured man."

"He was not tortured! He was a man of great personal happiness, who spread happiness to those around him!" Sheila Cartwright sounded like a religious fundamentalist whose belief was being challenged.

"I have evidence to the contrary," said Marla Teischbaum coldly. "And I will write nothing that is not fully supported by evidence. Now, if you'll excuse me, I'm going to pay a call on Graham Chadleigh-Bewes."

"I can save you the trouble, Professor. He's out for the afternoon, with his aunt. And they'll be back just in time for a meeting tonight at seven. So you won't have an opportunity to talk to him today."

"Then I'll have to find another day."

"He still won't tell you anything."

"We'll see about that." Professor Teischbaum's voice took on a new intensity. "You can't stand in the way of the truth, Mrs. Cartwright. My biography is going to be completed. It's going to be published. And nothing is going to prevent that from happening."

"Don't you believe it!" Sheila Cartwright now sounded dangerously out of control. "I'll prevent it from happening!"

"I think not." The words were spoken calmly, and the accompanying scuff of gravel suggested they had provided Professor Teischbaum with a satisfactory exit line.

Rather than being caught obviously hanging around listening. Carole moved forwards, making loud footsteps, as if she had just arrived.

As she rounded the corner, she saw the two strong-minded women taking a last look at one another. Though almost exactly the same height, they couldn't have been more different in style. Sheila Cartwright, her white hair sensibly short, looked what she was: an upper-middle-class Englishwoman in white blouse, navy suit, and sensible black shoes. Marla Teischbaum, the copper-beech of her hair gleaming in the sunlight, was wearing a symphony of autumn tints in linen and Indian cotton.

Suddenly it started to rain. Big, heavy drops thudded down onto the gravel. Marla Teischbaum lifted the briefcase she was carrying to hold it over the perfectly coiffed chestnut hair and, with a nod of acknowledgement to Carole, stalked off towards the car park.

Sheila Cartwright managed a curt "Good evening," and then she strode away towards the main house, no doubt to prepare for the emergency trustees meeting she had summoned.

Carole went into the Administrative Office to speak to the person who should have called the emergency trustees meeting.

But she couldn't forget the scene she had just witnessed between Sheila Cartwright and Marla Teischbaum. Or the flame of intense hatred that had burned in the eyes of both women.

21

It had been a bad day for Jude. She had been woken at half-past four by Laurence's coughing, which sounded worse than ever. It was. There was blood all over the sheets, and still dribbling from his mouth.

She had called an ambulance immediately. Though a great believer in the efficacy of alternative therapies, Jude knew when conventional medical intervention was required.

They had left Woodside Cottage before anyone else in the road was awake, and Jude had had a day of intense anxiety at the hospital while Laurence was subjected to a series of X-rays and tests, building up to a late afternoon interview with the consultant. Even though she had no official relationship with him, Jude reckoned she would have been allowed to sit in on that meeting, but Laurence didn't want her to, and she respected his wishes.

Even though the day, like most in hospitals, involved a lot of sitting around waiting, Jude was too preoccupied with Laurence's health to think of anything else.

She'd meant to ring Carole to discuss the previous night's news bulletin about the Bracketts skeleton, and to tell her about Mervyn Hunter's escape from Austen, but such intentions were swamped by worry about Laurence.

He was silent in the cab back from the hospital. Except for the occasional coughs, coughs that had taken on a new and ominous significance for Jude.

But as soon as he got back inside Woodside Cottage, he found his black leather jacket, took out a cigarette packet, and lit one up. Jude said nothing as she watched him gratefully drink in the smoke.

"Would you like a whisky?" she asked.

"God, would I like a whisky? I've spent this entire day only thinking how much I would like a cigarette and a whisky." His voice was dry and cracked after his ordeal. He looked paler and thinner than ever.

Jude waited till they both had drinks and were sitting in two of her shawl-draped armchairs. Then she said, "So?"

"So . . . what?" he echoed with a dusty giggle.

"Presumably the consultant didn't give you a clean bill of health?"

"I think, Jude, that would have been too much to hope for."

"Cancer?"

"He came up with a lot of longer words first, but then he made a concession to my ignorance and used that one. Always a problem for us academics. If it's not our speciality, we just don't know the jargon."

"And what treatment did he recommend?"

"Oh, there was chemo-this and radio-that. It all sounded distinctly unpleasant."

"Don't you think the alternative might be even more unpleasant?"

He shrugged languidly, tapped out the ash of his cigarette, and returned it to his mouth. "It all seems rather a fag," he said, ambiguous as to whether the pun was deliberate.

"Are you saying you're not going to have any treatment?"

"I'm saying that I've spent nearly sixty years of being me. That me is not a particularly admirable being. It certainly smokes and drinks too much. Its morals don't accord to the prescribed norms. It has probably caused unnecessary hurt to people — mostly women — who didn't deserve it. But that me has suited me surprisingly well. Having got this far through life, jogging along with myself amiably enough, I don't want to have a personality transplant at this late stage."

"So you think treatment for the cancer would change your personality?"

"I'm damned sure it'd change my life-style. There seems to be some rather tedious conventional wisdom in the medical world that chemotherapy and chain-smoking don't mix."

Jude couldn't help smiling. Laurence Hawker had always been a poseur, a lot of what he said purely for effect, but its mischievous knowingness still made her laugh.

"So you're saying you're not going to have any treatment? You'll let the cancer run its course?"

"Yes."

"And did the consultant say how long that course might be?"

Laurence Hawker shook his head, exhaling dubiously through pursed lips. "An inexact science, the prediction of longevity. But I get the impression that I should think in terms of short stories rather than novels. Certainly O. Henry rather than Proust."

There was a long, peaceful silence between them. Each took a substantial sip from their glass. Laurence reached across and affectionately took hold of Jude's hand.

"One of the things I like about you," he said, "is your lack of knee-jerk reactions.

Very few of the human species, after what I've just told you, could have resisted saying, 'But you must have the treatment, you must!' Whether they meant it or not. It's just one of those things people say instinctively, like 'Bless you' after a sneeze. Thank you, Jude, for not saying it."

She shrugged. "Not my place to say it. Your life. You're grown-up. You make your own decisions."

"Thank you."

The peaceful silence descended again. When Laurence next spoke, it was with greater briskness. "I'll be off tomorrow. This has been an extraordinarily pleasant interlude. I'm very grateful."

"Where are you going?" He shrugged. "To another of your women?"

"I don't think that'd be very fair. No, I'll find a base somewhere, and meet them on a daily basis, for nice, long, self-indulgent lunches."

"There is an alternative," said Jude.

"Sorry. I'm not going to sweat in a tepee, or only eat pulses, or have ginseng enemas. All those sound at least as undignified as the chemotherapy."

"That is not what I meant, Laurence. And you know full well that is not what I meant." He smiled acknowledgement of

216

her percipience. "I meant you don't have to go. You can stay here."

He was silent for a moment. "Jude, I know you never make offers you don't mean, but I think that's too much for you to take on."

"My decision, I'd have thought."

Another silence. "It's tempting."

"You've never had any qualms about giving in to temptation before. Why suddenly get picky now?"

"Hm." An even longer silence. "One thing. . . ."

"Yes?"

"If I do accept your very generous offer. . . ."

"Hm?"

"You won't tell anyone, will you?"

"Won't tell anyone you're here? That's going to be tricky. I'm afraid, amongst its many conveniences and amenities, Woodside Cottage doesn't feature a priest's hole."

"I meant don't tell anyone why I'm here. Don't tell anyone I'm ill."

"Oh," said Jude. "Not even Carole?"

"Particularly not Carole."

"Why?"

"Because, if ever I saw one of the 'But you must have the treatment, you must!' brigade, Carole Seddon is it."

Jude wasn't sure that he was right about her neighbour, and foresaw problems ahead. She visualised a lot of misunderstandings, when she would have to spend time caring for Laurence, and Carole would regard her preoccupation as a personal slight. But it was his illness and his decision, so she just said, "All right. Any other terms and conditions?"

"Just one other thing I'd like to clarify." A sardonic smile twitched his full lips. "If I am living here. . . ."

"Mm?"

". . . will I still be able to go out and meet my other women for nice, long, self-indulgent lunches?"

"Oh, yes, Laurence. I wouldn't dare try to change your personality. Don't worry, I'm way beyond that kind of jealousy," Jude replied, with a grin.

"Good. Both being grown-ups, eh? Two people who have been lovers and can still enjoy each other's company."

"And bodies."

"Yes. And bodies." He mimicked a prim smile of political correctness. "But only, of course, by mutual agreement."

"Of course."

"No pretence, though, that we're the great loves of each other's life."

Jude nodded firmly. "Fine by me."

"I think I need some more whisky," said Laurence Hawker.

After their talk, Jude rang Carole and got the answering machine. She didn't leave a message. She'd go round to High Tor the following morning.

Then she rang Sandy Fairbarns's number.

"Just wondered if there was any more news about Mervyn."

"Well, they haven't found him yet, if that's what you mean."

"How hard are they looking?"

"As hard as they would for any other escapee from an open prison."

"But not as hard as they would for a dangerous woman-killer who might strike again at any moment?"

"No, Jude. As you know and I know, that stuff was all in his head."

"I wonder what made him suddenly jump now? The police know he had nothing to do with the skeleton at Bracketts."

"I thought you said he'd talked of reoffending so that he gets another prison sentence, so that he doesn't have to face the real world so soon?"

"He did."

"An escape could achieve that quite neatly, couldn't it?"

"Yes. Except that an escape takes him out into the very real world that he's so scared of."

"Where he might be in danger of being alone with a woman, and the consequences he fears from that situation?"

"Exactly, Sandy. Anything else you've found out about him?"

"Only that he had another visitor."

"Oh? After me?"

"Yes."

"But he said he never had visitors."

"Then his luck's changed. He's had two in a week. Second one the day before he absconded."

"Who was it, Sandy? Who came to see him?"

"Someone from Bracketts . . . you know, the place where he was working."

"I know."

"It was Sheila Cartwright."

22

Having had the emergency trustees meeting set up around his commitments, when it came to the event, Lord Beniston couldn't make it. A six-forty call to the Administrative Office from his secretary conveyed his regrets that he'd been unavoidably delayed in London "by a business meeting that had overrun." In fact, though no one at Bracketts ever knew, the meeting had been a lunch at the Garrick (where the rules of the club do not permit the discussion of business) that had run on through the afternoon into an evening drinking session.

(In fact, Lord Beniston was beginning to have doubts about his involvement with Bracketts. The doubts had nothing to do with recent events at the house, but arose from the question he constantly posed to himself: "What am I actually getting out of this?" Bracketts was a relatively obscure setup, so few people were aware of the brownie points he should have been earning for his charity work. Also, he did have to go there in person to chair the meetings. He felt sure he could lend his name to the letterheads of other organisations that would raise his philanthropic profile higher and make fewer demands on him.)

Gina Locke, who had taken the call while Carole was in the office with her, immediately took the decision that, in the absence of Lord Beniston, she would chair the meeting herself. Though not a trustee, as director of Bracketts she would be the senior responsible person present, and she should be in charge.

Carole had no problem reading the subtext of this announcement. Sheila Cartwright had once again wrong-footed Gina by calling the meeting; she wasn't going to be allowed to reinforce her dominance by chairing it, too.

"Have you had many calls from the press?" asked Carole, remembering her interrogation by the intrepid boy reporter.

"Quite a few. Referred them all to the police. That's the official line, incidentally. We have no information here. When there is anything to say, the police will be the ones to say it."

"Any press actually turned up here?"

"One or two. All firmly turned away. As you know, the house and gardens have been closed to the public. And we've kept the gate from the car park locked right through the day. Only just had it opened, so that you trustees can get in."

"Have you seen Professor Teischbaum?"

"No." Gina looked surprised. "Should I have done?"

"She was here. I just saw her talking to Sheila."

The surprise on Gina's face turned to white-lipped anger. "She should have come to see me. If Marla Teischbaum comes to Bracketts, it should be to see the person in charge!"

Carole made no comment.

Attendance at the emergency trustees meeting in the sitting room at Bracketts was depleted. No Lord Beniston, and Josie Freeman's social calendar was far too rigidly set in stone to be altered for anything less than a family funeral — and even then her appearance would have depended on whether it was her own or her husband's side of the family. (In fact, that Friday evening had long been booked for her and her husband to attend a production of *Parsifal* at the Royal Opera House. He would be bored rigid throughout, and wouldn't understand the story — nothing to do with car parts — but it was the kind of place where his wife told him he should be seen, and he knew she knew about that kind of thing.)

George Ferris was at the meeting in ginger tweeds, looking more than ever like a smug inhabitant of Middle Earth. Graham and his aunt also attended, she as ever vague and quite possibly on a different planet, while he looked tense and fragile. Carole found herself wondering how real his suicide threat had been. There was an unnerving lack of stability about the man.

But of course the main adversaries at the table were the current director of Bracketts and the woman who thought she was still in charge of the place. They must have done some deal before the meeting started, though, because Sheila Cartwright meekly allowed Gina Locke to welcome the trustees and outline the main business on their agenda.

"I'm sure you all know by now that the discovery of the corpse in the kitchen garden is public knowledge. The skeleton is, literally, out of the cupboard, and some of you have no doubt already had approaches from the press about it. . . ."

Graham nodded agreement at this,

showing in his pained face what a hardship and intrusion this had been for someone as sensitive as he was.

"Well, it was bound to happen at some point. And," she went on, in a conciliatory tone, "we all owe a great debt of gratitude to Sheila for using her influence to keep the story out of the press for nearly a week."

Gina's rival gave a magnanimous nod of acknowledgement.

"So the main purpose of this meeting — and once again, may I say how much I appreciate your making time in your busy schedules to be with us tonight — the main purpose is to talk through how we're going to answer press enquiries . . . to see that we're all on-message and, as it were, singing from the same hymn sheet.

"What we're aiming to achieve is a uniform approach that will keep the press off our backs, but — very importantly — not antagonise them. There's already a degree of resentment from the media about the way the story's been kept from them and, whatever we do, we don't want to make that feeling any worse than it currently is."

Sheila Cartwright was unused to being silent so long, and the director's taking a breath gave her an opportunity to butt in.

"I think what Gina's trying to say —"

"I know *exactly* what I'm trying to say, thank you very much."

The look that accompanied this would have frozen a fire hose at a hundred meters, but it didn't stop Sheila Cartwright. "The important thing is that no rumours get around. Any dead body discovered in these circumstances is going to prompt speculation. It's up to us to ensure that such speculation is kept to a minimum."

"Thank you, Sheila," said Gina with commendable coolness. "Everyone at the meeting will get their opportunity to speak at the appropriate time." The edge in this line did momentarily take the wind out of her opponent's sails, and Gina took the opportunity to press on. "Now I have today spoken to the detective inspector in charge of the investigation, and at this time there is no further information the police wish to disclose about the body. Forensic tests are still continuing, and when there is something substantial to report, another statement will be made by the police."

"We know all that," said Sheila Cartwright unceremoniously. "The important thing is not what the police say, it's what *we* say. The casual use of a word like 'murder' by someone actually involved in the Bracketts setup could cause untold damage."

"We're all aware of that," said Carole frostily. Sheila was annoying her, and she reckoned Gina needed some support. "There's no need to talk to us as if we are schoolchildren."

Support came from an unexpected quarter. "I agree," said Graham Chadleigh-Bewes. "And, anyway, the danger from the press is considerably less than that posed to everything Bracketts stands for by the presence very near to us of one Professor Marla Teischbaum. The Teischbaum Claimant." The half-joke got no acknowledgement from the assembled meeting. "That woman's biography is going to be a complete hatchet job on the reputation of Esmond Chadleigh."

"Not necessarily," said George Ferris. Then, with a snidely sideways look at Graham, he went on. "Professor Teischbaum is at least a serious academic with a record of successful publication. I think she has considerable insight into Esmond. I was discussing him with her only this afternoon."

Sheila Cartwright flared up at that. "You shouldn't have been speaking to her. We've agreed that, as trustees —"

"I wasn't speaking to her as a trustee of Bracketts," he countered complacently. "I do have other hats, you know. One of which is advising the County Library and Records Office about research enquiries from visiting academics. I've even written a book on the subject, entitled *How to Get the Best from the Facilities of the County Records Office*." (This reminder was now so familiar that it prompted no reaction at all.) "Without in any way compromising my position at Bracketts, it falls within the domain of my responsibility to direct Professor Teischbaum towards available research sources, and I would be failing in my duty if I did not fulfil that function. I also —"

This local-government-speak looked set fair to continue for some time, had it not been cut short by a petulant outburst from Graham Chadleigh-Bewes.

"Professor Teischbaum's biography will be a travesty of the truth, and an offence to everything that we at Bracketts hold dear. And it must not be allowed to appear in print!"

George Ferris sniggered. "If your biography had been delivered when it was meant to be, we wouldn't have this problem. You'd have got in first and garnered all the available publicity for Esmond. Marla's coming out so soon after, would have vanished without trace."

Carole just had time to register the ex-librarian's use of the professor's first name before Graham began his predictable tirade. "Oh, yes, it's all my fault, isn't it? You have no idea how much work is involved in just looking after Esmond's literary estate. I have to go out and do talks in schools, I'm editing an edition of the letters, I have to try and persuade publishers to reissue the books. If there's any reason why the biography is late —"

"It's because," George Ferris cut in, "the job has been put in the hands of an idle dilettante!"

"How dare you call me a — !"

"Gentleman! Squabbling is not going to help anyone. Can we please be quiet!"

Gina Locke sounded surprisingly masterful. A grudging stillness fell. "Well done, girl," murmured Belinda Chadleigh.

But Gina wasn't allowed to take advantage of the silence she had won. It was immediately hijacked by Sheila Cartwright. "You're absolutely right, George," she said unexpectedly. "Previously the delay on Graham's biography didn't matter. Keeping it back to coincide with the centenary of Esmond's death made sense. But that was before we'd got the odious Professor

Teischbaum snapping round our heels. Now it's of paramount importance that the authorised biography is published before hers."

"It won't be easy for me," whinged Graham Chadleigh-Bewes. "There's still lots of research to do and —"

"I know it won't be easy for you," said Sheila. "In fact, I don't think there's a chance of your delivering a manuscript in the time scale that is now essential to us."

"Well, I could try, but —"

"Which is why," she steamrollered over him, "you are no longer writing the biography, Graham."

"What?" The word came from more mouths than just his.

"We should have made the change a long time ago," said Sheila coolly, "but it's not too late. I spoke today to Jonathan Venables."

Graham Chadleigh-Bewes was appalled. "You mean the one who did those tatty scissors-and-paste jobs on George Orwell and Hilaire Belloc? His research never goes beyond the clippings file."

"It will in this case," Sheila Cartwright continued relentlessly, "because you are going to hand over all your research to him."

"I wouldn't dream of doing such a thing."

"You will do it, Graham!" The would-be biographer quailed under her implacable eye. "I've talked to Jonathan Venables's agent, and he's drawing up a contract. The book will be delivered by the end of the year."

Now George Ferris joined the protest. "But he can't do a decent book in two months."

"He can, and will. More important, Jonathan Venables's book will be published long before Marla Teischbaum's."

Graham had risen from the table. Tears were pouring unchecked down his baby face. "You can't do this to me, Sheila."

"I'm sorry. It's done. This is an emergency. Someone had to take the initiative."

"Maybe," Gina intervened. "But if anyone should have taken the initiative, it should have been —"

"Be quiet," Sheila Cartwright commanded. "This is important. Bracketts is under threat, and I'm the only person who can save it."

The messianic light burning in her eyes made everyone round the table uncomfortable. After a moment's silence, Graham pushed his chair back so fiercely that it crashed to the wooden floor.

"You won't get away with this, Sheila," he muttered through his tears, as he stumbled out of the room.

Belinda Chadleigh looked up in bemused surprise. "Well, that was a short meeting," she said, and tottered off after her nephew.

23

The emergency trustees meeting rather ran out of steam after that. The announcement that Sheila Cartwright had taken the decision to commission a new biography of Esmond Chadleigh without even the illusion of consultation had knocked the stuffing out of Gina Locke. She had the look of a woman who'd contemplated throwing in the towel many times before, and had now been floored by the final body blow. On her small, dark face was an expression of resignation, and it looked as though a matching letter would soon follow.

She no longer maintained even the pretence that she was chairing the meeting, and listened while Sheila outlined her orders to the others for dealing with the press. The Old Guard had won. Sheila Cartwright was as much in charge of Bracketts as she had ever been.

The only resistance she encountered was from George Ferris, who echoed the doubts Graham Chadleigh-Bewes had expressed about the likely quality of a biography written by Jonathan Venables.

"It doesn't matter," Sheila responded tersely. "The important thing is that it's published as soon as possible, and spikes the guns of Professor Marla Teischbaum."

"We can't be sure it'll even do that," said the ex-librarian slyly. "I heard a rumour that the good professor is pretty well advanced in her researches. It could be a race to the line."

Carole would have put money on the fact that the rumour came from Marla Teischbaum herself.

"She can't complete it before the end of the year," said Sheila, countenancing no possible argument. "She's still got requests in to the estate for permission to quote from Esmond's works. We can spend a good while to-ing and fro-ing over that."

"Before finally saying no."

"Exactly." The word was accompanied by a thin, complacent smile. "Don't worry. We can delay Professor Teischbaum for quite a long time."

There was a flash of lightning outside. The rain that had been threatening on and off all afternoon came down with sudden force. Recalcitrant thunder groaned distantly.

Gina Locke and George Ferris had left

the house as soon as Sheila Cartwright pronounced the meeting closed, hurrying out in a break between the thunderstorms. Gina looked pale, in shock, and walked like an automaton towards the Administrative Office. George turned towards the car park. Carole felt sure he would be seeing or telephoning Marla Teischbaum before the night was out.

She found herself lingering with Sheila at the open front door by the gift shop. Outside the darkness was now total, heavy with the threat of another inundation. Remembering the suicide masquerade she had witnessed, she asked, "Do you think Graham will be all right?"

"Yes," came the curt reply. "His pride's hurt, that's all. He's no one but himself to blame. He's been promising that biography for years, and there's no sign of it."

"How near do you think he is to completion?"

Sheila Cartwright snorted. "No idea. Not very far, I imagine. He's just gone round in circles doing research. I should think the amount of actual writing he's done could be measured in tens of pages."

"Why was he given the job in the first place?"

"Because he was the obvious person. A

relative, obsessed with Esmond, with easy access to all the papers — and a good Catholic."

"Is Jonathan Venables Catholic?"

"No, but that doesn't matter. He'll do a workmanlike job."

"I still don't quite understand why Graham was appointed to write the biography . . . ?"

"Because it flattered his vanity . . . mostly. Also, I thought it would give him a big project, something to do. . . ."

"Keep him out of your hair?"

"Yes. That was another reason."

"You sound as if you didn't much care whether his book ever got completed or not."

The tall woman looked down at Carole. There was an uncompromising honesty in her eyes. "All right. To be quite honest, I didn't. I was keen on anything that might raise the profile of Esmond and Bracketts, but I wasn't convinced the biography would make that much difference. Maybe, coinciding with the centenary in 2004, but . . . I wasn't really that bothered . . . until Marla Teischbaum came on the scene."

"Right."

For a second the outside world was illuminated by a flash of lightning. The thunder followed hard on its heels.

"Do you mind if I ask if you're Catholic, Sheila?" Carole didn't like the woman; she didn't mind if she sounded nosey.

"No."

"Then why . . . ?"

"Why have I devoted my life to this place?" Sheila Cartwright's dark blue eyes suddenly focused on the pale blue of Carole's.

"All right. Why?"

The rain fell as though an overhead sluice had suddenly been opened. The two women looked at the spatters of water bouncing up from the ground outside.

When she spoke, Sheila's voice was barely audible above the roaring of the weather. "The reason I'm obsessed with Bracketts is very simple. Comes down to one poem. Esmond's most famous poem. I'm sure you know it."

" 'Threnody for the Lost' . . . ?"

The tall woman's head nodded once. "Nearly twenty years ago, I was all right. Happily married, one teenage son. Nick. My husband had a good job, I didn't need to work. Just spent the time ministering to my menfolk. Cooking dinner parties for my husband's friends, ferrying Nick from pillar to post. Squash court to rugby club to hockey pitch to yacht club. . . ."

She was silent for a moment. "Nick was drowned in a sailing accident. He was fourteen. His body was never found."

"Like Graham Chadleigh's?" asked Carole softly.

Another nod. "I was devastated. We were both devastated, my husband more than me. He's never really recovered. He'd invested so much hope in Nick, in Nick becoming a sportsman, in Nick achieving things he'd never achieved himself. It was a bad time."

Only the persistent drumming of the rain filled the silence.

"I tried everything," Sheila went on, "that might bring me comfort. Religion . . . therapy . . . antidepressants. . . . Nothing worked. The pain just got worse. And then, for the first time, on the recommendation of a friend, I read 'Threnody for the Lost.' At last I'd found something that spoke to me, somebody who had shared and empathised with my pain. So I started to read more of Esmond Chadleigh's work, to read about his life. I discovered that this house was no longer in the family and falling into disrepair and" — the shrug of her shoulders seemed to encompass everything — "that's how an obsession was born."

"And your husband? Was he involved, too?"

A brisker shrug. "No. As I said, he went to pieces." Like the way she hadn't graced him with a name, this dismissal confirmed her husband's irrelevance in her life.

"You mean he's hospitalised?"

"No, no, he's at home. But he's had nothing to do with Bracketts."

That seemed to be all she had to say on the subject of her husband. And the brief moment of vulnerability brought on by the mention of her son had passed, too. Sheila Cartwright moved briskly to the doorway and looked out at the sheeting rain.

"It's not going to let up. We'd better make a dash for it."

"You'll get soaked through," said Carole dubiously, feeling slightly smug for having brought her Burberry with her from the Renault.

"I'll borrow one of these." Sheila took down a "Bracketts Volunteer" waterproof from the pegs by the door. "We've got plenty of them."

"Some sponsorship deal, was it?"

"Yes. Very promising one. Didn't last, though. Company got taken over by one of the insurance big boys, and the new owners weren't interested in sponsorship

239

at this level. Wanted to entertain their corporate clients at golf tournaments, not writers' houses," she concluded bitterly.

"Still, the coats are good," said Carole.

"Oh, yes, got something out of it," Sheila agreed, zipping up the front and pulling the hood over her head.

"Shouldn't we lock up?" asked Carole.

"Oh, no," said Sheila Cartwright. "Gina's the director. That's her job."

24

As they walked towards the car park, the rain pounded down. Carole envied Sheila's hood, and wished she'd brought some kind of hat, as her hair was flattened against her head. The rain splashed up so much on hitting the ground that Carole's tights and shoes were instantly drenched.

"A good example of the pathetic fallacy," Sheila shouted over the din.

"I'm sorry?"

"When inanimate objects reflect people's emotions. Literary device Esmond used to use quite a lot. Him and the Romantic poets. So you have this rain and wind echoing the storminess of the emergency trustees meeting."

"You were the one who made it stormy," Carole couldn't help saying.

"Unavoidable, I'm afraid. Where the survival of Bracketts is concerned, any means are acceptable."

The moment of sympathy Carole had felt when Sheila talked about her dead son was once again replaced by irritation.

The woman was nothing less than a bully; all she cared about was getting her own way.

Suddenly the path around them was flooded with light. Long slanting lines of rain became solid in the beam. Carole looked up for the flash in the sky, but the light continued.

"Security lamps," Sheila explained. "Triggered by anyone walking towards the car park." Then her attention was distracted. "What the hell . . . ?"

Carole followed her gaze. They were walking along the wall of the kitchen garden, whose gates, locked since the day of the skeleton's discovery, now hung open on their hinges.

"What's been going on?" asked Sheila angrily, as she stepped forwards into the space designated for the Bracketts museum.

Carole saw no lightning flash, but there was a sharp crack of what she took to be thunder. In front of her, Sheila Cartwright shuddered and stood rigid for a moment. Then slowly, she toppled forward, face-down, to the ground.

Carole moved quickly towards her. From the tall body on the ground came a guttural gurgling.

The white beam of the security lamp

caught on the ridges of brown mud by the woman's head.

And on the red blood that was spilling from her hidden face.

25

Carole ran to the Administrative Office to summon the police. It was empty, no sign of Gina. The motherly voice on the other end of the line asked her if she was sure the woman was dead. Instinctively, Carole said yes. She was told not to touch anything, but wait until someone arrived. It shouldn't be more than ten minutes. There was a patrol car in the Fedborough area; wouldn't take long to get to South Stapley. Bracketts, the big house, right. Near the car park, fine. If Mrs. Seddon wouldn't mind waiting by the entrance . . . assuming, of course, that the weather wasn't too bad.

In fact the rain had stopped, as suddenly extinguished as the life of Sheila Cartwright. When Carole returned, the body was completely still, and the pool of blood seemed to have stopped increasing.

The beam of the security lights now showed another gleam of blood, on the dark wetness of Sheila's "Bracketts Volunteer" waterproof, right between her shoulder blades. Only very little had spilled through the small hole in the fabric; presumably a lot more had spread inside, between the coat and her punctured flesh.

It must have been a bullet. Nothing else could have made such a mark and had such an effect. Carole tried to remember exactly where Sheila had been standing when she had been hit, and from what direction the shot had been fired. Definitely not from the car park. The bullet had come from the cluster of buildings — Bracketts itself, the converted stable block that housed the Administrative Office, and Graham Chadleigh-Bewes's cottage. Or maybe the killer had been standing in the open somewhere between them. There was still no sign of anyone, apart from Carole and Sheila's body.

She moved closer to inspect the kitchen garden gates. There was no sign that they had been forced open. Someone had used a key.

As yet, Carole didn't speculate as to who that someone might have been. She was still too numb, too much in shock, to think of attributing blame for Sheila's murder. And, even though logic dictated that the weapon which killed her had been an old service revolver, Carole did not let her traumatised mind form the thought.

Uncertain what she was expecting, she looked fearfully towards the spot where the skeleton had been unearthed less than a fortnight before. There was nothing to see. No boxing-in with fabric structures, no police tape. So far as she could tell in the gloom of the wall's shadow, the ground where the body had lain had been neatly raked over. Whatever official investigations were still going on into that death, they were no longer taking place at the scene of the crime.

Sheila's great triumph, she thought, had been delaying the announcement of that little titbit to the hungry press.

But as Carole turned to face the approaching headlights of the police car, she somehow didn't think any amount of influence with the chief constable was going to allow Sheila Cartwright's murder to be kept quiet for long.

The police were very calming, and tried to make the process of questioning as gentle as possible. Carole was taken back to the Administrative Office, where Gina Locke had reappeared. The small, dark woman seemed to have grown in stature, a model of efficiency as she showed round and answered the questions of the investigating officers. The news of her predecessor's death had lifted a cramping shadow from her, instantly providing her with the space into which she could expand in her role as director of Bracketts.

It was Gina who suggested that the police take over the outer office used by her secretary as a temporary centre for their operations, and it was there that Carole was questioned. She had the sensation of being only half there. The death of Sheila Cartwright felt as though it had taken place in a different existence, and yet Carole's watch told her less than an hour had elapsed since she had made her call to the police.

There was a plainclothes male detective and a uniformed Woman Police Constable. They punctiliously gave their names, but the information did not take any grip on her shaken mind. She was in serious shock, and a part of her consciousness seemed to detach itself to observe the phenomenon. *Come on, you're Carole Seddon*, it urged, *you're the ultimately sensible person. In your Home Office career, you were respected for your control and objectivity. You shouldn't be disoriented by the sight of a little blood.*

But she had been. Of that there was no doubt. And the detached part of her wondered whether her agitation might have been caused by her proximity to Sheila Cartwright at the moment of death. Had the bullet strayed only a couple of feet to the left, it would have been Carole Seddon lying facedown in the mud. Perhaps that knowledge had caused the coldness and the involuntary trembling that twitched through her body.

All she knew, as she went through the basics of her name, address, and other personal information, was that she was not in control of the situation. Or of herself. And Carole hated not being in control.

The questioners, whose names she had so carelessly lost, asked her to describe the moment of Sheila Cartwright's death, and her answers felt dismally inadequate. Why hadn't she been concentrating? Why hadn't she noticed the exact direction in which the victim had stumbled? Why hadn't she looked back after the shot? Why hadn't she run back towards the house to see if there was anyone about? Why hadn't she listened for the sounds of a departing vehicle?

To be fair, this guilt-inducing tone of questioning was all her own. The police were much less hard on her, careful of her emotional state, grateful for the meagre titbits of recollection she could provide for them.

They took her gently back from the moment of murder to the events earlier in the evening — the emergency trustees meeting, the reasons for its calling, and the topics that had been discussed during it.

When asked to describe the business of the meeting. Carole felt an instinct for caution. Sheila Cartwright's overbearing manner had been particularly insulting to Gina Locke and Graham Chadleigh-Bewes. Wasn't giving the police a blow-by-blow account of this tantamount to providing them with two murder suspects?

But Carole was too traumatised to cope with duplicity. She could only tell the unspun truth. And, after all, she was giving information that the police would be getting soon enough from some other source. What did it matter?

The male detective indicated the end of the interview by saying, "Thank you very much, Mrs. Seddon. You've been most helpful, and we much appreciate your frankness at a time that must be very difficult for you. I'm afraid, inevitably, as our investigations continue, we will need to talk to you further, and I apologise for that now. Given the circumstances of the emergency trustees meeting you've just described, I'm sure I don't have to tell you to avoid discussion of this evening's events with any member of the press. All media contact will be handled by the police."

"Of course."

"Finally, Mrs. Seddon, there's one thing I do have to ask you. Though we await forensic confirmation, it would appear that what you witnessed tonight was a violent crime against Mrs. Cartwright. Can you think of anyone who might possibly have had a motive to kill the lady?"

Given the direct question, some of Carole's customary circumspection returned. "Sheila Cartwright had a very strong personality. She had her own ways of doing things, particularly so far as Bracketts was concerned. She seemed to regard this place as her personal fiefdom. As a result, she did tend to put a lot of backs up. But whether annoyance at Sheila's manner would be a sufficient reason for someone actually to kill her . . ." Carole shrugged. ". . . I have no idea."

"No. Well, thank you very much indeed, Mrs. Seddon."

"Now do you think you feel all right to drive yourself home?" asked the female constable solicitously.

"Yes. I was very shaken, but I feel a lot better now."

"We could easily make arrangements for. . . ."

"No. No, thank you, I'll be fine."

As the detective led her to the door, Carole could feel in his body language the urgency to be rid of her and move on to the next interview, but that didn't stop her from asking, "Would you imagine there's a connection between Sheila Cartwright's death and the discovery of the body in the kitchen garden?"

He smiled indulgently. "Mrs. Seddon, even if I knew the answer to that question, you know I wouldn't tell you. We are very early into the investigation of tonight's tragic event. Far too early to be making the kind of connections you suggest."

"Yes. Yes, of course," said Carole, as she left the Administrative Office.

But there was no doubt in her mind that there was a connection between the two deaths.

26

In the short time she had been talking to the police, the area around the kitchen garden gate had been transformed. Floodlights, a battery of vehicles, and equipment now surrounded the scene. And a white, tentlike structure had already been erected over the dead body of Sheila Cartwright.

A polite policeman in a bright yellow waterproof escorted her to the car park. This was only partly, she knew, from solicitude. His main purpose was to make sure that she did actually leave the premises.

Carole was a habitually cautious driver, but that night the white Renault went even slower than usual on its way back to Fethering. The trembling had left her body, but still threatened to flicker back into action at any moment.

Very cautiously, she reversed into the garage at High Tor. Then, as she crossed to her front door, she looked across at Woodside Cottage. She desperately needed to talk to Jude, to share the shock of the evening, and to feel the healing calmness of her neighbour's reaction.

The lights were still on, both downstairs and upstairs. Carole hesitated for a moment.

Then she heard the distinctive sound of coughing from the front bedroom.

Grimly, Carole put her key in the lock of High Tor.

"God, why didn't you come round last night?"

"Well, I. . . ."

"You must've seen the lights on. Laurence and I were talking till really late."

Carole couldn't think of anything to say. Jude had come bustling round from Woodside Cottage as soon as she'd seen her neighbour bringing Gulliver back from his early morning walk and, hearing of Sheila Cartwright's murder, couldn't believe that she hadn't been told about it the night before.

"I . . . I suppose I felt a bit shaken," said Carole inadequately.

"All the more reason to come and see me. I would have poured white wine into you until you calmed down."

"Yes. I know, but . . . well, anyway, I felt I needed to be on my own." There was no way she was going to reveal the real reason why she hadn't gone to see Jude, the threat to their intimacy posed by the presence of Laurence Hawker . . . even the danger that a late-night ring on the doorbell might *interrupt something intimate.* The thought of breaking in on some act of passion between her neighbour and her *boyfriend* . . . if "boyfriend" was the word. . . . The man seemed to have moved pretty fully into Woodside Cottage, so the assumption was reasonable that. . . .

Not for the first time, Carole wished she had more certainty about what was happening in Jude's life. Carole liked everything around her to be cut and dried, whereas everything that concerned her neighbour seemed in some mystical way joined-up and . . . whatever the opposite of "dried" was. . . . "Steamy," perhaps?

In the intuitive way that could sometimes be almost irritating, Jude sensed the way Carole's mind was moving. "Laurence is not around today," she said, with a friendly grin.

"Really?" Carole made it sound as if, though there might be many things on her mind at that moment, they did certainly not include Laurence Hawker. But then she let down the front of insouciance by asking, "Where is he?"

"He's away for the weekend. Got a cab

about half an hour ago. He's staying with a girlfriend."

Once again, so far as Carole was concerned, this was inadequate information. If Laurence was staying with a girlfriend, then presumably Jude wasn't his girlfriend. And if Jude wasn't his girlfriend, then why had she let him move into Woodside Cottage? Or was he a man who cultivated a great number of girlfriends? And if that were the case, and if Jude was part of that harem, how on earth did she tolerate the situation with such apparent equanimity? It was very frustrating not to have things defined.

But all Carole actually said was "Oh?"

And even if she'd wanted to say more, she wouldn't have been able to, because Jude hurried on, "Right, let me get us some coffee, and you give me your full murder witness routine, just like you did it for the police."

"I'll get coffee for guests in my own house, thank you." The instinctive spiky response was out before Carole could stop it.

But Jude just smiled. "All right. Sorry. *You* make the coffee. But may I come into the kitchen and listen to you while the kettle boils?" she added humbly.

Carole knew she was being sent up. Her insistence on the principles that a hostess made the coffee in her own house, and that the coffee, once made, should be consumed in the sitting room rather than the kitchen, was, she knew, old-fashioned and even ridiculous at the beginning of the twenty-first century. But that was the way Carole had been brought up, and this particular leopard was not about to change any more spots than were absolutely necessary. At times the way she was infuriated her, but that was the way she was.

While Carole moved the kettle between sink and Aga, Gulliver greeted Jude as if he had never seen such a wonderful human being since he left the rest of the litter in his mother's basket.

Then, perching on the edge of the table (why couldn't she use a chair?), Jude said, "So . . . tell me exactly what happened."

Carole had become so absorbed in her retelling of the previous evening's events that she didn't notice that they'd both ended up sitting at the kitchen table with their coffees.

At the end of the account, Jude let out a long "Well . . . ," then went on, "Are you sure you're all right? It must have been a terrible shock."

"Well, yes, it was. But I'm fine now.

Actually slept very well last night."

"Emotionally drained."

"Maybe."

"Still, it's a nice little murder mystery, isn't it, Carole? A victim with lots of enemies, and most of them conveniently gathered in the place where she was killed."

"I suppose so."

Jude rubbed her plump hands together gleefully. "Who've we got, then?"

"Sorry?"

"Suspects."

"Ah."

"From what you say, the two whom Sheila Cartwright really humiliated at the meeting were Gina Locke and Graham Chadleigh-Bewes. Both very definitely on the scene at the relevant time. And you said you'd actually seen Graham with the murder weapon?"

"If it *was* the murder weapon. . . ."

"Oh, come on. A handy World War I service revolver. How many more guns are there going to be around a place like Bracketts?"

"All right," Carole conceded. "But Gina would have known of its existence. As would old Belinda."

"Ooh, yes, don't forget the old lady."

"Though I'm not sure what motive

Belinda Chadleigh would have had to kill Sheila Cartwright. She seemed very much to approve of everything Sheila had done around Bracketts."

"*Until*," Jude suggested, with a gleam of mischief in her eyes, "Sheila committed the unforgivable sin of upsetting the old lady's beloved nephew."

"Maybe. I don't think it's very likely."

"Oh, come on, Carole, at this stage we're not concerned with what's *likely*. Just let's allow our ideas to *run* for a bit."

"All right." But Carole didn't really sound as though she approved of the proposal.

"And what about your ex-librarian?"

"George Ferris?"

"Yes. Was he still around when Sheila Cartwright was shot?"

"I don't know. He went off towards the car park, but I didn't actually see him leave."

"So he definitely stays on our list of suspects."

"Why?"

"Not being seen to leave is, by definition, a suspicious action. So — hooray — four lovely juicy suspects!"

Carole's pale eyes were not quite so disapproving as she looked at her neighbour and said primly, "I don't think you're taking this completely seriously, Jude."

27

"I wondered if we could talk." Gina Locke's voice sounded cool and authoritative. The call had come through early on Saturday afternoon.

"Yes, of course," Carole had replied. "How can I help?"

"Be easier if we could meet up . . . if that's all right with you?"

"Fine. When?"

"Sooner the better. I don't mind coming down to Fethering. Or we could meet somewhere for a drink or . . . ?"

"There's a nice pub near the seafront here. Called the Crown and Anchor. Meet there about six-thirty?"

She got a frisson from making the arrangements. The Carole Seddon of a few years before would never have fixed to meet someone in a pub, and certainly not in a pub with whose landlord *she had a history*.

"Yes, I heard about that business up at Bracketts. Couldn't avoid it. Regulars at lunchtime weren't talking about anything else."

259

Carole had deliberately arrived at the Crown and Anchor early for her appointment with Gina Locke. Deliberately so that she could have a word with Ted Crisp.

Though their brief relationship — Carole still had difficulty allowing herself to use the word "affair" — hadn't worked out, she was glad still to be in contact with Ted. Once the embarrassment of splitting up was over, she could once again find reassurance in his shaggy presence. He was once again all that he should ever have been — a good friend (and Carole never admitted to herself how influential Jude had been in restoring that state of affairs).

But looking at him that Saturday evening, Carole did find slightly incongruous the idea that Ted had ever been more to her than a good friend. He had sweated through a busy Saturday lunchtime at the end of the tourist season, and his hair and beard looked like flake tobacco, and there were white tide marks round the armpits of his T-shirt. Thank God at least he wasn't wearing the shorts. . . .

No, Ted Crisp would never really have fitted into the clinical neatness of High Tor. Or the matching neatness of Carole's life.

"What," she asked, as she sipped her

white wine, "are your lunchtime regulars saying about the murder at Bracketts?"

"How'd you mean?" He'd taken advantage of the lull to pull himself a half of lager and was sitting at the table with her.

"Well, I'm sure the Fethering gossips have already worked out whodunit."

"Plenty of theories, yes. But Bracketts is a bit far away. No one knows any of the people involved."

"You know one," said Carole, with the nearest her thin face could get to a mischievous expression.

"Do I?"

"I'm a trustee of Bracketts."

"Are you?" The look on his face did no favours to her self-esteem. "Why you, of all people?"

"Because of my successful career in the Home Office," she replied frostily (though, even as she used it, she had a little niggle of doubt about the word "successful").

"Oh. Right." Ted nodded the nod of a man who didn't know about that kind of thing. "So, if you're a trustee, you can give me all the dirt."

"Sadly, I can't. For two reasons. One — we've all been sworn to absolute secrecy. . . ."

"Ah."

"And, two" — she confessed sheepishly,

though not entirely accurately — "I don't really know any dirt." He nodded in sympathy with the unfairness of her situation. "So what your lunchtime regulars were saying, Ted, is probably at least as useful as anything I know. What were their speculations?"

"Oh, the usual suspects. A serial killer. They like serial killers, the old geezers who come in here. The Sanatogen and Stairlift Brigade. I keep trying to tell them that you can't have a serial killer responsible for a single murder. By definition, there has to be at least one more stiff before you can start using the expression. But will they listen?"

Carole grinned. Her previous life hadn't encompassed anyone like Ted Crisp.

"Then some of the old farts reckon the murder's down to local politics inside Bracketts. If they knew you was a trustee up there, then they'd definitely finger you for the job, Carole. Or again, there's the escaped convict theory."

"Hm?"

"Always very popular for any crime done round this locality. 'Cause we're so near to Austen, you see. Crime in a nice middle-class area like West Sussex — must've been done by a criminal, that's how the logic goes. And where are there any criminals

262

round here? H.M.P. Austen's bloody full of them. So there's your culprit. And, as it happens, a lifer did go over the wall few days back, so . . . there you are — bingo, hit the jackpot — he must've done it."

Carole nodded slowly, as the image came to her mind of Sheila Cartwright turning on Mervyn Hunter just after discovery of the skull in the kitchen garden.

There was a clatter from the door, and the sounds of a tired family entering after a chilly day on the beach. The wife wanted to go straight home. The husband was insisting on having a quick pint before they faced the drive back. The children had had enough.

Ted rose to his feet. "Better go and do my job, I suppose." He grinned down at Carole. "My regulars'll be dead impressed when I tell them you're a trustee up at Bracketts."

"What, because they haven't heard before about my distinguished career in the Home Office?"

"Nah." Ted Crisp shook his head in bewilderment. "Because there's been a murder up there."

The bickering family's arrival was quickly followed by that of Gina Locke. She asked for a white wine, and the two women were soon ensconced in a corner booth, well away from the Crown and Anchor's other customers.

The impression Carole had received the previous evening — and indeed on the telephone — that the director had been empowered by Sheila Cartwright's death, was accentuated by seeing her in the flesh. The charisma that had struck Carole on first meeting seemed to have paled during their subsequent acquaintance, but was now back in full force. She had never particularly noticed Gina's clothes before, but that evening was aware of the finesse with which the generously cut grey trousers and skimpy chocolate-coloured woollen top had been chosen. The brown eyes had an added lustre, and the short, dark hair looked newly sculpted. The murder of Sheila Cartwright had effected a makeover in Gina Locke.

"Reason for this meeting is a bit of a hymn-sheet one," she began.

"Sorry?"

"Hymn-sheet. See that we're all singing from the same one."

"Ah. Yes." Carole felt exposed and unfashionable. She had heard Sheila using the expression before; she should have caught on quicker.

"I think there could be an announcement from the police sooner rather than later, so I want all the trustees to be prepared."

"An announcement? Are you talking about an announcement of an arrest?"

"Yes. It's a pretty open-and-shut case. Even the notoriously thick British police force can't take long over this one."

It wasn't Carole's style to say "Whoa, whoa, hold your horses!" but she raised a hand, which had the same effect. "You're saying you have no doubt who killed Sheila?"

"Of course not. It was Graham."

"Why?"

"Well, he's the obvious suspect. You were there, you saw her humiliate him in front of the other trustees. You saw her take away from him his life's work — the biography of Esmond Chadleigh. If that's not sufficient motive for murder, I'd like to know what is."

"But —"

Gina was not about to stop. "What's more, he'd got the gun. Supposedly taken it for cleaning, but if you believe that, you'd believe anything."

Gina clearly shared Jude's conviction that the murder weapon was the gun from the display case, but Carole wanted more proof. "Have the police actually told you that Graham Chadleigh's service revolver was the one that was used?"

Gina smiled. "You say Graham Chadleigh's, but in fact there's some doubt about that."

"But it's in the display case with a card saying it belonged to Graham Chadleigh."

There was a cynical little shrug. "Truth is one of the first casualties of the heritage industry, Carole. If you counted up all the beds in which Queen Elizabeth the First slept, she'd've had to be using about three a night."

"Ah. Have you ever handled the revolver, Gina?"

"No," came the sharp reply.

"Graham told me it was in full working order."

"Must've been. And if he admits to knowing that . . . behold another argument for the fact that he shot Sheila."

"Ah, right. So, nothing else of interest you've gleaned from the police, Gina?"

"No, they've told me very little, actually. Not surprised, they've been so busy questioning Graham."

"Have they?"

"Yes. Apparently, he claims to have an

266

alibi for the time of the murder, but it's only old Belinda. And since she seems to be only half-conscious at the best of times, the police shouldn't take long to crack that. I think they'll arrest him in the next twenty-four hours."

"What makes you so sure, Gina?"

"Logic. The logic I've just outlined to you, and . . . Graham's character. He's not the most stable of people, is he?"

"No, true. But there's a big jump from being unstable to being a murderer."

"Depends on the provocation."

"Maybe. So you're of the view that we're all capable of murder, given the right provocation?"

"Yes, I think I'd go along with that."

Carole fixed Gina with her pale blue eyes. "You took quite a bit of provocation at the emergency trustees meeting."

"Yes." The director giggled, suddenly girlish. "Sheila had got me pretty furious, I don't deny it. Maybe I would have topped her myself . . . if Graham hadn't so conveniently saved me the trouble. Her death is certainly the best thing that's happened since I took over this job."

Carole must have shown some instinctive middle-class reaction of disapproval, because Gina went on, "Sorry, not the

267

right thing to say, is it, of a woman less than twenty-four hours dead? Don't speak ill, et cetera. . . . But I can't pretend in Sheila's case. That woman's sole aim was to make my life a misery. I am ecstatic to know that she is no longer around, and that I am now free to get on with my job as director of Bracketts."

A motive for killing Sheila Cartwright could not have been more straightforwardly expressed, and yet the insouciant baldness with which Gina Locke had spoken seemed instantly to rule her out as a suspect. Surely, thought Carole, no double bluff could be that elaborate.

But Gina hadn't finished. "I think what really annoyed me was that I'd been set up from the start."

"Sorry?"

"With the job. Sheila had decided a year or so back that she was taking on too much at Bracketts, and she needed to back off a bit, bring in someone else to do the administration. The trustees, some of whom had been getting a bit sick of her high-handed ways, agreed, and advertised for the job of director. Sheila wanted a yes-man — or yes-woman — someone to do the boring stuff and rubber-stamp her decisions. The trustees wanted someone with a bit more self-motivation and energy. I got the job. Sheila stood down, and became a trustee.

"Except, of course, she was no more capable of standing down and giving her successor a free run than Margaret Thatcher was. From the day I started here, it was clear that I was director in name only. I was still going to have Sheila leaning over my shoulder all the time, cherry-picking the best bits of the job. A potential major sponsor in the offing . . . did *I* get to go and do the pitch to them? Did I hell? No, they were used to dealing with Sheila Cartwright. They wouldn't be safe in the hands of someone my age — in spite of the qualifications I have in the arts, leisure, and heritage industries."

Gina took a long, satisfied sigh, and sipped from her glass. But Carole didn't say anything; she sensed there was more to come.

"Well, I don't need to tell you. You've seen her in action, Carole. She resigned as a trustee . . . which is in fact why there was a vacancy on the board for you to fill . . . and you're not going to believe the reason Sheila gave for resigning. 'I don't really think a trusteeship is the ideal role for me — it seems to involve responsibility without power.' " The tone with which she invested the words was uncannily evocative of the dead woman.

"Put it another way, being on the Board of Trustees meant she occasionally had to listen to the opinions of others about what should be done at Bracketts. So she ceased to be a trustee, and just continued to go her own sweet way, as if there never had been any change in the management structure."

Gina grinned gleefully. "But not anymore. I am now going to show what I can do in this job. I'm going to turn Bracketts round, and I am going to get that museum built."

"Have you got a sponsor, then?"

"I've got some very good potential names. Big companies. Sheila had set up meetings with them. I will go to those meetings, catch them when their guard's down and they feel they should be saying appropriate things about her death. There's nothing like death to put people in a charitable mood."

This sounded a painfully cynical approach to fund-raising, but Carole didn't question its efficacy. For some obscure reason, though, she felt moved to defend Sheila Cartwright, exonerate the dead woman from the full force of Gina's vilification. "Did Sheila ever tell you why she took up the cause of Bracketts so single-mindedly?"

Gina shrugged. The answer didn't interest her. But Carole still recounted the conversation she'd had with Sheila while they were waiting for the rain to ease off . . . in fact, just before the woman had been shot.

Still Gina wasn't impressed. "That may have been what started her. What kept her going was her pure megalomania. From which, thank goodness, none of us will ever have to suffer again."

There was a silence. The unchallenged director of Bracketts glowed. Having unburdened herself of that lot, the makeover was complete.

Then Carole said, "Which I assume means you won't go to Sheila's funeral . . . whenever that may be?"

"Don't you believe it. I'll be there."

"But if you hated the woman as much as you say. . . ."

"All the Great and the Good of West Sussex will be there." She made a little finger-rubbing money gesture. "Dosh. Potential sponsors."

"Right," said Carole, who was beginning to get a clearer idea about the ethics of fund-raising.

And that was about it, really. They finished their drinks, and Gina said she'd have to go. Which she did, leaving Carole wondering why this important face-to-face meeting had been set up in the first place.

All Carole was left with was the very strong impression that Gina hadn't killed Sheila Cartwright, but that Graham had.

Which perhaps, she reflected, was exactly the impression with which Gina had intended to leave her. And to give that impression had, indeed, been the sole purpose of their meeting.

28

Jude enjoyed a slow getting-up on the Sunday morning. She had had all the windows open most of the previous day, and only a residual tang of cigarette now hung about Woodside Cottage. It was a long time since she had cohabited with anyone for more than a night, and she couldn't deny her relief at having the house to herself.

The fact that she knew Laurence Hawker to be in the company — almost certainly the bed — of another woman could not have worried her less. For the first six months in Prague, even the suspicion of such a possibility would have reduced her to an anguish of doubt and pain. Now . . . the image of the other woman did not even enter her mind. Partly, she knew, this was because she had matured. And partly . . . it was because of Laurence's circumstances.

The shadow of his infidelity, which had hung over their previous cohabitation, had been replaced by the shadow of his illness. Jude tried not to think about it too much, and for much of the time could keep her mind fruitfully full of other thoughts, but every now and then the reality gate-crashed. Neither of them pretended that they were the great loves of one another's lives, but their rediscovered proximity was bound to aggravate the inevitable pain that lay ahead.

Occasionally, Jude's mind strayed to the possibilities of cure. She knew many heart-warming stories of success with cancer, using both conventional and alternative therapies. But every time she had such thoughts, she hit a brick wall; she couldn't take the idea further. It was Jude's deeply held belief that in all matters medical the wishes of the patient remained paramount. Even to raise the subject of treatment with Laurence would be a betrayal of the agreement they had made. Jude sometimes found it hard to live with that agreement, but she knew she must. If Laurence were to change his mind, the situation would be different. But she knew he was never going to.

Still, as she soaked in a bath fragrant with herbs and oils on the Sunday morning, Jude was able to displace morbid thoughts of one death with more cheerful thoughts of another. Since she'd never properly known Sheila Cartwright, the murder prompted an intellectual rather than an emotional reaction. Jude didn't have nearly as much knowledge of the principals in the case as Carole did, but she could still speculate. And ring Carole later, see if she fancied lunch at the Crown and Anchor, for a bit more speculation.

The phone rang. Fortunately, for once she'd remembered to bring the mobile with her, so she could answer it without getting out of her cocoon of bathwater.

It was Sandy Fairbarns. "I'm ringing because I heard about the murder up at Bracketts."

"Hard to escape it. Radio, television . . . I haven't seen any of the papers yet today, but I'm sure it'll be all over them, too."

"It is. And, listen, the police have been to Austen."

"Really? Why?"

"Asking some of the other inmates about Mervyn Hunter."

"Ah."

"Until Friday evening, the search for him was a kind of 'Circulate his details round the country, but he'll turn up in his own good time.' Now it's a manhunt."

"You mean he's a suspect?"

"Apparently he had a good few set-tos with Sheila Cartwright. Just the kind of bossy, demanding woman who'd get to him."

"Yes, but do you think . . . ? It would have taken planning . . . for Mervyn to make his way up to Bracketts, find the gun and —"

"No, I don't for a moment think he's anything to do with it. But the poor sap's tarred with that brush . . . you know, he killed a woman once, so. . . ."

"Of course he's going to go on killing women."

"That's the thinking, yes."

"But I'm sure when he's found, it'll be proved he had nothing to do with this murder."

"Hope so. I'm just worried about 'when he's found.' I'm afraid if the hunt got really intense and close, Mervyn might panic and . . . do some harm. . . ."

"To himself or to someone else?"

"Either. I'm actually more worried about him doing harm to himself."

"Hm. So what do you want to do, Sandy?"

"I want us to try and find him before the police do."

Jude let out a low whistle. "What are the chances of that? Do you have any leads?"

"Only one. There was a guy up at

Bracketts that Mervyn used to talk about. Sounded almost like he'd got a friend up there. Certainly closer to a friend than anyone he met round Austen."

Jude understood instinctively. "So you want me to go and talk to this 'friend'? See if he knows anything about Mervyn's whereabouts . . . ?"

"That's it," said Sandy.

"All right. What's his name?"

"Jonny Tyson."

Mrs. Tyson had answered the phone. She volunteered that her name was Brenda, but still sounded guarded. Yes, Jonny was at home, but he didn't like the telephone. What was Jude's call in connection with?

"It's about a friend of Jonny's. Someone he works with up at Bracketts. Mervyn Hunter."

"Ah." The name brought instant warmth to Brenda Tyson's voice. It seemed to come more naturally to her than the initial frostiness. "Yes, Jonny talks about Mervyn a lot. They seem to get on very well."

"Well, I don't know if you'd heard, but Mervyn Hunter has escaped and —"

"Escaped? I'm sorry, I don't know what you're talking about."

Oh, dear. Perhaps Mervyn had never mentioned his unusual accommodation arrangements. Or perhaps Jonny had not mentioned them to his parents.

Still, Jude had stepped too far in for retreat. If she was going to get to see Jonny, the truth would have to come out. "Mervyn Hunter's a prisoner at Austen. He works at Bracketts on a day-release programme they organise."

"I wasn't aware of that." But Brenda Tyson didn't sound too shocked by the news.

"Well, the fact is that Mervyn's escaped, and the police are looking for him. They haven't been in touch with Jonny yet, have they?"

"The police? Good heavens, no. Jonny's never had anything to do with the police."

"I'm sure he hasn't. I was just thinking, Brenda, that it might help if I came and talked to Jonny. . . ."

"Why?"

"So that, if the police want to talk to him — and I think they probably will — Jonny will at least know the background to what they're talking about."

"Yes. . . ."

"I thought it might be less frightening for him."

Jude's response to the uncertainty in Brenda Tyson's tone had exactly the right effect. "Good idea. Yes, you come and talk to him." Then, hesitantly, Jonny's mother asked, "Is this something to do with that poor woman up at Bracketts . . . the one who . . . you know . . . ?"

"There might be an indirect connexion."

"Then you'd better come over here as soon as possible."

A twenty-minute cab ride took Jude to the Tysons' house in Weldisham, a place that still had dark memories for her. A previous investigation in the village had led to Carole's kidnapping and a very real threat to her life. But most of the people Jude had met at that time had, for one reason or another, moved away.

That early October noontime, though, the very idea that the village might have a darker side was incongruous. The sky was a deep autumn blue, lazy lines of cloud straggled across the top of the grey-green Downs; the thatch and flint of Weldisham's houses acted out the fantasy of every tube-bound Londoner.

The cottage outside which Jude's cab drew up was the most idyllic of the lot. Old red brick with flint facing, thatch that came down low like a generous piecrust. The front garden was immaculate; no autumn leaf would be allowed more than a temporary sojourn on that fitted carpet of a lawn.

Brenda Tyson had clearly been waiting for her. The studded wooden door, over which climbing rosebushes had been artfully trained, was open before Jude came through the garden gate. A smell of Sunday roast emanated from the cottage, and the woman who stood in the doorway supplemented the image of English home and mother love.

She was in her late sixties, sturdy rather than plump, dressed in the kind of belted blue cotton dress that, never having been fashionable, did not look unfashionable. There were thick brown sandals at the ends of her stout legs. Grey hair was cut short in what was once called a pageboy style, and her ruddy face looked as if it had never bothered with makeup.

"Jude, so good of you to come. I'm Brenda, as you probably worked out. Jonny's in the garden. I haven't told him you're coming. It's often better if he doesn't have time to worry about things. Do come in."

Jude was led through an immaculate

hall, whose white-painted panelling was bright with highly polished horse brasses, trivets, and warming pans, into a sitting room from whose French windows a beautifully kept garden sloped down into a small valley. There was no sign of Jonny; he must have been working out of sight down at the bottom of the garden.

But there was someone else in the room. Propped awkwardly on an armchair with a footrest extension sat a thin old man, neatly dressed in cavalry twill trousers, a tattersall checked shirt, and a lovat green cardigan with leather-covered buttons. He appeared unable to move, though a flicker in his half-open eyes registered the new arrival.

"My husband, Kenneth. He's had a couple of strokes, but" — she smiled determinedly across to him — "you're on the mend now, aren't you, love?"

Brenda Tyson left a polite moment for some response, but there was none. "Do sit down, Jude. Can I get you a tea or coffee or something?"

"I'm fine, thanks."

At that moment Kenneth Tyson slipped slightly in his chair and was left hanging over the arm. While his wife straightened him up, Jude took in the sitting room. Like everything else about the Tysons' cottage, it was impeccably neat. Curtains with a design of ivy on a white background toned with the sage of the carpet and the darker Dralon of the three-piece suite. Kenneth Tyson's chair, though clearly a piece of specialised furniture, had been covered to match the rest.

And on every surface in the sitting room were celebrations of Jonny. Photographs of him as a baby, an infant, a child, a teenager, a powerful adult. The flattened face with its same huge smile beamed from every frame.

Brenda Tyson followed Jude's gaze and could not repress a smile of pride. "He's nearly forty now, you know. When he was born, they said there was no chance we'd have him that long. But the care has improved, and. . . ." She chuckled. "Mind you, when he was born, he was called a 'Mongol.' But we're not allowed to say that now. 'Down's syndrome' . . . I don't know why that's reckoned to be any better. I suppose it's all this political correctness — mustn't say anything that might be hurtful to the Mongol hordes. Though, having lived in this area all my life, I think it's only a matter of time before someone pops up and says 'Down's syndrome' is offensive to the South Downs. Doesn't worry me, though. Whatever name he's given, he's still basically just our Jonny."

There was tension in her smile as she finished, and Jude realised that, in spite of her relaxed mumsy exterior, Brenda Tyson was on edge. Her long speech had been displacement activity, putting off what she really wanted to say.

Jude was good at silence, and she let it extend until Brenda felt ready to confide in her.

"The fact is, Jude, I'm worried about anything that may upset Jonny." She gestured round the sitting room. "We've got everything settled here for him. He knows what to expect. He's calm. There's a rhythm to his life which suits him.

"The same up at Bracketts . . . not quite to the same extent, because there are a lot of other people up there . . . but he knows what's expected of him, and he works very hard for them in the garden." She couldn't resist a proud digression. "Jonny's wonderful with plants, you know. He really seems to understand them, be in tune with them." Her gaze shifted out through the French windows. "He does everything here, you know. It's all down to Jonny."

Brenda Tyson was again silent, still

having difficulty getting to the point she wanted to make.

"You're worried that this business with the police may upset his routine?" Jude suggested.

The woman smiled gratefully. "Exactly that. Most of the time, when he knows what's going on, Jonny's fine. He's a real ray of sunshine to have around the place. But when there's something he doesn't understand . . . he gets confused. He sort of has tantrums. And he's such a strong boy that. . . ."

"Are you saying he sometimes gets violent, Brenda?"

A firm shake of the head. She wasn't going to have that word applied to her son. "No. He gets confused, as I said. He becomes very truculent and uncooperative. Jonny's like all the rest of us — he likes to be liked. If he gets the impression someone dislikes him, if someone's harsh with him . . . I'm sorry, I know I'm overprotective . . . but I'm his mother, and I know him so well. . . . He's very trusting with strangers, but if someone's nasty to him — or shouts at him — or bullies him . . . he reacts very badly."

"Did Sheila Cartwright ever bully him up at Bracketts?" asked Jude tentatively.

She had feared Brenda Tyson might read

this as suspicion of her son, but that anxiety was immediately diffused. "No. Sheila was very gentle with him. With all the . . . oh, dear, what's the current politically correct way to describe them? 'People with learning difficulties,' that's probably it. Sheila set up that whole system, she saw the potential for cooperation between Bracketts and all the training colleges that look after . . . people like that. And she was always particularly good with Jonny. Very calm, let him take things at his own pace. Sheila had a son, too. She lost him. I think that made her extrasensitive to young people."

This was a new dimension to the image of Sheila Cartwright, but Jude did not disbelieve it. She could not imagine Brenda Tyson speaking anything other than the complete truth.

"Does Jonny know what happened to Sheila?"

Brenda shook her head, shamefaced. "I haven't dared tell him yet. And I've kept him away from news bulletins on the television and radio — not that he's ever much interested, anyway. No, he doesn't know anything." The face that looked up at Jude contained a mixture of apology and pleading. "It's the kind of news that'll really upset him, destroy his equilibrium.

And it'll make him angry with me. Jonny's never very good at distinguishing between the bad news and the messenger."

"Would you like me to tell him about Sheila Cartwright?"

Her open red face showed how much Brenda Tyson would like to say yes, how much she'd even been angling for the offer, but her sense of duty stopped her. "It's something I should do."

"I don't mind. He'll have to know, because of the things I need to ask him about Mervyn Hunter."

"It really should be me," Brenda insisted. "I'm his mother."

"You're his mother, and you've done brilliantly for him." Jude's gesture encompassed the whole cottage. "You've made this wonderful environment for him. You've made him safe and secure. Much better he should hear this bad news from someone else."

"Well, if you really don't mind. . . ."

"I don't make offers I don't mean."

As she sat back in her chair, some of the tension left Brenda Tyson's body. But its departure heralded a new sadness. She looked around the perfect sitting room and the perfect garden beyond. "And who's going to break the really bad news to him?"

"Which really bad news?"

She sighed. "When Kenneth dies. When I die. I've told him it's going to happen, every day I tell him it's going to happen, and he says he understands, but he doesn't. 'If you start dying, Mummy, I'll make it better. Jonny'll look after you.' He doesn't understand." A distant, pained look came into her eyes. "I know why people in this situation sometimes kill their children. It's less cruel than to leave them alone in a world that doesn't understand them."

Jude's response was stopped by the sudden change in Brenda Tyson's expression. Dashing away the incipient tear, she beamed broadly as she looked out towards the garden.

Framed in the French windows was the stocky, powerful figure of her son, whose face was irradiated by a huge smile.

"Jonny, darling."

"I'm jolly hungry, Mummy. Isn't lunch ready yet?"

"Not quite, love. Very soon. But first, I'd like you to meet Jude."

"How do you do?" Beautifully schooled, he reached his large hand across and shook hers.

"Jude'd like to have a little talk to you before lunch."

29

"Is this Carole Seddon?"

"Yes."

"Marla Teischbaum."

"Good morning."

"Listen, I'm sorry to interrupt your Sunday, but I wanted to talk about what happened at Bracketts on Friday."

"Fine." Carole remembered the caution that had been given to all the trustees about talking to the professor. But she was intrigued. Marla Teischbaum wasn't the sort of woman to phone her for no reason.

And so it proved. "I believe you were actually with Sheila Cartwright when she was shot."

"That's true, yes. We were walking to the car park together."

"So where was the shot fired from?"

"I'm sorry, I don't see what relevance this has to you. I've given an account of what happened to the police, and I think I should probably leave it at that."

"No, you gotta tell me. This is important!"

For the first time in their brief acquaintance, Marla Teischbaum sounded as though she were losing it. Carole had seen her angry before, during her exchange with Sheila Cartwright at Bracketts, but the woman had still sounded totally in control. Now she was nearly hysterical.

"Why's it important?" asked Carole, her own cool increasing as Marla grew more heated. "Are you planning to add an appendix to your biography about Sheila Cartwright's death?"

"No, I just . . . want to know." The professor slowed down, regaining mastery over her emotions. "All I'm asking is whether you can say exactly where the bullet was fired from?"

There didn't seem to be much harm in answering that. "Then the answer's no. It was dark, it was raining, we were walking away from the house. It took me a minute or two to realise that a gun had been fired, and that Sheila had been hit."

"Was she hit in the front or the back?"

"Back." Again that was hardly classified information.

"So the gun was fired from the house rather than from the car park?"

"From somewhere near the house, yes. From that direction, anyway."

"But you can't be more specific? You didn't see anyone with the gun?"

"I've told you. My first instinct was to find out what had happened to Sheila. It was only when I saw the blood that I realised she had been shot. By the time I looked back towards Bracketts, any self-respecting murderer would have been well out of sight."

"Yes. That's true." And the news seemed to bring some comfort to Marla Teischbaum. She certainly sounded more relaxed, less threatened, as she went on. "I was wondering whether recent events might have changed the situation . . . ?"

"What situation?"

"The situation with regard to cooperation on my biography from the Bracketts setup."

Carole was appalled. "Marla, Sheila Cartwright hasn't been dead two days. The trustees haven't met since the tragedy, and I think when we next do, cooperation with you on your biography may not be at the top of our agenda."

"Aw, come on, don't go all snooty on me. I'm American, I'm direct. If there's a question that matters to me, I ask it. The worst anyone can say to you is no."

"And I'm afraid, at the moment, that is

the only answer I can give you. Maybe, when the trustees next meet, the situation will be reassessed."

Carole knew she was sounding pompous, but . . . the sheer gall of the woman. Sheila Cartwright had been one of the main opponents of Marla's biography of Esmond Chadleigh. With Sheila conveniently — though tragically — out of the way, the professor was coolly asking whether she was now in with a chance.

On the other hand, if cooperation from the Bracketts trustees was the outcome she anticipated, it would have given Marla a very good motive to kill Sheila Cartwright. But, as with Gina Locke, the awareness of her advantage from the crime was so overt that surely she couldn't be the perpetrator. No self-respecting criminal would be quite that obvious.

"But I will, if you like," Carole continued, feeling she ought to offer some kind of sop to the professor, "ask Graham if there's any more Esmond Chadleigh material he's willing to part with."

"Forget it. If it's as useful — and as incompetently doctored — as the last lot, he can keep it."

"Fine. I was just trying to be helpful."

"If you're talking to Graham, by the way,

will you *thank him profusely* for sending me the material, and tell him I'm *not that stupid?* You can also tell him that I have found a new research source — through the County Records Office — that he knows nothing about, but that is providing me with some *wonderfully different* insights into the history of the happy Chadleigh family."

The emphasis with which Marla Teischbaum swooped on certain phrases was deeply ironic. Carole couldn't know whether the messages she was being given were true, or whether they were being sent just to upset Graham Chadleigh-Bewes. She thought that probably, given the battering Esmond's grandson had been given, first by Sheila at the emergency trustees meeting and now presumably by the police, it might be kinder to omit passing on the messages.

Carole was thoughtful after she had put the phone down. Both Gina and now Marla had been very keen to talk to her, and yet neither had used their conversation to do much more than spell out — in very blatant terms — the strong motives they had for wanting Sheila Cartwright dead.

Jude. She needed to talk to Jude.

But there was no reply from Woodside

292

Cottage. Carole returned to High Tor for a thoughtful but uninspiring lunch based on the remains of a fish pie.

Gulliver nudged hopefully at her knee, hoping to deflect her mind towards thoughts of walks, but she was too preoccupied to notice him.

There were one or two things Marla had said on the phone that prompted at least speculation, possibly even investigation. She'd talked about a new "research source." Perhaps that was a phrase academics used all the time, but the last time Carole could recall hearing it was from George Ferris at the emergency trustees meeting. On that occasion he'd also talked of speaking to Marla "this afternoon." Was it possible that he'd given her a lift over to Bracketts and they'd talked in the car? George lived in Fedborough; Marla was staying at The Pelling Arms in Fedborough; there would be a logic to it.

And if George had driven her to the house, did he also give her a lift back afterwards? Given that was the case, what did Marla do while the emergency trustees meeting was going on? Was she still at Bracketts when Sheila was killed?

Carole knew her mind was racing, making connections from insufficient facts, and she tried to curb its gallop. Come on, whatever else she might be, Carole Seddon was always *sensible*.

And there was something else she could do that was less speculative, more pragmatic. Marla Teischbaum had definitely spoken of the material Graham Chadleigh-Bewes had passed on to her as being "doctored."

Carole was glad she'd taken the photocopies. After lunch, immune to the deep misunderstood pathos in Gulliver's big brown eyes, she spread the documents out over the sitting room table.

30

Brenda Tyson left them discreetly alone, announcing that she had to get on with lunch, and maybe Jonny would like to show Jude round the garden. This he did, with great enthusiasm, pointing out the various features and the work he had done on them.

"Daddy used to do it all, and I helped him. Now I do it, just like he did," he said with pride. "Daddy can't do it, and I'm looking after it for him . . . until Daddy's better."

Oh dear, thought Jude, was this another example of Brenda Tyson trying to keep bad news from her son? Medical science would have to advance exponentially before the wreck she'd seen in the customised armchair would be once again looking after his own garden.

They had reached the bottom of the valley, where a tall, thick hedge marked the limits of the Tysons' property. An area had been flattened down there, and work had begun on paving it with huge slabs of York stone.

"This'll be a place for Mummy to sit in the evenings. It catches the last of the afternoon sun. It's a proper little sun trap." He spoke the words confidently, but he was clearly quoting his mother verbatim.

There was something strange about the way Jonny spoke. His voice was gruff, but had an adolescent's liability to crack from time to time. And he sounded as though he was modelling his speech on someone else's. But the model he had chosen was out of date, nearer the 1950s than the beginning of the twenty-first century. Maybe that was the effect of an upbringing cosseted by an ageing mother and lacking contact with his contemporaries.

"You're doing it beautifully," said Jude, looking at the half-finished patio.

"Yes. It's going to be very good for Mummy." Suddenly, ebulliently, he lifted up one of the piled York flagstones and laid it neatly on the prepared sand. He leapt back, waving his upraised fists in excitement, like a footballer who had just scored a goal, then jumped forward, landing his full weight on the stone to settle it.

He turned and smiled shyly at Jude. She smiled back, but all she could think about was Jonny's strength. He had lifted the solid flagstone as if it had been made of polystyrene.

The scene was idyllic. A warm autumn day in one of the most beautiful parts of the British Isles, the sun rousing smells of the garden, the distant flavour of a Sunday roast. And Jonny Tyson, beaming in the glow of Jude's approval.

But she knew she had to break the perfection. And quickly. She didn't want to disrupt the established routine of the Tysons' Sunday lunch.

"Jonny . . . ," she began.

"Yes, Jude," he said trustingly, proud of his command of her name.

"I want to talk about things that have been happening up at Bracketts."

"I work there." The statement gave him great satisfaction.

"I know you do. Listen, something rather unpleasant has happened. Someone at Bracketts has been killed."

"There's no need to tell me that. It was actually me who dug up the skeleton." Whatever shock may have been his initial reaction to the discovery had now been replaced by pride.

"I wasn't talking about the skeleton, Jonny. Someone else has been killed."

This puzzled him. "Someone else? Who?"

"Sheila Cartwright."

There was a long silence. Jude tensed, awaiting the outburst of a tantrum. But when Jonny finally spoke, he sounded bewildered, as he tried to piece together the logic. "Sheila Cartwright got me my job at Bracketts. . . ."

"I know."

"Does this mean I won't still have a job at Bracketts?"

"No, I'm sure it won't change anything about the running of the place," said Jude, without questioning the basis on which she made this assertion.

"Sheila Cartwright's dead." Jonny slowly processed the information. "Like Granny Tyson. I won't see her again."

"No. You won't."

The confusion in his face gradually melted into one of his huge smiles. "Mervyn'll be pleased," he announced.

"Mervyn Hunter?"

"Yes. My *friend*. Mervyn doesn't like Sheila Cartwright."

"Ah." The opportunity was too good to miss. "I did actually want to talk to you about Mervyn Hunter, Jonny."

"That's all right. He's my friend. And he lives at Austen Prison." These facts were produced like rich gifts.

"But he isn't at Austen Prison now."

"Isn't he? Have they let him go home early?"

"No, they haven't, Jonny. He ran away from the prison."

"Did he?"

"Yes. Last week." Jude looked into the slightly watery blue eyes. "When did you last see Mervyn, Jonny?"

"At Bracketts. At work. Last week."

"Do you know which day?"

Jonny shook his head dubiously, jutting out his lower lip. "I'm not sure." But then he remembered. "Oh, yes, it was Thursday. Late Thursday . . . because my friend Mervyn was doing a *special project*." He brought his voice down to a childlike conspiratorial level for the words.

"What kind of 'special project'?"

"It was something Sheila Cartwright had asked him to do. That's why he couldn't be seen by the other volunteers. Only me. I was the only one he trusted," said Jonny, once again as proud as Punch.

"Did he give you any more details about it?"

"No, he said it was secret. And if something's secret, that means you can't tell people about it." He looked at Jude reprovingly. "Which means I can't tell you about it."

"But do you actually know about it? Did Mervyn tell you?"

Jonny looked a little discomfited. "No, he didn't tell me. But if he had told me, I wouldn't be able to tell you about it. Because it was a secret."

Jude didn't want to bully him, so she shifted the angle of her questioning. "But it was definitely Thursday you saw him?"

"Thursday." He nodded emphatically. "And Friday."

"Oh?" The young man could not begin to know the impact of his words. "Mervyn Hunter was at Bracketts on Friday?"

"Mm. Because I gave him something on Friday."

"What did you give him, Jonny?"

"They don't do nice food at Austen Prison. My friend Mervyn used to have the same packed lunch every day he came to Bracketts. Not very nice. Not like the packed lunches Mummy does for me on my working days." The pleasure in his voice once again demonstrated the close relationship between Jonny and his food. "And I always said to my friend Mervyn, 'Why don't you have some of my lunch? Or, even better, why don't I get Mummy to do a nice packed lunch for you, too?' But my friend Mervyn always said no. Until last Thursday."

300

"He asked you to bring him a packed lunch?"

"Yes. On Thursday. He said the 'special project' he was on meant it was difficult to get his packed lunch from Austen Prison. So I asked Mummy, and she did two packed lunches for me on Friday." Awestruck by his own cunning, he went on, "I didn't tell her who it was for. Because my friend Mervyn had said it was a 'special project,' you see. And that meant it was a secret. And I had to meet him somewhere secret at Bracketts to give him his packed lunch."

"Do you know," asked Jude softly, "whether his 'special project' meant Mervyn couldn't go back to Austen Prison on Thursday night?"

"I don't know."

"That could explain why he wasn't able to get his food from the prison, couldn't it?"

Jonny looked confused. Clearly the idea had never entered his head. All he could produce was another "I don't know."

She smiled her most reassuring smile. "Don't worry about that. Mervyn didn't ever talk about the idea of staying at Bracketts, did he . . . ? Of having a secret place there that he could stay in if he wanted to . . . ?"

"Yes, he did," said Jonny in innocent surprise. "How did you know that?"

"I just wondered."

"You're very clever, Jude." He looked at her with increased respect. "Yes, my friend Mervyn did say there was always somewhere he could hide at Bracketts." A belated caution came into his wide blue eyes. "But he said it was a secret. And you can't tell people about secrets, can you?"

"Well, sometimes you can. If someone's going to be hurt by something being kept secret, then telling the secret might be a good thing . . . because it would be stopping that person from getting hurt."

This ethical argument seemed too difficult for Jonny to understand. Anyway, as he explained, he didn't need to understand it. "My friend Mervyn didn't tell me where his hiding place was, so I haven't got the secret, so I can't tell anyone."

He looked troubled at the end of this, so Jude soothed, "It's fine. Don't worry about it."

"No." He was silent for a moment, organising his thoughts. "Sheila Cartwright's dead . . . ?"

"Yes."

"So she won't come back . . . ?"

"No."

"Mummy says nobody comes back when they're dead."

"That's true."

"She says when Daddy dies, he won't come back." He seemed to be testing the ideas against some abstract standard in his mind. "Mummy says when she dies, she won't come back." The anxiety in his voice resolved itself into confidence, and his huge smile returned. "I'll look after Mummy. I won't let her die."

"Listen, Jonny, it's not as simple —"

But that was as far as she was allowed to get with her explanation. Brenda Tyson came hurrying over the brow of the garden towards them. And the expression on her face suggested she was announcing something more weighty than the readiness of Sunday lunch.

"Jonny, you are popular today. Some other people have arrived who want to talk with you."

For the first time Jude saw petulance in his face as he said, "I don't want to talk to anyone else. I want to have my lunch."

Though pained by the situation, this time his mother could not let him have his own way. "You'll have to talk to them, Jonny. The people who've arrived are from the police."

Jude's first thought was that she'd only got there just in time.

Her second was more compassionate. She just prayed Jonny Tyson's next interviewers would be as gentle with him as she had been.

31

Carole was so absorbed in the papers on her sitting room table that she didn't hear the cab driving up to Woodside Cottage. The first she was aware of Laurence Hawker's return was when the bell rang and there he was, standing on her own doorstep.

He looked thinner and more haggard than ever. As ever, a lighted cigarette dangled from the corner of his mouth, defying the attempts of his coughing to dislodge it. He was dressed in his usual black with the leather jacket — what Carole regarded as the complete poseur's kit.

"Ah. Good afternoon. Is Jude not there to let you in? I do have a key, so, if you like —"

"No. She gave me a key." He smiled the boyish smile that rarely failed to thaw the most frosty of women. It had no effect on Carole.

"What I actually wondered was whether you've got any whisky . . . ?"

"Whisky?" she echoed.

"Yes. I drank the last of Jude's Friday

night. I meant to pick some up at an off-licence over the weekend, but, what with one thing and another. . . ." He shrugged helplessly.

Carole was torn. Her first instinct was to deny his impertinent request and close the door in his face. But the atavistic middle-class tradition of good manners told her that one should be polite to friends of one's friends, even if one didn't particularly care for them.

Breeding won. "I believe I may have some left over from Christmas," she said primly.

"If I'm not depriving you of supplies. . . ."

She knew how prissy she sounded when she said, "I'm not a habitual whisky drinker. It's in the cupboard in the sitting room," she went on, and was then faced by another social dilemma. She wanted just to get the bottle, hand it over, and close the door on him. But the entrenched middle-class rules about how one treated guests were too strong. She stood back from the doorway. "Won't you come in?"

He lounged after her into the sitting room, coughing again.

"So how was your weekend?" asked Carole, punctiliously polite as she opened the drinks cabinet.

"Not so dusty," he drawled. Which seemed a strangely archaic reply. And, given the fact that he'd spent the night with a woman other than Jude, an inadequate one.

The bottle was nearly half-full. Carole had bought it three Christmases before. She very rarely drank spirits, just the occasional glass of white wine (though, since she'd met Jude, the occasions had gotten closer together). She held the whisky bottle out towards Laurence Hawker.

"Great." He looked at it wryly. "Keep me going for a couple of hours. Jude can get some more when she comes back."

He didn't say that walking any distance was becoming increasingly difficult, so that the stroll down to Allinstore, the supermarket in the High Street, would have been beyond him. For Carole, the impression of his cavalier male chauvinism was reinforced.

With no attempt at concealment of his interest, Laurence Hawker was looking at the photocopies spread over the table. By Carole's middle-class standards, such behaviour came under the definition of "nosey."

"Esmond Chadleigh memorabilia," he observed, compounding his offence, revealing that he had actually read someone else's papers.

"Yes." Carole's curt monosyllable was meant to precede her suggestion that, now he'd got his whisky, perhaps he'd like to return to Woodside Cottage and consume it. But another thought came into her mind. Her own perusal of the documents had revealed nothing; she didn't have the background knowledge of Esmond Chadleigh and his world to make them meaningful. But she did actually have in her sitting room an academic who — although she had considerable reservations about him as a person — would know a lot more. She remembered the details he'd filled in for them on the Bracketts guided tour.

The reservations were put on hold. "Would you like to have a look at the material, Laurence?"

He agreed with relish, drew up a chair to the table, and, without asking permission, lit up another cigarette.

"I think I've got an ashtray somewhere," said Carole tautly.

But Laurence Hawker was uninterested in such domestic details. "If you happened to have a glass, too, and could pour some of the whisky into it, that would help enormously."

Biting her lip — if Jude wanted to be treated like a doormat by this man, that was up to her — Carole did as he suggested. She put a full glass and the bottle to his left, and an ashtray to his right. Taking alternate sips and puffs, Laurence Hawker was silent, except for the regular coughing, while he read through the documentation. Carole quietly drew a chair up to the table, feeling like a visitor in her own sitting room.

After about twenty minutes, he sat back, and let out a cough even louder than the previous ones. When he'd recovered his breath, he said, "Interesting. Where did you get this stuff from?"

"Graham Chadleigh-Bewes. I was to deliver it to Professor Teischbaum."

Laurence let out an ironical laugh. "That makes sense."

"You know her?"

"By reputation. In the academic world you hear about what most people in the same field are up to. I know Marla Teischbaum's working on a biography of Esmond Chadleigh. And I think hers will have rather more intellectual rigour than the one written by Graham Chadleigh-Bewes" — he tapped the photocopies on the table — "in spite of his delaying tactics."

"What do you mean?" Carole remembered the word Marla had used on the telephone. "Are you saying that this stuff has been *doctored?*"

"Yes. And not very subtly."

"When she last rang me, Marla accused Graham of doing it."

"I should think she's right. You said he issued the material, didn't you?"

"Yes. What kind of 'doctoring' has been done, Laurence?" The longer he was there, the easier she was finding it to use his name. She still disliked and disapproved of him, but she couldn't fault his intellect.

"There's been a bit of fiddling with the dates. Don't know why." Instinctively, and without asking, Laurence Hawker topped up his empty glass. "I suppose he just hoped Professor Teischbaum would publish the misinformation in her book, and then be discredited for getting her facts wrong. But she'd be too canny to fall for that. I'm not even an expert on Esmond Chadleigh, and yet I saw instantly what had been done. No, I'm afraid all this stuff does is to show up the sad incompetence of Graham Chadleigh-Bewes. Incompetence as a forger, certainly — and probably incompetence as a biographer, too."

Carole moved closer to the table. "Can

you show me exactly what you're talking about?"

Proximity strengthened the smells of cigarette smoke and whisky, but she was starting to find them less offensive as her interest in the documents mounted.

"Well, take a look at this." He picked up the photocopy of the letter from "Pickles" to "Chadders." "Perfectly ordinary schoolboy letter, thanking his friend for letting him stay at Christmas. Dated '29 December 1917.' And yet there are a whole lot of references in it that make that date sound wrong."

"Like what?"

"Look at this."

Her eyes followed his finger to the sentence in which "Pickles" referred to his aunt: *I don't think she likes anyone — certainly not me or Mr. Lloyd George, so she's in an even sourer mood than usual.*

"O.K., Lloyd George was still prime minister in 1917, but he actually took over the job in December 1916. Wouldn't his appointment be what made the aunt 'sourer than ever'?"

He raised a hand to curb objections. "All right, that one's arguable, but these two references to the Somme seem very odd."

Again his finger found the relevant passages.

I'd like to get a bit of revenge for all those chaps Strider lost on the Somme. He seemed raring to go back, didn't he, champing at the bit to get back and finish the job?

and

Did you hear, incidentally, that old "Rattles" Rattenborough, School Captain of a couple of years back, has died of wounds he sustained during that Somme fixture? Bit of a damper when you hear about chaps you know, but it seems to be happening all too often these days.

"Now the Somme offensive started in July 1916 and, O.K., it was dreadful, left deep scars on the country. But by December 1917, the Third Battle of Ypres — all the horrors of Passchendaele — had happened. Surely those'd be more in the mind of a war-watching schoolboy than the events of nearly eighteen months before? And can you really believe that it had taken eighteen months for 'Pickles' to hear about the death of a school captain?"

"Ah, that one's not certain," Carole pointed out. "He died of 'wounds sustained during that Somme fixture.' We don't know how long that process took."

"Take your point." Laurence Hawker nodded in appreciation. Then his finger moved quickly to another line. "But look at this. This is the clincher."

Carole read,

Now our boys have got those new-fangled tanks out there, it shouldn't take long.

"British tanks were introduced to the Battle of the Somme in September 1916. Surely fourteen months later our schoolboy wouldn't be describing them as 'new-fangled'? Three months later, maybe."

Coughing lightly, he sat back with an air of triumph, and took a long drag from his cigarette.

"So what are you saying, Laurence?"

"I would stake my reputation as an academic — or even something of real value" — he interpolated a self-depreciating grin — "that the date on this letter has been changed from 1916 to 1917."

"But why would Graham Chadleigh-Bewes want to do that?"

"Don't know . . . unless, as I said, it was a feeble attempt to make Professor Teischbaum's research look iffy." He reached forward. "But this is designed to have the same effect."

What he picked up was the photocopied page from Felix Chadleigh's diary, which began:

12 November 1917
The Lord and all the Holy Saints be

praised! After all the exhausting uncertainty of the last few months, we did finally today take possession of Bracketts.

"This is an even cruder forgery," said Laurence. "I don't know who Graham Chadleigh-Bewes thought he was going to fool with this. He's just written in '1917' over that blotch of ink."

"And are there internal inconsistencies?"

"Yes. If this was written only a fortnight after his son's death at Passchendaele — I think we can assume the family would have heard the news by then — saying 'Here we will put our griefs behind us' seems somewhat understated."

"Yes. And you think Graham did this for the same purpose as the other one?"

"Must've done. For some reason best known to himself, the authorised biographer of Esmond Chadleigh was trying to make the unauthorised one believe that the Chadleigh family moved into Bracketts a year later than they actually did."

At that moment their researches were interrupted by a ring of the doorbell. It was Jude.

32

Carole ushered her neighbour into the sitting room. Laurence Hawker didn't rise from his seat or acknowledge Jude with more than a casual wave. He was preoccupied with the photocopies on the table. There was anxiety in Jude's face as she looked at him — hardly surprising, thought Carole. Any woman would look anxious if she knew her lover had just spent the night with another woman.

Laurence looked up for a moment. "I came round because your house is completely devoid of whisky."

"How disastrous for you." To Carole's mind, the remark should have been said more sardonically; and then Jude compounded the offence by saying, "Don't worry, I'll go down to Allinstore and get some later."

Carole knew her neighbour had taken many roles in her relationships with men, but never imagined that one of them would be that of doormat. Why did Jude seem to be in thrall to this man who — even

315

though Carole had warmed to him a little over the previous half-hour — remained an egocentric poseur?

"Since we're all having a drink . . . ," Jude hinted.

Carole didn't point out that in fact only Laurence was having a drink so far, but went to open a bottle of white wine. She didn't entirely condone the concept of drinking through a Sunday afternoon, but Jude was her guest. . . .

While she was in the kitchen, she could hear a whispered exchange between Jude and Laurence . . . well, she could hear that there was a whispered exchange, though frustratingly she couldn't make out any of the words. Jude's tone was concerned rather than — as it should have been — admonitory, and Laurence's replies were weighed down with his customary languor. Carole wondered what was going on. Whispering was out of character for Jude.

She came in with the open bottle of wine and two glasses on a tray. (Trays were another of the inescapable legacies of her middle-class upbringing. Food or drink should be carried into a room on a tray — and then, in an ideal world, placed on an individual small table beside the chair of each guest. Carole still felt a slight frisson of audacity in dispensing with the individual small tables.)

"Has Laurence been telling you about his detective work?" she asked as she poured the wine.

"No. Why, what's happened?"

Laurence lit up another cigarette, and let Carole provide the recap on his discoveries.

". . . so the biggest question we're left with," she concluded, "is why Graham would want Marla Teischbaum to believe that the Chadleigh family moved into Bracketts a year later than they did."

"Yes. . . ." Jude gave the problem a moment's thought, and then shook it out of her mind, setting the blonde bird's nest of hair quivering. "Sorry, I can't think about that. My mind's too full of what I've been doing this morning."

"Yes, I wondered where you'd been," said Carole, not quite managing to iron all of the reproof out of her tone.

"I had a call from Sandy Fairbarns, my contact at Austen Prison. . . ."

"Has Mervyn Hunter been found?"

Jude raised a plump hand. "All in good time. She put me in touch with a friend of Mervyn. Down's syndrome boy named Jonny Tyson, who works as a volunteer up at Bracketts."

"I remember meeting him. He was the one who actually uncovered the skull in the kitchen garden."

"Right, Carole. That's him. Anyway, Sandy thought Jonny might have some idea where Mervyn was, so I went to see him."

"And did you get anything useful?"

"Nothing absolutely definite, but I'm pretty certain Mervyn spent last Thursday — and quite possibly Friday — at Bracketts."

"If he was there on Friday. . . ."

"Exactly, Carole." Jude grimaced. "Maybe Graham has to relinquish his prime suspect status."

"But I thought you said you couldn't imagine —"

"Oh, no, I'm sure Mervyn didn't do it, but I'm not sure the police are likely to be so imaginative. They tend to think in pretty straight lines. If you have a convicted murderer at the scene of a crime — and you happen to know that that murderer has a particular dislike of the victim. . . ." She completed the logic with an eloquent shrug.

As the revelations built up, a gleam of excitement grew in Carole's eyes. She had almost forgotten Laurence Hawker was in the room. She and Jude were together again on an investigation. "So where did Mervyn hide at Bracketts?"

"Don't know. Jonny wouldn't tell me. Or, to be more accurate, I don't think he actually knew."

"The priest's hole?"

"I know it was designed as a hiding place, but it's a pretty obvious one. Every visitor to Bracketts has it pointed out to them."

"But the house was closed on Thursday and Friday, after the press got hold of the story of the body in the kitchen garden."

"I know that, Carole, but there were still staff and people around. Maybe Mervyn could have actually spent the night there, but during the daytime he must've been somewhere else.

"Anyway . . . ," Jude sighed wearily, "it may all turn out to be academic. From our point of view, at least. If they're interested, I'm sure the police will be able to persuade Mervyn to tell them himself where he spent the time."

"What do you mean?"

"They've caught him."

"Oh?"

"Yes. Had a tip-off from someone who'd seen a suspicious figure skulking round a remote barn up on the Downs. Mervyn Hunter's back in custody."

"How do you know that?"

"The police were only just behind me in visiting Jonny Tyson. I was just leaving when one of the detectives took a call on his mobile. It was the news about Mervyn's recapture."

"Oh."

"He didn't make any trouble, apparently. Gave himself up as meekly as a lamb."

"What will happen to him?"

Jude shrugged. "You know more about the Prison Service than I do, Carole. But I would imagine that — even if he doesn't get done for the murder of Sheila Cartwright — he'll get something added to his sentence . . . and he'll have to complete it in a higher-security nick than Austen."

Carole nodded thoughtful agreement.

"Which," Jude went on, "is quite possibly what he wanted. Why he went over the wall in the first place."

There was a silence while they both processed the new information. Then, after a preparatory cough, Laurence Hawker said lazily, "Something else of interest I've found in this lot. . . ."

Carole was instantly alert. "What?"

"This business about the priest's hole.

We've all seen it, haven't we?"

"We went together," said Jude.

"Of course we did. And I think we'd all agree that, though the room's a fine bit of building work, and the sliding panel is well concealed to someone who's unsuspicious, anyone who was actually *looking* for a priest's hole in Bracketts would find it within five minutes."

Jude nodded. "So what's your point, Laurence?"

He picked up the photocopied sheet in the handwriting of Felix Chadleigh. "Given that, there's an odd thing here in the diary entry of Esmond's father for the day they moved into Bracketts." Laurence Hawker paused to cough before continuing, "He speaks of 'a cunningly hidden and complex priest's hole.' "

33

"Maybe you should have a more detailed look around the priest's hole at Bracketts . . . ," Laurence Hawker went on.

"See if there's another secret hiding place Mervyn could have used?"

"Something like that, Jude, yes." He tapped the pile of papers on the table. "Interesting, this lot. I wouldn't mind finding out a bit more about Esmond Chadleigh's murky past."

"Do you think he had a murky past?" asked Carole.

He smiled at her mischievously. "I'm sure we all have murky pasts, don't we?"

She didn't grace that with an answer. Carole certainly did not have a murky past. Wistfully, she sometimes wished she had.

"Where would you find out more information?" asked Jude. "Up at Bracketts?"

"Suppose there might be something up there." He coughed, stubbed out a cigarette in Carole's rarely used ashtray, then immediately lit up another. "I'd be tempted to start with more traditional research sources."

"Is the Internet traditional?"

"I'm sure I'll get on to that. But I was thinking of starting with local libraries, the County Records Office."

That reminded Carole. "Marla Teischbaum's been working there."

"Oh?"

"When she last rang me, she said she'd found out an interesting new approach to Esmond Chadleigh, from research she'd been doing in the County Records Office."

"Oh." Laurence smiled. "Well, I might meet her when I go down there. Find out what she's on to."

"Talk to her, do you mean?" asked Carole, with her upbringing's knee-jerk reaction to the idea of addressing anyone one hasn't been introduced to. "Do you know her?"

"No, but it's always easy to start a conversation with an academic."

"Oh? How?"

"Appeal, Carole, to the vanity that is common to all of us. I look up her details on the Internet, then, on seeing her, say, 'Excuse me, aren't you the Professor Teischbaum who wrote that brilliant paper on Darwinian imagery in Gerard Manley Hopkins's later poems, which was published in the 1997 *Sprachphilologische*

Ephemeriden der Litteratur Festschrift . . . ?'
— or whatever it happens to be — and I'm
her friend for life."

"Clever."

"Oh, I guarantee it works."

Jude's eyes were sparkling. "Do you really reckon, Laurence, that you could find
out something useful at the County Records
Office?"

"I should think so." He indicated the papers on the table. "Given this lot as a
starting point."

"But what would you be looking for?"
asked Carole.

"That's the beauty of academic research
— you never know. You always find the
best bits when you're looking for something else. Some people never find what
they're looking for. Very distinguished academic careers have been built on the foundation of never having found anything at
all."

"When are you going, then? Tomorrow?"

"Maybe, Carole." Laurence Hawker exchanged a look with Jude. "If you're free to
take me there. . . ."

"I think I could probably manage that."

He sighed helplessly. "I've never been
very good with public transport."

Honestly, Carole thought, *he is so lazy.*

Never lifts a finger. Seems prepared for Jude to do everything for him. And she just seems to accept it all. Where's her spine? Where's her feminist solidarity?

"Are you going to come, too?" asked Jude.

"No, I'd better not. Marla knows me. She'd think we were up to something if she saw me round the County Records Office. No, I'm going to get on to Gina."

"Find out if we can have a snoop round the Bracketts priest's hole?"

"Exactly."

"Right." Jude tapped her chin thoughtfully. "So where do we stand on suspects for the murder of Sheila Cartwright?"

Carole felt a slight resentment that Laurence seemed now to be included in their deliberations. But it wasn't as great a resentment as it would have been an hour earlier. He had definitely proved himself to have skills that would be useful to them.

So, putting her reservations on one side, she enumerated: "Graham Chadleigh-Bewes, Mervyn Hunter, Gina Locke, Belinda Chadleigh, possibly Marla Teischbaum, if she stayed around Bracketts that evening . . . and I suppose George Ferris could be in the frame, too, because I don't know how soon he left after the emergency trustees meeting."

"Right." Jude nodded. "And the police's prime suspect seemed to have shifted from being Graham Chadleigh-Bewes to Mervyn Hunter."

"We don't know that. We're guessing."

"Yes. As ever. I think it's really mean the way the police don't keep us informed about the progress of their investigations."

" 'Twas ever thus, Jude," said Laurence, ironically sympathetic. "Keeping the amateurs informed has never been high on the police's priorities."

"Presumably, now they've got Mervyn Hunter, they've stopped questioning Graham?"

"Who knows, Carole?"

"I'll ask Gina when I get in touch with her. She's got her ear closer to the ground."

"And you said she's convinced that Graham killed Sheila Cartwright?"

"That's certainly what she wanted me to think. But who knows . . . she may have had a hidden agenda of her own."

Jude nodded ruefully. "That's the trouble. All the suspects seem to have hidden agendas."

"Almost by definition," drawled Laurence Hawker.

"What?"

"Well, come on, no self-respecting murderer's going to have an *overt* agenda, is he? Otherwise you'd know whodunit straight away."

The West Sussex County Records Office was in Chichester, at the end of West Street, the site of the cathedral. An old building had been refurbished and considerably extended to house a wide range of local archives.

Their cab dropped them directly outside. They were later than intended, around eleven-thirty. Laurence had had another minor bout of bleeding just before they'd intended to leave, which had delayed them about an hour. Jude and he walked into the Reception Area of the Records Office. She carried a shapeless straw basket; he had his soft Italian laptop case under his arm. Jude was worried about how much effort each step seemed to cost him, and about the rasp of his breath even when he wasn't coughing. Laurence, though, behaved as ever. In spite of coughing up blood, he'd breakfasted on whisky, and had been smoking continuously since Jude woke up that morning. In fact, since he was now getting very little sleep, he'd probably smoked through most of the night, too.

"They won't let you smoke in there — that's for certain," said Jude, gesturing through the glass to the Reading Room.

"I know," Laurence wheezed. "Bloody uncivilised country we live in. I'm just going to check if she's in there, while I suck down a few more precious lungfuls of smoke . . . assuming, of course, one is allowed to do that even in here."

The frosty look from the woman behind the Reception desk suggested that one wasn't. Jude wandered across towards her, browsing through the various leaflets and local publications on display. Laurence meanwhile was surreptitiously comparing the people he could see through the glass at desks in the Reading Room with the printout in his hand. He'd downloaded a lot of information about Marla Teischbaum, including a photograph that looked more like a glamour shot than an academic's I.D. picture.

Jude was actually making a purchase from the suspicious-looking woman at the Reception desk when she heard Laurence wheezing towards her.

"What are you getting?"

She showed him. *How to Get the Best*

from the Facilities of the County Records Of-fice, by George Ferris. "Might come in useful."

"I can't think where."

"Here, I would imagine."

"Are you suggesting, Jude, that I don't know my way around a Records Office?"

"No, I wouldn't dare."

"Glad to hear it. The academic life may not bring much in the way of practical benefits, but it does make one a dab hand round libraries and archives."

"I'm sure it does," said Jude as she took her change and moved away from the desk.

She heard the rasp of Laurence's breath close against her ear as he murmured, "Got a winner straight away. She's in there."

"Marla Teischbaum?" He nodded. "What are you going to do — go straight up and congratulate her on her Festschrift?"

"Not immediately, no. Start a bit of re-search of my own . . . and maybe peer over her shoulder and see what she's digging into."

"O.K. You're the academic, Laurence. And who am I — another academic?"

"By no means. You are my research as-sistant."

"I seem to recall you using that description quite a lot back in Prague. For those pretty young students who were so essential to your work when you went off to conferences."

"Oh, yes." He smiled fondly, without a scintilla of guilt in his expression. "You're joining a very distinguished list, you know, Jude."

"And do I get the same bonuses all the other research assistants used to get?"

"If you play your cards right" — he winked — "you might be in with a chance."

But his pose of the Great Seducer was destroyed by another bout of coughing. He waited until it had passed, then immediately screwed his cigarette back into his mouth for the final drag. The woman at the Reception desk approved of him even less.

The cool of the air-conditioning hit them as soon as they walked into the Reading Room. Also in the air was the vague mustiness of old documents. One or other — possibly both — brought on a renewed spasm of coughing from Laurence. At the end he panted, "Can't take this for long. Twenty minutes top-weight, then I'll have to go out for another cigarette."

He gestured to the back view of a tall

figure in an elegant linen suit, her head of neat, copper-beech hair bent forward over documents, and gave Jude a meaningful wink.

"What are we going to do?" she murmured.

"What do you think? Research."

Instinct and long experience with libraries pointed out to him exactly the right person to ask and the right material to ask for. He gestured Jude to a chair and drew out of his leather bag the photocopies he'd taken from Carole's house.

"You'd better have a look at these, get up to date," he breathed at her.

"Why?" asked Jude, with slight irritation.

"Because that's what research assistants do." He turned to leave.

"What are you going to do?"

"Have a smoke while they fetch our stuff." And he went out to antagonise the woman at Reception even more.

Jude read through the photocopied material he'd left her. She found it engrossing. Old documents always moved her. She could sense the characters of the people who had written them, feel the strong but invisible link between her own time and the moment when the pen had first marked the pages.

The volumes Laurence had ordered were soon delivered to the desk and, seeing their arrival through the glass, he came back in, once again coughing at the assault of the air-conditioning. To Jude, as he came towards her, he looked impossibly thin.

"One thing this tells us," he murmured as he sat beside her, "is that Marla Teischbaum's well ahead of us."

"Sorry?" Jude whispered back.

"This stuff is to check the date Esmond's father actually took possession of Bracketts. She's already done that." He looked speculatively across at the neatly coiffed woman on the other side of the Reading Room. "I wonder what she's on to now."

The documents Laurence had ordered were bound copies of Land Registry documents, photocopied parish registers, and census forms. They all confirmed his conjecture. Felix Chadleigh had moved into Bracketts and written his celebratory diary entry on November 12, 1916.

With practised skill, Laurence Hawker removed his laptop from its leather case, started it up, and began to key in information. Jude was intrigued to see he had already opened files named "Bracketts," "Chadleigh Family," and "Esmond Chadleigh." Maybe that's what he had been doing, as well as smoking, during his long, sleepless night.

He was certainly absorbed. Jude hadn't seen him working for a long time, since Prague in fact, and she was reminded what an indissoluble link there was between the man and his studies. Women might come and go in Laurence Hawker's life; his real passion would always be his work. If Jude had recognised that fact earlier, she might have accepted with more equanimity his diversions with the series of "research assistants." No one woman would ever possess Laurence Hawker.

She once again felt a strong urge to argue with him in favour of treatment. Maybe there was no dominant reason in his personal life to keep fighting, but to be able to continue with his work for longer. . . . Even as she had the idea, she rejected it. Laurence Hawker's life was his, to dispose of as he saw fit.

He was so caught up in what he was typing that he didn't see the newcomer in the Reading Room. Though unprepossessing, short, and bearded, the man moved with assurance, on his own patch and wanting everyone to be aware of the fact. His arrival had an immediate effect on one of the County Records staff, who

greeted him sycophantically and introduced him to a younger colleague. "You
haven't met George Ferris, have you?"

That's handy, thought Jude. *Another suspect.*

The younger colleague was suitably ap-
preciative of the honour bestowed by introduction to the former assistant county
librarian. "Of course," she said. "You
wrote *How to Get the Best from the Facilities
of the County Records Office.*"

They were the right words. The Hobbit
face beamed. Jude found herself idly wondering whether, beneath the thick grey
socks and stout brown walking shoes, there
was hair on the top of George Ferris's feet.

After a little more condescending badinage, the great man brought the librarian
talk to an end. "Someone I've got to see,"
he said, with a man-of-the-world wink.

Jude tapped Laurence's arm and they
both watched George Ferris move across
towards Marla Teischbaum. There was
something of a turkey strut in his walk; he
got a charge from knowing an attractive —
even exotic — younger woman.

"I was wondering, Marla," Jude and
Laurence heard him say, "whether I could
lure you out for a spot of lunch . . . ?"

34

George Ferris's luring proved effective. Leaving the documents she was working on open on her desk, Marla Teischbaum scooped up the elegant leather bag by her side, and the two of them left the Reading Room. As they walked out, the Tolkien imagery seemed reinforced: he, a rustic bumpkin from the shire; she, some elegant, exotic creature from an elfin master race.

Jude looked across at Laurence, mouthing, "What do we do?"

"You follow them," he whispered back.

"And you?"

"I'll try and get a peek at what she's been researching."

Jude nodded and, gathering up her straw basket, moved towards the Reception area. Through the glass she could see George Ferris lingering there, waiting. Marla must have gone off to tidy herself up in the ladies' room. Jude showed great interest in a framed map of eighteenth-century Sussex boundaries.

Her conjecture proved correct. Marla

emerged a moment later, patting her recently brushed hair with satisfaction. Jude remembered Carole saying something about the woman being in love with herself, and particularly with her hair.

She gave the ill-matched pair a moment to get out of the Records Office, and then slowly, almost lackadaisically, followed.

It wasn't a difficult tailing job. In the bright October sunshine, which pierced the threatening clouds of autumn, George Ferris and Marla Teischbaum walked along West Street towards the cathedral. But they didn't go far, soon crossing the road and entering the first available pub, rather imaginatively named The Cathedral. Jude wondered whether Marla had insisted on lunching close by so that she could return quickly to her studies; or, more likely, that the pub had been George's regular in the days when he had worked for West Sussex Libraries.

There were enough people in The Cathedral at half-past twelve for Jude's entrance to be inconspicuous. From the bar she located her quarries at a table in the window. Marla had a glass of sparkling mineral water; George Ferris, a pint "in a jug," from which he drank with much elaborate beard-wiping. He'd used the word "lunch," so Jude reckoned she was safe to order herself. An unashamed lover of fry-ups, she went for the all-day breakfast, and took her glass of white wine over to a table next to theirs. Neither had met her before, so, with her back to them, Jude felt suitably invisible.

But to make her earwigging less blatant, she needed something to read. She riffled through the options in her straw basket. The recently purchased *How to Get the Best from the Facilities of the County Records Office* would be far too much of a giveaway, as would the copy of Esmond Chadleigh's *Vases of Dead Flowers*, which Laurence had asked her to carry for him.

The thought of Laurence made her realise that he didn't know where she was, and so would be unable to join her. No great problem, though. He was less of a lunch eater than ever, and if he didn't come into The Cathedral by chance, there were plenty of other places in Chichester where he could top up his whisky intake. Besides, his clothes and coughing made Laurence Hawker a much more conspicuous figure than Jude; his presence might inhibit the conversation at the adjacent table.

In the bottom of her bag she found a

book a friend had written about herbal antidepressants, which she had promised to read for some time. Her eyes skimmed over the words, and she reminded herself to turn a page every now and then, as, filtering out the ambient sounds of barroom banter and Muzak, she focussed her hearing on the next table.

The first bit she heard didn't promise great revelations. "Oh, damn," Marla was saying. "It's started to rain, and I don't have an umbrella with me."

"I've got one . . . ," said George gallantly.

"Good."

". . . but it's in the car."

"Then that's not much use to me, is it?" Marla snapped.

"No, but it's not far back to the Records Office."

"Huh. Far enough to get my hair totally mussed."

"Ho-ho. You ladies and your hair. . . ."

This jocular male chauvinism was not the approach most calculated to appeal to an independent woman like Marla Teischbaum. "I'm not a lady. I'm a woman."

George still didn't get the message. "Oh dear, dear. I always think that's so inelegant. When I was growing up, a lady was a lady, and we respected her for it."

"Nothing to stop you respecting women, George."

"No, no, I agree," he replied archly. "But I find it hard to think of the beautiful ones as women. Some women will always be ladies in my mind."

"Fine. So long as you keep it in your mind, you won't offend anyone."

"My mind's getting a rather full place." There was a new wistfulness in George's tone. Slowly, the appalling realisation came to Jude that he was actually chatting up the professor. Trying to sound boyish and winsome, he went on, "My mind is full of thoughts of one beautiful woman in particular. . . ."

"Well, lucky her." Clearly Marla hadn't caught on to his meaning as quickly as Jude. "Oh, Gard," she growled, "that damn rain."

"Not as wet as it was on a certain other evening. . . ."

If George was trying to prompt fond recollections, he failed. "Whaddya mean? What evening?"

"When we last met," he said softly. "At Bracketts."

That silenced her. Jude wished she could turn round to see what expression was crossing Marla's face, but she didn't dare draw attention to herself.

"Yes." When the professor finally spoke, her tone was more subdued, even anxious. "Have you had anything more from the police . . . since we last spoke?"

"No. So I think they believed me."

"That you drove straight back home after the meeting?"

"Yes. There's no real reason to think I'd done anything else. I certainly drove straight out of the car park after the meeting."

"Right." Marla was still thoughtful, not entirely reassured. "They didn't ask you anything about me?"

"Your name wasn't mentioned. Relax, Marla. The police have got a suspect."

"Oh?"

"Apparently there was some escaped prisoner with a grudge against Sheila Cartwright."

"He's in custody?"

"So I believe. Which means the police aren't going to bother double-checking on anyone else. They've bought your story about getting a cab back to The Pelling Arms before the emergency trustees meeting started."

"I hope they have."

"Of course they have." George was en-

340

joying his role of masculine reassurance. He winked roguishly. "And no one will ever know that you had a knight-errant waiting in his car at the front of the house to whisk you away."

"True, they won't. I was grateful for that, George."

They were interrupted by the arrival of their lunch. "One tuna salad on granary, one all-day breakfast."

Marla Teischbaum got into a discussion with the girl who'd brought the food about available dressings for her salad, but The Cathedral's range proved inadequate to her demands. "Gard," she said, as the girl went back to the bar, "when're you going to get some concept of service in this country?"

"Well, we are a bit old-fashioned in some ways," George conceded.

"Old-fashioned? Antediluvian, more like."

"I'm quite old-fashioned, you know," he said earnestly. Once again, Jude reckoned, he was moving into chat-up mode. "Yes, I'm a bit of an old fogey, but that doesn't mean I'm an automaton. . . ."

"What?" asked Marla distractedly, through a mouthful of tuna salad on granary.

"I'm not a person without feelings," he explained. "I like helping people with their academic research, obviously . . . that's part of my job . . . under my, as it were, consultancy hat . . . sharing the expertise I've gained over years in the Library Service with people who can benefit therefrom."

"Sure." Marla sounded uninterested. She certainly wasn't aware that he was coming on to her. Probably the idea that a man like George Ferris might come on to her was so incongruous that the thought didn't even enter her head.

"But . . . ," he went on, his earnestness becoming more sincere by the minute, "I like it even better when I can share my expertise with someone I'm interested in. . . ."

"Yeah, it's good when people have research interest in common." Marla was still paying more attention to her lunch than to her companion. "So the fact that I'm doing Esmond Chadleigh, and you're a trustee of Bracketts, well, that's kinda neat."

"But there's more to it than that," said George in an intense whisper. "You know there's more to it than that."

"Sorry?" Now she was listening to him.

"These last two weeks have been the most important of my life, Marla."

"What?"

342

"Helping you has given a meaning to my life."

"What are you talking about, George?"

"You know how we get on, how we see eye to eye about things. . . ."

"We haven't had any arguments, but then you've only been helping me through the issue system in your libraries, for Gard's sake."

"There's been more to it than that," he murmured in a voice that he must have imagined to be sexy.

"George, you've given me some useful leads, and I've been grateful. But the fact remains that most of my research I've done for myself. That's how I work. And do you know," she went on mischievously, "I've even managed to crack through the conspiracy of silence at Bracketts. Everything seems a lot more relaxed there now Sheila Cartwright's off the scene. I'm going to pay a visit there tomorrow."

"Surely Graham hasn't agreed to see you?"

"No, not Graham. I've circumvented him and made a direct approach to his aunt. Belinda Chadleigh has very gracefully agreed to see me tomorrow."

"She's totally gaga."

"I'm not so sure about that. I think she

has an interesting story to tell. She's Esmond Chadleigh's sister, for Gard's sake. And I think she could be a lot more generous with information than her nephew is."

"Well, good luck with her." George was not to be deflected from his declaration. "Listen, I'm not claiming to have done your research for you. I've just given you some useful pointers, that's all. But what I'm really talking about" — his voice lowered — "is what's happened between *us*."

"Nothing happened between us."

"Don't pretend, Marla."

"Pretend what?"

"That you don't feel it, too."

"Feel *what*, for Gard's sake!"

"Love."

"Love?"

"We're meant for each other, Marla. And I know I'm still technically married to Geraldine, but —"

"George, you are talking total garbage!"

"No, I'm not. Listen, don't fight it, Marla."

His voice was now more earnest and intimate than ever, and her next line explained why.

"WILL YOU TAKE YOUR HAND OFF MY KNEE!"

She intended to silence the pub, and she succeeded. Only the Muzak continued to trickle through the awkwardness that followed.

Since everyone else was looking at them, Jude felt justified in turning round herself.

George didn't notice. He was in a world of his own. His hand stayed on Marla's knee, as he went on, "I've never been so sure of anything. And, although you deny it, I know you really feel the same. After all we've shared, Marla —"

"Oh, for Gard's sake, you stupid little man!" she said, lifting his hand from her knee and firmly slamming it back into his lap. "I'm not interested in you."

"Oh," said George Ferris, at the moment that his fantasy of sharing his retirement with a glamorous mistress was not so much faded out, but instantly switched off.

"I am very happily single, thank you very much. And if I did ever go for a man, it wouldn't be some sawn-off, knee-high dork like you, George Ferris."

With that, Marla left The Cathedral. She swung her leather bag over her shoulder, picked up the remains of her tuna salad on granary in her left hand, and one of the laminated menus in the other, and stalked out. On the street she held the menu over her precious hair, and strode back towards the County Records Office.

It was quite an exit, and it made an impression on everyone in the pub.

But the impression it made on Jude was probably the greatest. Because in the course of her conversation with George Ferris, Marla Teischbaum had virtually admitted to being at Bracketts at the time Sheila Cartwright was shot.

Another murder suspect had joined the growing list.

35

Since she'd moved her chair round to witness the parting scene, Jude didn't turn it all the way back and, over her book, monitored George Ferris's reaction to the collapse of his romantic dreams.

He looked considerably less than devastated. After the initial embarrassment of the row — the English are so upset by raised voices in public — the pub's other customers returned to their drinks, food, and, slowly, conversations. At first George Ferris did very little. He just sat there, looking straight ahead, perhaps in shock. But after a few moments he visibly relaxed. Amongst the many emotions his body language could have been presenting, the dominant one was relief. Maybe the fantasy to which he had been gearing himself up, the transformation of his life through a passionate affair with Marla Teischbaum, had rather frightened him. Sinking back beneath the unrippled surface of his retirement (with Geraldine) was perhaps a more attractive prospect.

There was also anger in his demeanour. He was on his own patch, after all, and that woman — whom he'd gone out of his way to help — had made him look a fool there. Jude could see him mentally justifying his feelings of ill-treatment.

She watched him down the remains of his pint, then turkey-strut across to the bar for a refill. "Bloody women, eh?" he said to the barman, whom he clearly knew.

The barman produced one of those jocular, commiserating responses that go with the job, and George returned to his table. After an initial dubious look at the remains of his all-day breakfast, he clearly made the decision that no bloody woman was going to put him off his food, and tucked back into it.

Jude's had also arrived, and she ate hers, too, keeping an eye on George's progress and wondering what her next move should be. She already had some new information to share with Carole and Laurence, but was hopeful that, if she played her cards right, she might get even more.

George finished his fry-up, and Jude tensed, prepared to follow if he left the pub. But he didn't. Instead, with relish he drank the last of his second pint and went up to the counter for a third. This time his badinage with the barman included the phrase "Perdition to all women." He was doing running repairs on the punctures Marla had made in his considerable self-esteem.

He sat back at his table, sipped at his beer, and looked quite benign. His body language seemed to say that he'd had a narrow escape with that bloody American woman, and was well out of it.

Jude decided that Laurence Hawker's recipe for starting conversations with academics was at least worth a try. And it wasn't as if she didn't have the relevant prop to hand. Extracting from her basket the copy of *How to Get the Best from the Facilities of the County Records Office*, she turned towards his table and said tentatively, "Excuse me, you aren't by any chance George Ferris, are you?"

His first instinct was suspicious, but then he saw the book in her hand. Like sun through trees, a wide beam broke through the foliage of his beard. "Well, yes, I am, actually."

Jude blinked with naive enthusiasm. (She was particularly good at naive enthusiasm — her eyes became bigger and more trusting by the moment.) "Someone in the County Records Office pointed you out to me."

"Ah." He preened himself in the glow of her adulation. "Yes, well, I am quite well known there."

"I do think" — she tapped the book in her hand — "that this is simply wonderful. Such a help in sorting through the complexities of the archives and what-have-you. . . ."

His beam grew even wider. "Well, yes. I saw a gap in the market. I thought, here we have this wonderful research resource here in Chichester, and yet people waste so much time making the wrong approaches, going through the wrong channels. What is needed is a simple, straightforward guide which — without in any way 'dumbing down' — presents the necessary information in a way that is accessible to the general public."

"You've certainly done a wonderful job," Jude cooed. "Have you written lots of books?"

He considered the question sagely. "I have quite a lot of books *in me*. There are many projects that I've been working on for some time, and that probably will end up in book form . . . but this is the only one I've had published . . . at the moment."

"Oh, it must be great to be so talented." Jude wondered if she was overdoing it, but the complacent grin on the Hobbit face showed that it was impossible to overdo praise of George Ferris. He lapped up everything that helped to support his own self-estimation. Jude realised why he had bounced back so quickly from his apparent humiliation by Marla. In his own mind he'd already turned round the balance of guilt in their encounter. Marla had been the one who'd made a fool of herself. She wasn't worthy of a man like him.

And, of course, he was probably thinking, *She's lesbian, which explains it all. That's what she'd meant by being "very happily single."* There was no other explanation. Any woman who could resist the charms of George Ferris would have to be a lesbian.

Having softened him up, Jude moved on to what she really wanted to talk about. "Who was that rather rude woman who was with you earlier?"

"Oh," he replied airily, "just some American professor I've been helping out with her research."

"She didn't seem very grateful for your help."

"No. Well, a rather ungracious nation, the Americans, I often find. And" — he let out a discreet, self-deprecating little cough — "in that case, there was a personal agenda, too. . . ."

"Oh, really?"

"Yes. I always try not to mix business with pleasure" — he grimaced wryly — "but can't always be done." He smiled in apology, regretting what a dog he was, and how often his fatal attractiveness had led him into this kind of situation. "As Byron put it, 'Hell hath no fury like a woman scorn'd.'"

Jude happened to know that the line was from Congreve rather than Byron, and that George had in fact misquoted it, but she didn't draw attention to his errors. She needed to keep him sweet for her next question.

"So what kind of research was that American woman doing?"

"She's writing a biography of Esmond Chadleigh. Have you heard of him?"

"Didn't he do those children's poems about the nurse?"

"*Naughty Nursie's Nursery Rhymes.*"

"That's it."

"Yes. And of course a lot more."

"Oh, so she's writing about Esmond Chadleigh, and she came to you as an expert on the subject?"

The description pleased him. "Yes. I've given her some very useful leads. Not, of course, that she'll acknowledge my input." He sighed at the selfishness of the academic world, in which true genius was so often ignored, then nodded knowingly. "No, I think there'll be quite a lot of stuff in Professor Marla Teischbaum's book that she'd never have known about if I hadn't set her on the right track."

"What kind of stuff?" asked Jude innocently.

"Oh, some unpublished private collections of letters, that kind of thing."

"Letters from members of the Chadleigh family?"

"No," said George self-importantly. "Anyone'd know where to look for those. But if I hadn't given Professor Teischbaum the lead, she'd never have looked for the Strider family letters."

"Oh," said Jude, as if she'd never heard the name before.

"In my role as a consultant to the County Records Office" — he bathed in self-admiration — "I often check through documents that have been offered by members of the public . . . decide which ones should be kept, which ones justify use of the limited storage space we have available to us."

"And the . . . what did you say . . . Strider family letters? Those did seem worth keeping?"

"Very definitely, yes."

"So when Professor Teischbaum's biography comes out, and it gets wonderful reviews, really the credit should go to you . . . ?"

"Oh, I think that would be excessive." Though his manner suggested he didn't, really.

"Well, I think she's behaved very badly. To be so ungrateful after all the help you've given her."

"I would have given her more . . . if she'd played her cards right," he added coyly.

The image appeared in Jude's mind of George rationing out gobbets of research to Marla in exchange for sexual favours. It was too revolting to contemplate.

"So you do have other information . . . that you didn't give her . . . ?"

"Oh, yes. As I say, with my consultancy to the County Records Office hat on, I do have access to all kinds of private documentation" — he sniggered — "and, without my pointing her in the right direction, there are certain connexions she's never going to make on her own."

"It must be a very responsible job," said Jude, still apparently awestruck by his brilliance.

"Well, yes," he agreed. "I do have to

make some pretty important decisions. For instance," he went on, in case she still hadn't taken on board quite how important he was, "there was an old lady came to see me last year, name of Hidebourne. She had some letters, didn't want them to get chucked out when she died, did I think there'd be a place for them in the County Records Office? She showed me a few, and I thought they would be very interesting, particularly because" — he smiled at his own cunning — "and this is the bit I didn't tell Professor Teischbaum . . . there was a connection with the Strider family. Some letters from a Lieutenant Strider, who had a connexion with Esmond Chadleigh. So . . . old Miss Hidebourne didn't want to hand the documents over then and there . . . she still enjoys reading them . . . but it's all been sorted out legally . . . and, soon as she pops her clogs, the letters will come here . . . to the County Records Office, that is."

"And *you* sorted all that out?"

"Oh, yes," he replied airily.

"Fancy," breathed Jude, tapping her copy of *How to Get the Best from the Facilities of the County Records Office*, "being able to do all that, and write books, too."

"Just something I do."

He made a self-deprecating, wide-handed shrug, then looked at Jude closely. He seemed to realise for the first time that she was an attractive woman.

"Maybe I could get you another drink . . . ?"

Though thwarted in his pursuit of Marla, a man as attractive as George Ferris wouldn't have to go long without female company. Maybe it was time to strike out in a new direction. Jude could see the thoughts going through his head.

Deciding that she had maintained her masquerade quite long enough, she politely made her excuses and left The Cathedral. Just as she was about to enter the County Records Office, she looked back and saw George Ferris also leaving the pub and moving, a little unsteadily, in the direction of the car park.

Jude found Laurence Hawker sitting in the Reception Area. He was coughing, of course; and continuing to smoke, of course. In fact, he took the cigarette out of his mouth only to take swigs from the half-bottle of whisky he held in his other hand.

The frosty woman behind the counter was clearly having a problem with him. She disapproved of his smoking. Now that he'd added drinking to his crimes, her disapproval was even greater. But his appearance made her uncertain as to what she should do. She knew the protocol for ringing security to get rid of the usual type of drunk or dosser from her domain. But this visitor looked too elegant, too cultured, to be dealt with in that way. He confused her, and she didn't like being confused.

Laurence looked up languidly at Jude's entrance. "I knew you'd come back eventually," he said, and coughed.

She sat beside him and asked in a low voice, "Did Marla come back?"

He nodded, jerking his head back towards the Reading Room. Jude looked through the glass and saw the back view of Marla. She was once again bent over her books, absorbed in her research. She gave no signs of being affected by her recent encounter with the mistakenly amorous George.

"Did you get any useful information, Laurence?"

"You bet."

"Me, too."

"Let's go and have a drink somewhere, and pool what we've got."

The Cathedral was the nearest source of alcohol, and Jude had seen George Ferris leave, so she felt safe to return there. From Laurence's slow pace of walking, the rattling and rasping of his breathing, he wouldn't have been able to make it much further, anyway.

After the lunchtime rush, the pub was fairly empty. Jude got another white wine for herself, and a quadruple Scotch for Laurence. No point in rushing back and forth to the bar every five minutes.

"You go first, Laurence. Did you manage to get a look at what Marla had been studying?"

"Oh, yes. It's an academic skill you don't lose. Get very used to peering over people's shoulders in libraries, finding out what the opposition is up to. Sadly, though, I fear it's a skill that won't be valuable for a lot longer. As more and more research is done through the Internet, a dying art" — he grinned — "probably see me out, though."

Jude didn't react to the morbid joking. "What was she looking for, then?"

"The lovely Marla appeared to be following up on the history of the Strider family."

"Strider as in Lieutenant Hugo Strider, who was mentioned in those documents?"

"I imagine so. She had some letters. And from the other stuff she had out — parish records, Land Registry documents — I'd say she was trying to trace any living descendants of Lieutenant Hugo Strider."

"But you don't know whether she'd found any?"

He shook his head, sardonically regretful. "Rather thoughtlessly, she hadn't left a notebook open on the desk with the name and addresses of the people she was next going to talk to."

"And even if she had," said Jude, "there'd be one very significant name and address missing from the list."

"Oh?"

"An old woman who has in her possession some letters written by Lieutenant Hugo Strider. Her name's Miss Hidebourne."

36

"I've spoken to Gina," said Carole. "She's quite happy for me to have a look around Bracketts tomorrow."

"To inspect the priest's hole?"

"Yes. I'm going over about twelve."

"The police haven't been there yet?"

"Apparently not. Maybe they've got more important questions to ask Mervyn Hunter than where he spent the nights he was on the loose. Will they actually be questioning him in Austen Prison?"

"No way." Jude shook her head. "I asked Sandy. Anyone who's captured after an escape from an open prison goes straight into a Cat B or C one, at least initially. Mervyn'll probably be in Lewes . . . if he's not still with the police."

"Maybe he did kill Sheila Cartwright," said Carole, with an air almost of despondency.

"Don't even think it. I'm sure he didn't."

"Where's Laurence?"

The question was posed casually enough, but Carole really wanted to know the answer. Although her attitude to Laurence Hawker had thawed a little, she'd still be glad to receive the news that he'd left Woodside Cottage for good.

"He's having an early night. Wasn't feeling so hot." That was an understatement. The day out in Chichester, following on his weekend away, had taken a lot out of Laurence. He'd coughed up more blood after the cab brought them back. Jude was beginning to wonder how much longer he could continue without being hospitalised. But it was not a subject to raise over a glass of wine in the neatness of Carole's kitchen.

"Incidentally," said Carole. "One detail I got from Gina . . . about the first body in the kitchen garden. . . ."

"Oh, yes?"

"Still been no official identification, but Gina had found some old letters about one of the Bracketts stable boys who'd disappeared about the right time. Named Pat Heggarty. Son of the Chadleighs' housekeeper. The thinking at the time was that he'd done a runner to escape conscription. I don't know. It's a thought."

"Yes, that body seems rather to have paled into insignificance since the death of Sheila Cartwright."

"True. I wonder if there *is* a connexion between the two deaths," said Carole thoughtfully. "When Sheila died, I was convinced there was. Now I'm not so sure."

"I think there is a connexion . . . at least through Bracketts. Something that's happened in this house was important enough to make someone commit a murder. . . . By the way," Jude went on, "am I included in this invitation?"

"Invitation?"

"For priest's hole exploration."

"Well . . . ," Carole began awkwardly.

Jude picked up the hint very quickly. "Say no more. You're wangling your way in as a trustee. Justifying bringing a friend along might prove more difficult."

"That, I'm afraid, is the situation exactly, Jude."

"Don't worry. I've got things to do tomorrow." Trying to persuade Laurence to see a doctor being one of them, she thought grimly. But she said, "There's an Esmond Chadleigh lead Marla's been following up. Some letters from Hugo Strider."

"Did you get to see them?"

"Laurence had a quick look after the professor had left. They'd been written to a distant cousin while he was living at Bracketts."

362

"Useful stuff?" asked Carole eagerly.

"Not really. All very correct and British and giving nothing away. I'm afraid upper-class English gentlemen between the wars didn't go in for baring their souls much. Laurence says he'll go back and have another look at them, but he wasn't very hopeful of finding anything."

"Another blind alley, then?"

"That one may be, but there's something else," Jude announced proudly. "Another Strider connexion about which Marla knows nothing at all."

"Really?"

So Jude told Carole about what George Ferris had told her. "And, because Laurence is such a whiz at research and positively zipped around the County Records Office, I now have an address and telephone number for Miss Hidebourne."

Even as she spoke, Jude was keying numbers into her mobile phone.

When Carole arrived at the Bracketts Administrative Office at noon the next day, Gina Locke was still in her post-Sheila Cartwright pomp. Her brown eyes sparkled, and her confidence was almost overweening.

"Had a really brilliant day yesterday, Carole. Went to see a major potential sponsor. Better not mention the name, because everything's still a bit under wraps, but they are seriously big. Multinational food company, I can tell you that much. Anyway, they've had a bit of a battering in the media recently, because one of their American subsidiaries used a lot of genetically modified produce, and basically they need a mega public relations makeover. To show how caring they really are as a company, how involved in the local community and the arts. And I think I've persuaded them that sponsoring the museum here at Bracketts would give them just the kind of image transplant they need."

"Well done."

"Yes. As I say, it was a good day. You know, some days you feel really competent and fluent, like you could take on the world. . . ."

Carole didn't have many days like that, but she still nodded, not wishing to interrupt Gina's flow.

"I saw the guy Sheila had been cultivating, but I think I was probably more effective than she would have been. He clearly had an eye for the ladies and the younger woman. . . ." She grinned. "Have to be prepared to use any wiles to get sponsorship these days, you know."

"And did you use the 'what a tragedy about Sheila' wile?"

"You bet I did. Damn nearly got his condolences in the form of a cheque. No, I said all the right things . . . how much she'd enjoyed her meetings with him . . . how optimistic she'd been about a happy outcome to their discussions . . . how the museum would become like a memorial to Sheila Cartwright . . . and how good it would be for the compassionate image of any company involved in such a project."

Had Jude been there, Carole would have exchanged a raised eyebrow with her, but as she was on her own, she just nodded.

"So" — Gina rubbed her hands gleefully — "with a bit of luck I might get the whole museum paid for by this one company. An exclusive sponsorship, just what I need. And, if it goes through quickly, we could open the museum in 2004, on the centenary of Esmond Chadleigh's birth."

"Will there be time for that?"

"You bet. The architects' plans were drawn up over a year ago. The planning permission's sorted. Only waiting for the money to make it happen."

"Well, congratulations on a day well spent yesterday."

"Thank you." There was no humility in

the director's response. She was just taking the praise that was her due.

But the wrapping up of that part of the conversation did enable Carole to move on. "I was very interested in what you said on the phone about that stable boy . . . Pat . . . ?"

"Pat Heggarty."

"Right." Carole was remembering a previous encounter, in the Crown and Anchor, when Gina had been very firmly trying to direct her thought processes about the body in the kitchen garden. "Who told you about him?" she asked diffidently.

"Graham. He's the great repository of all knowledge about everything that's ever happened at Bracketts."

"Funny he didn't mention it before . . . when the body was first discovered."

"Odd, yes." But Gina didn't sound that interested; her mind was moving ahead to the next step of her museum-building project.

"Straight after Sheila's death . . . ," Carole persisted.

"Yes?"

". . . you seemed to be convinced that Graham had killed her."

"Mm, I remember saying that."

"Presumably you don't still think he did?"

"No. Just seemed to make sense at the time. Now the police have got hold of this escaped convict . . . well, I must have been wrong." But there was no apology in her tone, no sense that there was possibly something reprehensible in bandying around accusations of murder.

"Right." Carole stood up. "If you're sure you don't mind my having a look at the priest's hole. . . ."

"No, of course not." Gina took a large set of keys down from a row of hooks on the wall. "I've got a few follow-up calls to make on the sponsorship. Do you mind letting yourself in?"

"Not at all. If you're sure that's all right. . . ."

"Look, you are a trustee. You're hardly going to walk away with the exhibits, are you? If there was somebody I didn't know wanting to get into the house, that'd be different."

Probably, thought Carole, it was just as well she hadn't brought Jude along.

Carole had a logical mind; all her colleagues at the Home Office had recognised that. And logic dictated that before she went inside Bracketts, she should look at the exterior of the house.

She recalled the words of the white-haired, kilted lady as their guided tour had reached the priest's hole: "From the outside of the house no windows are visible, but comparisons of the exterior dimensions and the measurements of this landing demonstrate that there is a space within the walls unaccounted for."

It was a bright, bold autumn day, with a whiff of wood smoke on the air. Carole, warm in her Burberry, moved over the dampish grass, orienting herself by the large landing window. To the right of this was the angle of the house that, on the first floor, had no corresponding concave angle inside. That's where the priest's hole was.

Nothing looked odd from outside. The lack of windows in the relevant part of the structure raised no questions; there weren't that many windows in the rest of the house. But, Carole noticed with a little spurt of excitement, there were no windows in the ground-floor section directly beneath the priest's hole either.

She didn't rush, but continued to work logically. She went up to the house and, producing the tape measure she had brought specially for the purpose, took a reading from each side of the distance from the edge of the nearest window to the corner of the house. She tried to make out what lay inside, but the windows were curtained to protect the elderly furniture from the sun.

Controlling her excitement, Carole walked round to the front of the house and let herself into Bracketts.

She went straight to the ground-floor area directly beneath the priest's hole. This involved going through a door marked PRIVATE into a part of the house not included in the guided tours. But what the hell? She was a trustee. She could go where she wanted.

Disappointment stared her in the face. Her best fantasies had been of a jutting pair of walls, matching the area of the priest's hole above. There'd either be another sliding panel, or maybe the hidden space was accessible only from the first floor.

But, instead of walls, she was confronted by cupboards, large cupboard doors on either side of the projecting right angle. When she opened them, she found an array of vacuum cleaners, brushes, mops, and other cleaning equipment.

Oh, well, it had been a nice idea. Carole

was about to close the doors, when a thought struck her.

Yes, they were cupboards all right, but they were surprisingly shallow cupboards. The vacuum cleaners fitted in fine, but there was space for only one row of them. Carole once again took the tape measure out of the pocket of her Burberry.

The cupboards both sides of the right angle were of the same depth. Two feet. According to Carole's recollection, the dimensions of the priest's hole were about twelve feet by eight. So behind the cupboards, depending on the thickness of the walls, there could be a space of up to ten feet by six.

She felt the walls behind the vacuum cleaners, the suspended mops and brushes. She tapped them. There was no false backing; they were solid stone.

Punctiliously, Carole closed the cupboard doors and, deliberately slow, went upstairs. Sufficient light came through the landing windows to show the dummy panel that led to the priest's hole. And over the years enough fingers had pressed against the relevant part for a shallow indentation in the wood to indicate the locking mechanism. The hands that started this erosion, Carole estimated, must have belonged to Catholic priests shaking with panic and the fear of imminent discovery. Now the pressure on the panel was applied by white-haired, kilted ladies, caught between a genteel sense of duty and total boredom.

She pushed, and the panel slid aside.

The priest's hole had been emptied for the winter. The low table was still in place, which was hardly surprising since it was bolted to the floor. However, the cloth, candlesticks, and book that had adorned its surface were gone.

Ever provident, Carole did have a torch in her pocket, but she felt sure there must be a light switch somewhere. Sure enough, there was, tucked away on the panelling inside. The concealed lighting came on, illuminating the intricate carved ceiling, and once again rendering the space solemn and ecclesiastical. She climbed over the step into the room. There was a low creak as the floorboards took her weight.

Cunningly hidden and complex. That was what Felix Chadleigh had written in his diary on the day he moved into Bracketts. *It is a source of great pleasure to me that there is a cunningly hidden and complex Priest's Hole here, a sign that for many years this has been a home to good Catholics.*

Carole ran her eye along the floor. Each dark board ran the length of the room, from the landing opening to the far wall. They were uneven, a little warped with age, but rubbed to the smoothness of glass by centuries of sweeping and polishing. She got down on her knees and lay with her cheek flush against the wood, trying to spot some break or irregularity. But all was universally smooth.

Once again planning ahead, Carole had put on shoes with hard, stubby heels. She stood up, and started to tap her way along the floorboards. She did it systematically, moving back and forth down the length of the room.

There was something. Definitely. A bubble of excitement started within her, but she dourly swallowed it down. Double-check, always double-check. So she repeated the whole exercise to be sure.

There was no doubt about it. The sound on two sides of the room, near the landing and along the right-hand wall, was dull and solid. But over the remaining rect-angle, into the far corner, the floorboards sounded hollow, as if there were a space beneath. A space that would have been en-closed by the cupboards on the ground floor.

The bubble of excitement returned, and this time it was irrepressible.

But how on earth could anyone get into the space beneath?

Carole stood up, and once again tried to bring her logic to bear on the problem.

The walls were solid and smoothly plastered, leaving no possibility of a hidden entrance. There were no visible breaks in the length of the floorboards either, which ruled out the chance of a section being lifted out, like a trapdoor.

Then the only possible way for access to the space beneath was for a whole length of floorboard to shift.

Carole moved backwards towards the landing as she pondered this. She heard a creak, just like the one when she had entered the room. She looked down at her feet. Yes, there was a slight give in the floorboards there.

Suppose one floorboard . . . or two floorboards . . . or a central section of floorboards . . . could be lifted out . . . or released downwards . . . or pivoted . . . ?

Excitement bubbled again, but was primly curbed.

She moved to the far end of the room and looked under the fixed table. Disappointingly, the ends of the boards were tucked neatly under the skirting. But there was a marked creak and an almost imperceptible bounce underfoot at that end, too.

Carole went back towards the landing, and knelt down to inspect the flooring by the entrance. Here again the ends of the boards disappeared under the solid beam that framed the bottom of the doorway.

But if that beam could be removed . . . then the boards would be freed. . . .

Carole put both hands on the solid rectangle of wood and tried to pull it towards her.

Nothing. Locked solid.

She squatted back on her haunches, defeated and frustrated.

As she did so, she heard the mocking creak of a floorboard.

And she knew exactly what she had to do.

She put her full weight on the floorboards as near to the landing as she could. They gave. Only a little, but enough to release the lock on the step.

Carole reached down to the beam once more. This time it moved easily towards her, pivoted in the corner of the room. Carefully she stepped over the beam, as she swung it out in a wide arc until it lay parallel to the floorboards at the left-hand side of the room.

Her full weight was still on the floor-boards at the landing end. Carefully, she stepped to one side.

The balance was finely judged, one end of the seesaw only slightly heavier than the other. Three parallel floorboards moved together on their hidden fulcrum, lifting slowly next to Carole and, at the table end, tipping down into the darkness beneath.

The bubble of excitement burst, and filled her body.

She let out a long, satisfied exhalation of relief. Then she switched on her torch.

Its beam revealed metal rungs fixed on the exposed wall below floor level.

In spite of her excitement, Carole, being Carole, was worried about how dirty the space beneath might be. So she removed her precious Burberry, and left it neatly folded on top of the table.

Then, with her torch held firmly between her teeth, Carole lowered herself into the secret, "cunningly-hidden" section of the priest's hole.

37

Jude hadn't prepared any cover story. In spite of the frailty of her voice over the telephone, Miss Hidebourne had sounded strong-willed, not the kind of woman to mess about with. And when Jude said she was interested in her collection of letters, particularly as they related to Lieutenant Hugo Strider, Miss Hidebourne had said she was welcome to come and discuss them . . . "though you'll have to come here, I'm afraid, since I don't get out as much as I used to."

Jude hadn't succeeded in persuading Laurence to go to the hospital or see a doctor — which didn't surprise her — but he had agreed to spend the day in bed at Woodside Cottage. That might save some of his energy, which, given the difficulty he was having moving around, would be a good thing, but Jude didn't delude herself that he'd do anything else mildly healthful. When she got home, she expected to find the ashtrays full and the whisky bottles empty.

Miss Hidebourne lived in a small village just to the north of Lewes, where the South Downs flatten out and lose the lushness of West Sussex. Jude travelled by cab, and said she'd call a quarter of an hour before she wanted to be driven back to Fethering. She justified the expense on the grounds that she didn't want to leave Laurence on his own for too long.

The old-fashioned voice on the phone had led her to expect a country cottage, but Miss Hidebourne lived in a modern block of flats for the elderly, right in the middle of the village. There were slopes for wheelchairs at all the entrances, round handrails on every wall.

The woman who opened the door looked in the last stages of time's erosion. Her angular back was bowed; on her crooked hands the veins and bones vied for prominence; and her sticklike legs tottered on bandaged feet in large Velcro-flapped slippers. But she was neatly dressed, her thin white hair had been recently whipped by a hairdresser into a neat meringue, and there was no vagueness in the sharp brown eyes embedded in her wrinkled face.

"You're Jude, I take it. Come in."

Hearing the voice again, Jude was aware of how upper-crust it was, a voice from another era, redolent of Angela Brazil's school stories.

"Incidentally," said Miss Hidebourne, as she led her into the tiny, neat sitting room, "I can't just call you 'Jude.' Sorry, it's the way I was brought up, to use people's proper names. Can't stand the way all these nurses and people who've never met you before insist on calling you by your Christian name. So what is your full name?"

Meekly, because she rarely mentioned it, Jude said, "Jude Nichol."

"Right. So is it Mrs. or Miss Nichol?"

" 'Miss' will do fine," replied Jude, retaining a little of her mystery.

"Now, I'm sure you'd like a cup of tea."

"Oh, I wouldn't want to put you to any trouble."

"It's no trouble," the birdlike figure said firmly. "I was just about to have one myself. Do just sit down, and I'll bring it to you."

"Isn't there anything I can do to help?"

"No, there certainly isn't." The tone used by Miss Hidebourne suggested that a serious breach of etiquette had just been committed. As she sank obediently back into her chair, Jude couldn't help being reminded of Carole. A certain generation of middle-class British had tea rituals at least as elaborate as anything witnessed in Japan.

"While I'm getting the tea ready, Miss Nichol, you may care to peruse those documents I've put on the little table there. They'll tell you something of Gerard."

"Gerard?"

"My brother. He was with whom Lieutenant Strider used to correspond."

"Ah, thank you."

Jude watched the agonising slowness with which Miss Hidebourne made her progress out of the room. If the tea-making was going to be conducted at the same pace, then she could be alone in the sitting room for some time.

The documents Miss Hidebourne had prepared for her were in a buff cardboard folder, a collection of neatly clipped-together papers, a few letters and some news cuttings. It was soon clear that most of them dated from 1984, the year of Gerard Hidebourne's death.

The newspaper cuttings were obituaries. Born to an eminent Catholic family in 1889, he had gone to Oxford in 1908 (one of a small minority of his faith, because Catholics had been banned from English universities until 1897). Subsequently,

Gerard Hidebourne had trained as a priest, being ordained in 1913. He appeared to have taken no part in the First World War, and continued working as a parish priest until his retirement in 1964. For the remaining twenty years until his death, he had lived with his sister in Lewes.

"Not a very exciting life, was it?"

Jude looked up in surprise to see Miss Hidebourne edging into the room with a tea tray balanced precariously on her arthritic hands. Everything must have been prepared in the kitchen, even the kettle boiled, before her guest arrived.

As Miss Hidebourne teetered towards her, Jude watched with trepidation. The entire contents of the tea tray looked as if they might at any second be tipped into her lap, but she knew better than to cause offence by making an offer of help.

By sheer willpower, Miss Hidebourne managed to secure the tea tray on the small table by her chair. Then she sat down, with a smile that suggested the exercise had been no effort at all.

"Now you've moved the file, you'll be able to use the small table beside you," she said, once again reminding Jude of Carole.

While tea was solemnly dispensed, Jude

picked up on Miss Hidebourne's entering remark. "You say your brother's life wasn't very exciting."

"Would you describe a life spent administering meaningless sacraments to uncomprehending parishioners as one packed with interest, Miss Nichol?"

"It certainly wouldn't suit me, but then I don't have faith."

"Nor did Gerard," Miss Hidebourne almost snapped. "He started with faith. His early letters glow with faith. But the Great War started the rot. He lost so many friends . . . so many friends . . . not to mention two brothers."

"I'm sorry. I didn't know."

"Why should you? Don't worry, I never met them. I was born after the war. 1922. My parents' attempt to replace part of what they'd lost. A big responsibility for me. Imagine the pressure of going through life with that over your head all the time."

"It can't have been easy."

"You have a gift for understatement, Miss Nichol."

"So your brother lost his faith. What about you, Miss Hidebourne? You were presumably brought up a Catholic, too?"

"Yes, and I lost mine. In my early twenties, inevitably, when contraception became an issue. I am still sometimes appalled when I stop and think how much harm, how much total destruction, the Catholic Church must have caused in human sexual relationships."

"But they say, 'once a Catholic. . . .' "

"And I believe, Miss Nichol, they intend the tag to be finished '. . . always a Catholic.' Not in my case. For me, being 'Once a Catholic' has made me daily more aware of what a pernicious creed it is."

Miss Hidebourne, Jude had by now pieced together, was not a woman who had problems about speaking her mind.

The old brown eyes focused on her guest. "Do you have a religion?"

"I have . . . beliefs."

Miss Hidebourne shrugged them quickly away. "Not the same thing at all. Beliefs don't have rules. With beliefs you can change them at will. They don't have a whole meaningless superstructure of rituals and rewards and punishments."

Jude did not entirely agree, but she didn't take issue. "So are you saying you think your brother's life was wasted?"

"Absolutely. He devoted his life to something for which he had no aptitude, and which for most of his life he didn't even believe in. He was not a man with the common touch. As a result, for his parishioners he was always a kind of joke. And, because of Gerard's choices, I am the last of the Hidebournes. When I die — and it won't be long now — that will be the end of the family."

"Was this why you wanted your papers to be kept at the County Records Office?"

"So that there's something left, yes. Gerard should have married. He would have been much happier with a wife and children. And the name would have carried on. Don't get me started on the subject of celibacy of the priests. A totally ridiculous principle, based on no scriptural authority at all, introduced first as an economic measure so that the Catholic Church would not be responsible for the upkeep of all the brats spawned by their staff, and the cause of more misery than. . . ."

She caught Jude's eye and, surprisingly, smiled. "As I said, don't get me started on that. . . . No, Miss Nichol, that is not why you are here, is it?"

"Not really, no."

"The subject of the harm done by the Catholic Church must wait for another occasion." The old lady rubbed her misshapen hands together. "You said on the telephone you were interested in the letters to my brother from Lieutenant Hugo Strider."

"Yes. It's in fact in relation to some research a friend's doing on Esmond Chadleigh."

"Ah, another victim of Catholicism." She raised her hand mischievously, as if to curb her tongue. "Don't worry, I'm not about to fulminate again. Hugo Strider, yes. He and Gerard met at Oxford. There weren't that many Catholics there at the time, so they bonded deeply. Kept up a correspondence until Hugo's death."

"When was that?"

"Early Thirties. 1933 . . . 1934 . . . I was little more than a child, but I remember hearing that Gerard had been terribly upset. Though, of course, Hugo Strider had never really been the same after the war. He was hideously injured at Passchendaele. Lost the power of speech and . . . I think his death was probably a long-delayed, but merciful, release. He died at Bracketts."

"Did he?"

"Yes. Felix Chadleigh, Esmond's father, offered him a home, and he went there after the medics had patched him up. Spent the remainder of his life at Bracketts. A miserable time, if his letters to

384

Gerard are to be believed."

"Miserable because of his physical sufferings?"

"He hardly mentioned those. No, it was his conscience that hurt him." The old woman smiled sardonically. "I'm sure I don't need to tell you that guilt is another destructive speciality of the Catholic Church."

"So I've heard. But tell me, Miss Hidebourne, what had Hugo Strider got to be guilty about?"

"He was guilty about his involvement in the death of Felix Chadleigh's son, Graham."

38

Little light spilled down from the chamber above, but Carole's torch revealed the dimensions of the tiny secret cell. Pointing it upwards, she could see, through the cobwebs, a fine ceiling decorated with carved Tudor roses. On the floor lay a tattered rug, a candle in a holder, a couple of old books, and an empty biscuit packet. Unlike everything else in the space, these were not dusty, and Carole felt certain they were signs of Mervyn Hunter's recent occupation . . . though how he'd come to know of the hiding place she had no idea. As she had the thought, however, she recalled Jude mentioning Mervyn's reading about the house's history in the Bracketts library. Maybe he'd found some reference to the double priest's hole and investigated it for himself.

The conjoined floorboards that had seesawed to allow her entrance stayed in the open position, and she had to make her way around the downward-projecting end to see what lay on the far wall. As she passed, she turned the torch beam up towards the bar or beam on which the boards pivoted.

A solid iron rod stretched the width of the ceiling. It was fixed in place by huge metal fittings whose ornate working, picking up the rose motif carved on the beams, suggested they dated from the time of the house's construction. A very simple, but neat and effective, feat of engineering.

Though not given to flights of the imagination, Carole couldn't help wondering how many Catholic priests had quaked down here in desperate prayer, listening as the sound of searching footsteps boomed around the house. Her excitement was diluted with uneasiness.

Nor could she quite suppress a shudder of claustrophobia. Locked down here, she thought, you'd be completely at the mercy of someone else. When the floorboards were back in place, the locking mechanism could be released only from above. The cell would be the perfect place in which to immure an unwanted visitor. She wondered if its history had encompassed the slow death of some unfortunate who had offended one of Bracketts's owners.

To displace such uncomfortable thoughts, Carole turned the beam of her torch onto the far wall, revealing a collapsing bookcase loaded with cardboard storage boxes. They were of antiquated design, probably Thirties office equipment, and over them the dust lay as thick as felt.

Carole wished she had gloves, but they were in the pocket of her Burberry, and she was too excited to bother going up to fetch them.

She reached forward to one of the cardboard boxes, lifted the lid, and shone her torch inside.

It was full to the brim of handwritten papers.

The paper was unlined, and the further down the page the small, awkward handwriting progressed, the more its lines tended to drift upwards to the right.

Whatever Carole was looking at had been written by Esmond Chadleigh.

Miss Hidebourne riffled through a neat box file of letters, one of many, each labelled with dates and details of its contents. When they were finally handed over to the County Records Office, the papers would be in excellent order.

"The same theme recurs in many of the letters, amidst a certain amount of Bracketts domestic trivia and news of old Oxford friends." The old lady held one out to Jude. "This'll give you an idea of the sort of thing, Miss Nichol. Dated 1933, the year before Hugo Strider died. Read that paragraph."

Jude obediently followed the swollen-knuckled finger.

I know I keep harping on about this, Gerard, but I do still feel huge guilt about Graham Chadleigh's death. I have never been to confession about what I did. I know I should have done, and I know the confidentiality of the confessional is supposed to be absolute, but some deeds are too dreadful to be spoken. (A betrayal of my mental state, perhaps, that I, who have lost the faculty of speech, should use the word "spoken.") It is not just the terror of the confessional that holds me back in this matter. There is also a promise I gave to F, that I would never breathe a word about it to another human soul. I cannot disobey. For so many reasons, F has power over me. He is perhaps the only one who knows the magnitude of the crime that I have committed.

"I don't suppose," asked Jude, "that you have any idea of the nature of the crime which Lieutenant Strider committed."

The small, white-haired head shook. "No idea that I can prove, no. But it's clearly nothing venial, is it?"

"No."

"And in the heat of the battle, in a hell on earth like Passchendaele, with men armed to the teeth, all kind of things could have happened, couldn't they? With nobody any the wiser?"

"Are you suggesting that Lieutenant Strider murdered Graham Chadleigh?"

"Well, it's a thought, isn't it?" said Miss Hidebourne with a sweet smile.

Carole was sitting with her back against the wall of her cell. Around her spread a litter of open, dusty boxes. She was totally absorbed in the riches she had unearthed.

She focussed her torch on a letter in the neat copperplate handwriting of Felix Chadleigh.

Dear Esmond,

I am writing this in confirmation of what we agreed last night. Your sisters will be receiving similar letters, and I want you to keep them in a safe place for ever. When I am dead, you will still be able to look at this, and remember the vow you made last night.

We all know what the truth is, the new truth, the truth we will all stand by. Hugo, after some misgivings, has agreed to support that truth, too.

Do not let me down. Any of you. I am not so melodramatic as to talk in terms of father's curses, but if anyone in the Chadleigh family lets me down in this matter, he or she will earn my eternal hatred, a hatred that will instantly cut through all ties of parental affection and that — believe it or not — I guarantee will continue from beyond the grave.

Your Father.

What on earth could it mean? What was he talking about?

Carole riffled through the contents of the latest box. She found another unlined sheet in Esmond Chadleigh's distinctive hand. There were scratchings-out and words inserted, a draft of something he was working on.

She read:

I'm writing to you at the request of my commanding officer who had a request from Lieutenant Strider for anyone who witnessed what happened to his men. . . .

Carole heard a sound from the main priest's hole above. Her heart leapt in shock, as she looked guiltily upwards.

The beam of a strong torch invaded her hideaway, coming to rest on her face, blinding her.

39

Jude was thoughtful as she left Miss Hidebourne's flat and stood waiting for her taxi. The old lady had, reasonably enough, not allowed her to take any of the letters with her, but had given permission for further research visits if required. If he was fit enough, Jude wanted to get Laurence to come and look through the material. Though the image of him dripping his cigarette ash over the neat surfaces of Miss Hidebourne's flat was incongruous, his instinct for research would quickly lead him to what was important.

Jude had found some useful detail in the letters, and pieced together a kind of chronology for Lieutenant Strider's life in 1917. Writing to Gerard Hidebourne, he had told how he'd used his influence from Flanders to get a commission in his own regiment for the eighteen-year-old Graham Chadleigh. There were a few mentions of the young man's officer training, details passed on in letters Strider had received from Felix Chadleigh, and the lieutenant's clear view that such minimal preparation was inadequate for someone about to face the horrors of the Ypres Salient.

Then, at the beginning of October 1917, Strider wrote to his friend from Bracketts. He'd been given two weeks' home leave, and since he had no close living relatives, the natural course was to spend that time with his old friend Felix Chadleigh and his family.

Jude recalled how the letter had captured the atmosphere of suppressed tension in the house.

Felix and Mrs. Chadleigh are understandably anxious about what the future holds for Graham. I, knowing the full horror of some of the possibilities, exercise great control over what I say, trying to infuse into them a spirit of optimism about the War which I cannot really claim to feel myself. The younger children are in a state of high excitement, running round the house in endless games of mock-battles, in which Esmond is always the British hero, overcoming incalculable odds, while his poor sisters are conscripted into the thankless roles of Boche soldiers. I would find it charming, were I not constantly comparing their innocent play to the reality that lies across the Channel.

There is no escaping the War, though some try. The son of the housekeeper at Bracketts, a lad called Pat Heggarty, who worked as a stable boy here, received his papers last week. Stories he had heard from the Front put the boy into such a blue funk that he ran away . . . the Lord knows where to. Living rough up on the Downs, I imagine, maybe with a rabble of other cowards who refused to answer the call of King and Country.

The incident has put poor old Felix into a serious quandary. Mrs. Heggarty has been with the family many years. She's a devout Irish Catholic and a good worker; neither Felix nor Mrs. Chadleigh has ever had cause to reprimand her about anything. And yet can they continue to employ a woman whose son has offended against every moral principle that exists? Felix has not yet made up his mind, though I do not see how he can possibly keep Mrs. Heggarty on, under the circumstances.

The days pass quickly, and soon I will be back in Hell. At the weekend Graham comes home for two days with his family . . . oh, dear, how nearly I wrote two last days with his family. I devoutly hope that is not the case, and yet when you have seen as many comrades as I have, die horribly before your eyes, pessimism is a difficult trap to avoid.

Graham and I both travel back to France on Monday. I doubt we will be in the same transport, but being in the same regiment, we will undoubtedly meet up on the other side.

Needless to say. I have promised the boy's father and mother that I will "keep an eye" on him, though they cannot know how ineffective would be a whole battalion of guardian angels in the mud of Flanders. They are proud of Graham, as they should be. They hope he will cover himself with glory, and return home a victorious hero. My ambition for the boy is more modest — the hope that he will survive. I used to have the same lofty ambition for myself, but now I am so sick of the sight of death, so bone-deep weary, that at times I hardly care.

I'm sorry, Gerard, an unworthy thought. Our religion warns us especially against the counsels of despair, and thank God my faith is still strong. If it had not been, my will would have been broken by the horrors I have witnessed during these last three years. . . .

After that letter, there had been a long

gap in the correspondence between Lieutenant Strider and Gerard Hidebourne. It was not resumed until March 1920, by which time the doctors had done all they could for the crippled man and he was staying as a permanent invalid at Bracketts.

From the moment this new stream of letters started, the guilt was in them. Jude had read a few more, but they hadn't added a lot to the first one Miss Hidebourne had shown her. Hugo Strider was deeply troubled by something dreadful he had done, something so dreadful he couldn't tell his closest friend, so dreadful he could not even breathe the secret in the anonymity of the confessional. And the crime was in some way related to the death of Graham Chadleigh.

"You're not meant to be down there," said the owner of the torch. "Nobody's meant to go down there."

"But I'm a trustee," protested Carole. In the circumstances, her assertion sounded rather feeble.

"I'm coming down," said Graham Chadleigh-Bewes. And, with considerable puffing and wheezing, he lowered himself down the rungs into the cell below.

His wide torch beam sought out the opened boxes around Carole. "You shouldn't be looking in those."

All Carole could think of was to repeat the fact that she was a trustee, but there didn't seem much point.

"This material's all secret. It's been down here since Esmond died. No one's allowed to look at it." He sounded as if he were repeating a formula learnt by rote, a pupil in detention reciting the school rules.

"Do you mean even you haven't looked at it, Graham?"

He shook his head. "It's forbidden."

"Is this the first time you've been down here?"

"Yes. I heard rumours of the existence of a second priest's hole, but I've never been here."

"Well, as Esmond's biographer, I think you should have been." Carole gestured towards the boxes. "I've only glanced through it, but the little I've seen suggests that a revisionist view of Esmond Chadleigh is at least a possibility."

"Esmond was a good man. He did his best, according to his lights . . . according to the values with which he was brought up. He never harmed anyone."

"He may not have harmed anyone, but

he was certainly involved in covering something up."

"What do you mean?"

Carole held out the letter from Felix Chadleigh to his son. Graham's fat face showed the struggle between two conflicting intentions. Then he made his decision. "I recognise the letter," he said.

Suddenly he snatched it from her, together with some of the other papers she had been looking at, and stuffed them into his pocket.

"You mean you *have* been down here?" asked Carole. "You have seen all this stuff?"

Caught out in his earlier lie, he nodded. "Yes."

"But you're still not planning to include it in your biography?"

"Some skeletons are best left undisturbed."

"Some of them refuse to stay undisturbed, Graham. That one in the kitchen garden that Jonny Tyson uncovered, that refused to be undisturbed, didn't it?"

"Yes. But nobody seems to know who it belonged to. It was nothing to do with the Chadleigh family."

"No? That's certainly what you wanted people to think. You wanted people to think the body was buried before the Chadleighs moved here. Which is why you falsified the documents you gave to Professor Teischbaum, to try to put her off the scent."

"Maybe," he said sourly.

"I think you were overreacting, Graham. Forensic science couldn't say exactly whether a body was buried in 1916 or 1917, so what you did was only going to cause a temporary confusion. The truth would have come out pretty quickly. All you achieved by your crude tampering with the documents was to reveal that you knew something about the body in the kitchen garden. And that you knew the body did have something to do with the Chadleigh family."

"Well, if it did, it was most likely the housekeeper's son. Pat Heggarty. He went missing around that time."

"So how did Pat Heggarty come to have a bullet hole in his head? Did one of the Chadleighs shoot him?"

"No, of course not!" Graham sounded flustered and confused.

"All right. Let's put that on one side for the moment. What about the other skeleton that refuses to stay undisturbed? Sheila Cartwright?"

He shook visibly at the mention of her name.

"What about her? Who killed her, Graham?"

"The police have arrested this convict, haven't they?"

"They've recaptured him. They're holding him in Lewes Prison. But, so far as we know, that's just because he escaped. They haven't charged him with murder."

"Only a matter of time."

"Do you think so? Did you know, incidentally, that the convict, Mervyn Hunter, actually hid down here after he escaped?"

"Really?"

Carole indicated the rug and candles. "He left those."

"Good God! How did he know the place existed?"

"From some book he read in the library here, I think. But presumably you know the contents of the Bracketts library inside out . . . ?"

"Well . . . ," he prevaricated, "I can't claim to have read everything."

"Tell me, Graham," said Carole, suddenly direct, "what did you do immediately after storming out of that emergency trustees meeting on Friday?"

"What the hell do you mean?" He was

full of a weak man's ineffectual bluster. "Are you accusing me of murdering Sheila?"

"I'm asking you what you did straight after the emergency trustees meeting. If you have nothing to hide, I see no reason why you shouldn't tell me."

"Because it's none of your business!"

"I may be being nosey, Graham, but I'm not accusing you of anything. If, on the other hand, you don't answer . . . well, that would make me suspicious."

There was a silence, then he put his hand against the suspended floorboards in the middle of the cell, and mumbled truculently, "I went back to the cottage and straight to bed. I was very upset. Anyone'd be upset if they'd just had their life's work rejected."

"Yes, of course. Are you sure you went *straight* up to bed? You didn't go into any of the other rooms in the house?"

"No. . . ."

Carole pounced on the slight hesitation in his voice. "Did you go into the study, Graham?"

"Why should I have done?"

"That's where you had Graham Chadleigh's service revolver."

"No, I didn't go in there," he snapped.

"So you went straight upstairs to bed?"

He wilted under the ferocity of her gaze. "Well, no. . . ."

"Where did you go, Graham?"

"Only into the kitchen. I got a tin of biscuits. I get very hungry when I'm upset."

Looking at the girth of the pathetic child-man in front of her, Carole Seddon could well believe that.

"But tell me, when did you . . . ?"

Her words trickled away. A new panic fluttered her heart. There was a sound of footsteps on the floor above them. And of voices.

40

Jude got home to find that Laurence had suffered another haemorrhage. Since he was unconscious, he couldn't argue about being hospitalised.

She sat anxiously in a corridor, waiting for the news that he'd come round. Though in theory she knew the seriousness of his condition, the haemorrhage had brought home its implacable reality. The threat to the life of someone she loved took priority over the deaths at Bracketts.

Jude's mind was too full to think about the case. And if anything urgent came up in that connection, Carole had got her telephone number.

The voices from above were those of Belinda Chadleigh and, surprisingly, Marla Teischbaum. Even more surprising, there seemed to be an atmosphere of considerable cordiality between them.

"This is very good of you," the professor was saying, as they approached. "I'd really given up hope of ever getting any cooperation from anyone at Bracketts."

"I think you have to be realistic." Belinda Chadleigh's voice sounded much more focused than before. The vagueness had gone, to be replaced by a brusque practicality. Observing the displaced floorboards, she said, "Well, goodness me, not the first visitors of the day. Graham, are you down there?"

Graham admitted that he certainly was.

"So am I. Carole Seddon."

"What a busy priest's hole we have today. Are you another researcher after knowledge, Mrs. Seddon?"

"In a way, I suppose I am."

"Hm. Graham, you'd better come out of there."

"Very well, Auntie," he said with childlike docility, and started laboriously to pull his heavy bulk up the rungs to the surface.

"I've just been talking to Professor Teischbaum," Belinda Chadleigh went on, "and I've made a decision."

"Oh?" he puffed, heaving himself up to the next level.

"I think we should allow Professor Teischbaum to see the archive down there."

"What!" Graham was appalled. "But after all the trouble we've gone to to protect it . . . Auntie, you're going against everything you've believed in all your life."

"Then maybe the things I've believed all my life were wrong. I've come to the conclusion, Graham, that the truth cannot be suppressed."

"I'm so glad to hear you say that, Miss Chadleigh," Marla cooed. "Truth is the goal of all academic —"

"Nobody asked your opinion!" Graham snapped.

There was a silence, and though she couldn't see them from down in the cell, Carole could sense the drop in temperature as the two rival biographers faced one another.

"Auntie, you can't let this woman invade our family's most precious secrets. I thought you swore to your parents that you'd never let anyone see this material."

"Yes, I did, Graham, but I think there comes a time when you have to question the hold the past exerts over the present. Maybe all these oaths and secrecy have done the Chadleigh family more harm than good over the years. Maybe in some way they contributed to the death of Sheila Cartwright. I don't know. All I do know is that I've decided Professor Teischbaum should have access to these hidden archives."

"But, Auntie, you can't —"

"That is what I have decided, Graham."

The strength in her words, and the silence that followed them, showed the power the old woman exercised over her nephew.

"Now," she said, continuing to take control, "I'm sure Professor Teischbaum would like to have a quick look at the riches on offer."

"I sure would love that."

"Mrs. Seddon, you seem to have made a start. Maybe you'd be so kind as to show the professor what you've discovered so far."

"Of course."

Carole had been initially surprised by Belinda Chadleigh's sudden cooperation with the American, but she quickly rationalised it. The old lady seemed such a peripheral figure that she was easily ignored. All of Professor Teischbaum's previous approaches had been made to the more dominant trustees. Perhaps from the start all that had been needed to break the deadlock was a direct approach to Belinda.

"I can't thank you enough, Miss Chadleigh." Already Marla's elegantly trousered legs were making their way down the rungs into the lower cell.

"Just have a quick look now. The archive

will be open to you whenever you need to consult it in the future. When you're ready, come over to the cottage for a cup of tea . . . and I dare say we could all manage a nice slice of ginger cake . . . ?"

"You bet, Auntie."

Marla had been kitted out with a Camping Gaz lamp that spread light throughout the small cell. As she straightened up to her full height, Carole could see the gleam of triumph in her eye.

"Oh, Mrs. Seddon," she heard Belinda Chadleigh call from above, "I just met Gina Locke on the way over here, and she was asking if I knew who owns a white Renault car in the car park."

"It's mine."

"Apparently it's in the way of some big trailer the local farmer's trying to manoeuvre into a field."

"Shall I come and move it?"

"Don't worry, just throw the keys up. Graham'll move it."

"Will I?" he grumbled.

"Yes, you will."

"Oh, very well. Chuck them up here."

Carole did so. The two women in the cell looked at each other in silence, as they heard the pair of footsteps above recede into the silence of the old house.

Then, with an even more triumphant beam, Marla announced, "I did it! I knew if I stuck at it, I'd get there. It was a matter of getting past bloody Graham. Gard, every time I tried to get through to the aunt, he'd stand in my way. But then I found out which days Graham wasn't there. . . ."

"Who did you find that out from?"

"Gina. She set it all up for me. Told me the right time to ring Belinda, Belinda agreed to see me, and" — she gestured flamboyantly around the small space — "here I am."

"You got off lightly, Marla. I virtually had to break in."

"Don't worry, I'd have broken in too . . . if I'd known the damned place existed. If you want to get information, you have to reckon on a bit of breaking and entering."

"You mean you've done it before?"

The tall American shrugged. "Hardly breaking and entering when the door's left open, is it?"

Carole had a sudden insight. "That's what you did during the emergency trustees meeting, didn't you? As soon as you saw Graham and his aunt come over to Bracketts, you walked into his cottage and started going through his research notes."

"Now that'd hardly be ethical, would it?" But the way Marla said it convinced Carole that her conjecture had been right.

"So when they came out of the meeting so early, they must've caught you snooping."

"No, they didn't." Realising she'd given something away, Marla smiled easily. "O.K., I was there. What the hell? I wasn't getting information any other way. Yup, and it did give me quite a turn when I heard Graham coming back into the cottage. It was raining so hard, I didn't hear footsteps or anything, just the front door opening. I stood there in the study, trying to think what clever explanations I'd come up with when he walked in. But I was lucky, he didn't. I heard him going into the kitchen, then he just stumped off upstairs. Tell you, I didn't need no second invitation. I hightailed straight outta that place."

"And went to wait in George Ferris's car?"

"Oh, you are clever," said Marla mockingly. "Well done."

"Just a minute, though. The rain. I've never seen it raining like it was that night. And when I saw you earlier, you didn't have a raincoat. You never went out of Graham's cottage and risked your precious hair in weather like that."

"I did too. I borrowed a coat. There was a great bunch of them hanging up in the hallway."

"Was it a blue coat with a hood and some logo on the front?"

"Sure. Why, it wasn't yours, was it? You're not accusing me of stealing your damn coat?"

Carole shook her head, hardly hearing Marla's question. Her mind was too full of the new possibilities that had just been opened up. Everything suddenly slotted into place.

Two tall female figures in identical hooded waterproofs. Carole and Jude had been wrong all along. They shouldn't have been trying to work out who killed Sheila Cartwright. The murderer's intended victim had been Marla.

This thought only just had time to register when the women's attention was attracted by a creaking noise from above.

Both looked up in horror. Carole leapt forward, as if she could do something to change their fate.

But she couldn't. Colour drained from both their faces as they saw the seesaw floorboards slowly arc back into place.

They were trapped.

41

It was late afternoon before Jude was told that Laurence had recovered consciousness. He was deathly pale and wired up to various machines like an undernourished early experiment of Dr. Frankenstein.

"Jude, my dear," he croaked incorrigibly. "I suppose a cigarette's out of the question . . . ?"

The nursing staff said he was stable, and Jude could detect an undercurrent of annoyance that they should have to deal with someone whose illness was so patently self-inflicted. They said Mr. Hawker's condition was unlikely to change much overnight. She could stay if she wanted to, but it'd probably make more sense if she went home.

As she left the hospital, she tried Carole on the mobile. Answering machine. Back at Woodside Cottage, she went round next door. But there was no reply.

Jude felt restless. The hospital had her mobile number; they'd call if there was any change in Laurence's condition. She had a nasty feeling that if they did call, it would not be with news of a change for the better.

She looked around her cluttered sitting room, amazed at how much Laurence Hawker had imposed his identity during the short time he had been with her. He was a man of few possessions, and yet he left a trail wherever he went of open newspapers, literary journals, books, and cigarette ends. Every fabric in the house was impregnated with the tang of his tobacco.

And she knew, in a way, that it hadn't worked, the idea of their cohabiting for the last stage of his life. The cohabitation wasn't the problem, it was the illusion that they could achieve it while maintaining the same bantering, affectionate disengagement with which they entered the agreement. She wasn't sure whether Laurence felt the same, but Jude had realised that she couldn't live with someone and not love them. However light and semi-detached they kept their relationship, the latest haemorrhage had brought home to her how much she loved Laurence. It wasn't the kind of love that would worry about him being with other women; but it was a love that would miss him terribly when, inevitably, he was no longer there.

With an effort, Jude stopped her emotions from going too far down that road.

She decided that if Carole didn't come back, she'd treat herself to supper down at the Crown and Anchor. Ted Crisp was a restful companion, surprisingly sensitive when things were going badly. And that evening Jude didn't want to be alone.

They still had light, but that was all they had. They certainly didn't have hope.

"God, I was so stupid!" Carole fumed. "To give away my car keys. Everyone'll think I drove myself away. Then, when they find the car abandoned miles from anywhere, that's where they'll start looking for me. Not here."

"But surely lots of people know about this priest's hole?" Tension made Marla's voice sound even more nasal and whiney. *God,* thought Carole, *if I am going to die here, I'd have chosen another companion to die with.*

The thought of never getting out of her prison brought to her the image of Gulliver. Poor, stupid, big, endearing dog, standing by the Aga, waiting for the mistress who was never going to come home. The thought physically hurt her.

"Lots of people must know about it," Marla whinged on.

"Lots of people know about the priest's

hole. Very few, so far as I can gather, know about this hidden bit beneath it."

"But people will be in and out of the house. They'll hear us if we holler."

"I'm not so sure they will. The walls of this place are pretty thick. Anyway, Bracketts is closed for the winter. Cleaners do their stuff about once a week, I think. Apart from that, nobody comes in here."

"Except for the people who locked us in?"

"And who do you think they are?"

"Well, I don't know. I'd kind of assumed it was Graham. He's never made much secret of the fact that he despises me. And now his aunt's given me access to the archive, he might want to get some kind of revenge. He's a funny guy."

"Yes. Or it could be the aunt herself. Maybe her agreeing to opening the archive for you was just a ploy to get you down here, so that she could lock you in."

"Why would she *do* that?" Marla had that unawareness shared by many insufferable people of just how insufferable she was.

"Or it could be both of them together. Then there's Gina," Carole continued thoughtfully. "She certainly facilitated my visit here today, and you say she set everything up for you. . . ."

"Couldn't have been more helpful."

Carole tapped her teeth. "And it was Gina who asked for my car to be moved, which was why I handed over my keys. . . ."

Marla wasn't listening; she was riffling through her mind for some shreds of hope. "Maybe this is just someone's idea of a joke. Your famous English sense of humour. Someone gives us a fright for an hour or so, and then. . . ."

"Maybe," said Carole grimly.

But Marla didn't believe her own fantasy. Slowly, pathetically, she started to cry.

"Oh, for heaven's sake!" Carole snapped. "That's not helping anything."

"It's helping me," the great professor wailed like a two-year-old.

"You should be ecstatic." Carole gestured ironically to the shelves of dusty boxes. "You've spent so much of your adult life wanting access to Esmond Chadleigh's private archive, and look — you're in it!"

"Yes, I want to be in it," Marla howled, "but I don't want to die in it!"

"I don't suppose," asked Carole coolly, "that you by any chance have a mobile phone . . . ?"

The tears vanished instantly. The confidence and the smile returned to Marla as she reached down to her bag and crowed, "I do!"

"Your bloke gone back, then, has he?" asked Ted Crisp.

"He's in hospital."

"Ah. Didn't think he looked too clever last time he come in."

"No."

"Haven't seen your mate Carole in here much recently either. . . ." Even so long after their brief relationship, there was still an awkwardness when he said the name.

"I'm sure she'll be in soon."

"Yes. Yes. Sure she will." He appeared to put the subject out of his mind. "Now, can I get you another of those white wines?"

The lifeline had gone. Either Bracketts' remote situation or the thickness of the walls that encased them prevented any signal from reaching the mobile. Marla had tried and tried, stabbing emergency numbers with increasing ferocity into the unresponsive unit. Finally, she had given up and lain down on the stone floor, sobbing like a child.

Where's your gung-ho, can-do American spirit now, thought Carole bitterly. Still,

417

having Marla crying was marginally preferable to having her talking.

Once again the reproachful image of an abandoned Gulliver was conjured up in Carole's mind.

She could feel panic rising in her, threatening to overwhelm her body and mind, but she swallowed it back and tried to concentrate on the facts she knew about their current situation.

The thesis made sense that she and Marla had been lured to Bracketts, so that they could be disposed of. Or it made some sense. In her case, she had hardly been lured. She had suggested a time to visit the house, and Gina had said, yes, that was fine.

Marla's situation was a little different. If Carole's theory was correct, then the incarceration was a second attempt on the American's life, the first one having mistakenly killed Sheila Cartwright. Marla's visit to Belinda Chadleigh had been set up by Gina Locke. Either one of the women — or, indeed, both working together — could have engineered its outcome.

And that still didn't include as a suspect the person whose animus against Marla was strongest — Graham Chadleigh-Bewes. He it was who had been rudest about her, he whose fear of the threat she represented to his precious biography had become almost pathological. He had certainly wanted Marla dead.

But then, after what happened at the emergency trustees meeting, he had probably wanted Sheila Cartwright dead, too. . . .

Carole found it was all very confusing. And difficult to concentrate when facing the imminence of a long, lingering death.

Oh, well, at least they still had light. Marla's Camping Gaz was burning steadily. They'd wait till that ran out before they switched the torches on. Fortunately, Graham had left his down there, so light was not an immediate problem.

Nor was food. Yet. Death by starvation lay a long way off, though Carole was already uncomfortably aware of not having had any lunch. She looked at her watch. Nearly eight in the evening. The minimal chance of anyone other than their captors coming into Bracketts had dwindled to nothing.

She stood up to ease the incipient cramp in her legs and, as she did so, felt her foot scuff against some fabric on the floor. She looked down to see the tattered blanket that Mervyn Hunter must have used.

A new thought started in her mind. A hopeful thought.

Mervyn Hunter had used the secret cell as a hideaway. When he'd first come to Bracketts after his escape from Austen, he couldn't possibly have known that the house had been closed to the public. So he must have assumed that guided tours would still be clattering through on a regular basis. Which meant he couldn't have risked leaving the concealed floorboard entrance open. He'd have been found straight away.

So, unless he'd had an accomplice. . . . And that seemed unlikely. Jonny Tyson was the only potential candidate, and from what Jude had said, Jonny's only involvement had been supplying one of his mother's packed lunches.

Mervyn Hunter must have known a way of getting out of the secret cell from the inside.

"Has anyone you've loved ever died, Ted?"

He gave his beard a pensive scratch. "Yes. Not while I was still with her. Girl I used to know on the comedy circuit. Clever she was, Jude, sharp as the crease on a car salesman's trousers. Doing well. I

420

kept bumping into her round all these upstairs rooms of pubs, and that. Then one evening . . . as the old music hall gag goes, one thing led to the other. . . . We had . . . I suppose . . . six weeks together. Then she moved on. Didn't dump me, just let me down softly, like when you got a slow puncture in an airbed. I felt a bit . . . you know, wistful, but . . . got on with things.

"Then two years later I heard she'd been killed in a car crash. Not even hot news. Heard about it from a mutual friend, had happened four months before. I was surprised how much it hurt."

"Mm." Jude nodded slowly. She had known Ted Crisp would be the right companion for that evening. She didn't need to break her word and tell him Laurence was dying. Ted understood.

At the bar of the Crown and Anchor a sad but complicit silence stretched between them.

Carole dropped to her knees and picked up one of the old books that had been left near Mervyn's candlestick.

"What're you doing?" Marla whined. "There's no point in doing any research if we're never going to get out of this place."

"I think certain research may be well

worth doing," said Carole.

The book was thin, leather-bound, probably eighteenth century. Its title page read *Some Oddities of Construction in the House Known as Bracketts Near South Stapley in the County of Sussex.*

She flipped feverishly through the pages until she came to "The Second, or Hidden, Priest's Hole." There was a diagram of the seesaw floorboards, showing how they pivoted and how they were locked in place by the step in the doorway from the landing.

The next page revealed a sketch of the second priest's hole's ceiling, with its lines of carved Tudor roses.

And then there was an enlarged detail of one corner, pointing out a single rose.

"Come on, Marla, get up! I'm going to need your help."

"You don't need my help. There's nothing we can do. We're going to die down here!" the professor wailed.

"You can die down here if you like. I'm not going to. Come on, I need you to hold these shelves steady."

Reluctant, still protesting, Marla nonetheless did as she was told. The bookshelves were rickety, and Carole wondered whether they would hold her weight.

But she reassured herself that they had not collapsed under Mervyn Hunter, and climbed on up.

It was the rose in the corner, and felt reassuringly smooth to the touch, as if it had been handled many times over the centuries. The book had said it should be turned in a clockwise direction.

Carole tried to twist, but the wood felt rigid and unyielding in her hand.

It wasn't going to work.

Jude got back to Woodside Cottage before nine. Her mobile had been silent all evening, and there was nothing on the answering machine at home.

Nothing from the hospital.

Nothing from Carole either.

Jude felt a little flicker of anxiety.

"Gard, what the hell're you doing up there?" whined Marla. "I can't hold on to this forever."

"You can bloody hold on a bit longer!"

Her anger gave her strength. This time, as she strained against the wooden rose, Carole felt a little give, a hint that it wasn't fixed, that it could be moved.

She released her grip, shook her hand to restore circulation, then once again cupped it around the wooden rose.

This time there was a definite, if reluctant, turn. The pommel moved a little, like the head of an old, embedded screw.

Unsteady on top of her bookcase, feeling the strain through her entire body, Carole continued to push the rose around.

Suddenly she felt it ease. And at the same moment she heard a welcome sound from above, a slight rumble as the locking doorstep eased from its mountings and started its long arc across the floor above.

"I'm going to have to let go. I'm —"

Carole bellowed through the thin voice from below. "You stay exactly where you are, Marla! And just watch out you don't get hit when the boards come down."

A final turn, the blissful sound of a click from above as the floorboards became free. And then, so finely weighted that they moved almost in slow motion, the seesaw tipped to the vertical, and they could climb out of their prison.

42

Though Carole knew how long they had been incarcerated, she was still surprised to find near-darkness when they emerged from the front door of Bracketts.

There was enough light for her to look up towards the car park and see that her car was gone. That brought home the reality of the threat to her and Marla. Had the car still been there, the American's suggestion of a practical joke was just about feasible. The fact that it had been driven away confirmed that their enemy — or enemies — had not intended them to emerge from the priest's hole alive.

"I'm not quite sure what we do now . . . ," Carole whispered.

"Just call a cab and get the hell out of here." Marla had her mobile out of her bag and was once again stabbing at it. "Damn. No signal here either."

"I think we're still in danger, Marla. There's someone round this place who wants us dead."

"Another good reason to get the hell out."

Carole was tempted. Part of her wanted only to get back to the comfort of High Tor, to give a big hug to Gulliver, who, though he would have no idea why he was being hugged, wouldn't mind.

But the part of her that wanted to get at the truth was stronger. "I'm just going to have a look around."

"Hell, you're crazy."

But Marla didn't want to be left alone, and she followed as Carole moved cautiously towards the Administrative Office. There were no lights anywhere in the stable block, no sign of life. Whoever had been working there had presumably gone home for the day.

But there were lights coming from the cottage Graham Chadleigh-Bewes shared with his aunt. Carole stepped towards them.

"We don't want to mess with those two anymore. Get the hell out, go to the police and —"

"I want to know what's been going on here." Carole spoke softly, but in a voice that would brook no argument. Finally, she was the dominant woman at Bracketts.

The door of the cottage was, as ever, open. Carole pushed it gently inwards, a reluctant Marla in her wake.

The door to Graham's study was also ajar, and through it they could hear a woman's voice very distinctly.

Carole moved soundlessly forward and put her eye to the crack between the door hinges. She saw a familiar service revolver in a woman's hand. It was pointing directly at Graham, who cowered behind the untidy desk, which was crowned by a plate containing a half-eaten slice of ginger cake.

"Why did you bring those papers from Esmond's archive, Graham?" the woman asked evenly.

"I just picked them up. That Seddon woman had got her hands on them. I took them away from her."

"Nothing's meant to leave the archive, Graham."

"I know that."

"Are you sure you haven't been having second thoughts?"

"About what?"

"About the kind of biography you're going to write? Now that dreadful American woman is permanently silenced, the opposition's gone, hasn't it? But maybe she's given you ideas. . . . Maybe you think you could have a go at a biography of Esmond that includes all the details that are never going to be revealed."

"No, I don't think that."

"Then why did you bring these sheets of paper over here?"

Her voice was hard and fierce, and it frightened him. "I told you," he gibbered, "it was just a mistake. I was never going to use them."

"No? If I for a moment thought you would, Graham. . . . You know the tradition of this family. Felix Chadleigh told his son Esmond how to behave, and Esmond passed that down to his daughters, to me and your mother. She, I'm sure, passed it on to you."

"Yes, she did, Auntie, she did!"

"It's a matter of good faith, Graham, telling the story right. Justifying, glorifying Esmond's memory. And the memory of his brother, whose name you bear."

"I know that."

"The Seddon woman and that American got too close, too close to telling the story wrong. That's why they had to die."

"And why Sheila Cartwright had to die, too?"

"You know that was a mistake." Belinda Chadleigh spoke of the murder as casually as if it had been a misdelivered letter. "Anyway, you can't complain. Sheila is no longer around to commission an author-

428

ised biography of Esmond from someone else. I've conveniently put both your rivals out of the way."

"Oh, Auntie. . . ." His voice was deep with despair. "I just wonder whether it's worth doing the biography."

"*Worth* doing it? That is your role in life. That is what you have to do. To preserve the memories of Esmond and Graham."

"But suppose I did something more truthful . . . ? Suppose I did use some of the stuff from Esmond's archive . . . ? After all, it's not him who comes out of it badly. If there is a villain in the piece, then his father, Felix —"

"Don't you dare talk about villains in the Chadleigh family . . . you . . . you traitor!"

The gunshot was so unexpected, and so loud, echoing through the enclosed space. In the moment of shock that followed its impact, Carole and Marla rushed into the room. They easily managed to disarm and immobilise the old lady.

Belinda Chadleigh gave them a look of undisguised, cold-blooded fury. They threatened what she held dearest in the world, the reputation of the Chadleigh family.

It was too late for Graham, though. He lay slumped back in his chair, redness spreading over his shirtfront. His eyes were wide with surprise, and there was a crumb of ginger cake on the corner of his mouth. In death, as he always had done in life, he looked slightly ridiculous.

43

Laurence Hawker survived his latest health scare and left hospital, his ears ringing with the dire prognostications of the staff. Unless he seriously amended his lifestyle, they could no longer be responsible for him. The very slender chance of his condition improving lay entirely in his own hands.

As soon as he got back to Woodside Cottage, he lit up a cigarette and reached for the whisky bottle.

But not for long. After a few weeks, he did start to moderate both his smoking and his drinking. The reason was that he had been given a project, an academic project which so intrigued him that he became determined to live long enough to see it finished.

The idea came from Carole. Now that the Esmond Chadleigh archive had been found beneath the priest's hole at Bracketts, it could not be unfound. While only the family was aware of its existence, the secret might be preserved, but with Marla Teischbaum knowing it was there,

there was no way she was going to keep quiet about the subject.

Carole therefore suggested to Gina Locke that a report on the archive should be prepared for presentation to the trustees, so that they could take a decision on what should be done with it, and to whom access to the material should be granted. She said that the ideal person to make the report would be an academic of her acquaintance, an expert on twentieth-century Catholic literature named Laurence Hawker.

Gina thought this was an excellent idea and, with the new confidence she now brought to her role as director, announced that the decision to commission the report should not be referred to the trustees; she would make it herself. (It may have been a harsh experience in many ways, but she'd learnt a trick or two from working in close proximity to Sheila Cartwright.) Besides, as she pointed out, the Bracketts Board of Trustees was somewhat diminished. Sheila, who acted like a trustee though she wasn't one, was dead. So was Graham Chadleigh-Bewes. And Belinda Chadleigh was under arrest, being investigated for the murder of at least one of them. There was nothing to be gained from consulting such a depleted body.

So Laurence Hawker was given the job of checking through Esmond Chadleigh's hidden archive and, where appropriate, Miss Hidebourne's collection of Lieutenant Strider's letters to his brother.

Jude would always have happy memories of the weeks during which he prepared his report. She nursed him unobtrusively, loved him, cuddled him, and watched with pleasure as his mind engaged with its final challenge. At first he would have letters and files and boxes scattered all over her sitting room table, while he sat with his laptop, keying in the relevant data. Later he would operate from her bed, propped up on a mountain of pillows, frequently working through the night, snatching odd minutes of sleep amidst the chaos of research.

The security at Lewes Prison made clear to Jude why there were so few escapees from Austen. She almost lost count of the number of doors that were opened and locked behind her on the way to the Visiting Room. The prison officers also seemed more brusque and watchful; there was no comfort in this regime. The customary prison smells of sweat and disinfectant were more concentrated in the enclosed space.

Jude had felt oppressed before she even

entered the place. Lewes always had that effect on her. There was something gloomy and introverted about the town, a feeling of hidden evil that had lasted through many centuries. Jude never arrived in Lewes without a psychic shudder.

The atmosphere of the Visiting Room was also in stark contrast to that of Austen. She didn't know whether children were forbidden, but there were certainly none in evidence that afternoon. And the process of checking visiting orders was stringent and unsmiling, compared to the laid-back attitude she'd encountered on her last visit to Mervyn Hunter.

He looked paler, but sat with the same defensive body language. The tables were all boxed-in rectangles, so that no drugs could be passed beneath them. The prison officers who sat behind the visitors did not relax their vigilance.

"How're you doing?" asked Jude.

Mervyn shrugged. "O.K. I'm more used to this kind of nick than I was to Austen."

"Yes. You heard they found who murdered Sheila Cartwright?"

He nodded. "You get the news in here. Radio. Television news, too, except most of the time people want to watch something else."

"Sandy Fairbarns sends her best wishes." He didn't seem that interested. "Mervyn, I've come to see you because I want to ask about your escape."

"Why?"

It wasn't a question for which she'd prepared an answer, so, characteristically, she told the truth. "A friend and I got interested in Sheila's murder. There are a few details we wanted to fill in, and we thought you might know."

"I didn't have anything to do with it."

"I know that, Mervyn. I never thought you did."

"The police did. You've got one conviction, that's it — obviously you've committed every other crime they haven't stitched someone else for." He sounded almost too weary for bitterness. "Which doesn't offer me much hope for when I'm back out in what they laughingly call 'the real world.' Better off in here."

Jude disagreed, but didn't pursue it. "Sheila Cartwright visited you the day you escaped, didn't she?"

"Yes. That was another reason the police thought I'd topped her. I ended up shouting at her during the visit."

"Why did you shout at her?"

"Because she kept on at me. She always

435

did keep on at me. Always ordering me around, she was, telling me what to do."

Jude could have told him he was not the only one to have suffered such treatment, but it wasn't the moment. "What did she keep on at you about?"

"About the body . . . you know, the one Jonny dug up. She said the press'd found out about it, and I wasn't to say anything to anyone. How she thought the press was going to get into the nick, I don't know."

"And that was all?"

"Yes, but the way she went on at me. I . . . it made me think. . . . It reminded me of. . . ." His words trickled away in pained recollection.

"So why did that make you want to escape?"

"Just to get away from her. The thought that I was kind of locked in the nick, and she could get at me any time she wanted . . . I couldn't stand it. Anyway, I'd been thinking about going over the wall for some time."

"So that you'd be recaptured?" asked Jude gently. "So that you'd end up back somewhere like here?"

"Maybe." He looked at her defiantly. "This is only temporary. They haven't sorted out yet where I'm spending the rest of my sentence, but it won't be Lewes."

"Still be the same security level, won't it?"

"Yeah. Not an open nick. I've been recategorised." There was almost a level of pride in his voice.

"Mervyn, if you so hated Sheila Cartwright, why did you go straight to Bracketts, the very place where you were most likely to find her?"

"I knew she wouldn't be there that Thursday night. She mentioned something else she was doing. And it was late afternoon when I walked out of Austen, so I knew I had to find somewhere close for that first night."

"And you thought of the priest's hole at Bracketts?"

He was genuinely surprised. "How do you know that?"

"We worked it out," Jude replied mysteriously. "My friend found the secret cell underneath, and saw evidence that you'd been there."

"Did she?" Mervyn Hunter sounded impressed. "Yeah, I'd read this book about the place and checked it out one lunchtime when I was working over there. Always useful to know a hiding place."

"Listen, Mervyn, I can understand why

you went there on the Thursday night . . . but why did you stay through the Friday?"

"For one thing, I'd got a mate to organise some grub for me."

"Jonny Tyson."

"Here, you know bloody everything, don't you?"

Jude shook her head. "Sadly, no. But you were still there in the evening, weren't you?"

"Yes. I'd just made this one quick trip out of my hiding place to get the grub from Jonny. Did that lunchtime, when I knew there wouldn't be anyone around. Then I laid low till I thought everyone had gone for the day. But when I got out of the house, I see there's bloody cars in the car park, and I look in through the window and there's a meeting going on in the dining room. Well, no way I was going to risk them hearing me getting back into the priest's hole, so I scarpered."

"You went straight away? You left the grounds immediately? You didn't do anything else?"

"For Christ's sake, you're just like the bloody police!"

"I'm sorry. But there's something else that needs explaining. Did you go to the kitchen garden?"

Mervyn Hunter let out a long sigh, and nodded. "I knew where there was a spare set of keys in the Admin Office. Easy to break in there, without anyone noticing. That's how I'd got into the main house. And just when I was leaving, I remembered there was a key to the kitchen garden on the bunch too, and I . . . I wanted to have a look at where the skeleton was found. So I unlocked the gates."

"Why?"

"I don't know why. It was . . . something. . . . A dead body . . . something about seeing a dead body. . . ."

Jude remembered Carole's description of how he'd reacted when the skull had first been uncovered. "But of course there was nothing there," she said.

"No. Don't know why I thought there would be. I knew there wouldn't be. . . ." He shook his head, and turned it despairingly against the wall, in exactly the same posture as when Jude had first encountered him in the Visiting Hall at Austen.

"Mervyn," she said very softly, "all of this . . . this fascination with the dead . . . this fear of what you might do to women . . . this . . . *fear of women*. . . ." She had hesitated before she spoke the last three words, but he did not contest her analysis.

"It all goes back to Lee-Anne Rogers, doesn't it?"

The silence was so long, she began to fear he'd never break it, but finally he spoke. "I was very young, young for my age. Immature, probably, a bit stupid. I'd never been with a girl, though all my mates — well, people I knew, didn't have that many close mates — they all talked about it, and everything on television talked about it, and how you had to get your end away and . . . I was in this club, and this girl come on to me very strong, and I'd been drinking — wasn't used to that, either — and. . . . Anyway, I thought this was it, I thought I'd hit the jackpot. And then she wants me to go out with her in her car, and I'm still thinking this is good. . . . And she stops in this lay-by, and she gets in the back of the car and invites me to join her. She knew what she was doing, been through the routine lots of times before. . . . So I get in the back with her and. . . ." The tension within him was now so strong he could hardly get the words out. "And she starts telling me what to do. . . . Not loving, not caring, just greedy. She starts telling me what to do . . . she starts telling me what to do. . . ."

"Just," Jude suggested very gently, "like

your mother used to tell you what to do?"

He nodded slowly, then suddenly averted his head, not to let his eyes betray his emotion. "I don't remember exactly what happened next. But I know I killed her. I must have killed her."

"Yes."

There was a long silence, isolated amidst the mutter of other prisoners and visitors.

Then Jude spoke. "Not all women are the same, Mervyn. Not all women want to bully you."

"No?" He sounded sceptical.

"No. The psychiatrists have said it, and I'm saying it, too. You are not a danger to all women."

"I must be."

"No. Look, we're talking all right, you and me, aren't we? I don't feel you're a danger to me."

"No, but we're not alone. There's people here."

"When you finally are released, Mervyn," Jude said slowly, "I want you to come and see me . . . on my own. . . ."

"But I . . . I mean, if you want me to. . . ."

"I don't want you to do anything. I just want you to come and talk to me."

"I wouldn't trust myself to —"

"You're the one who's afraid of yourself, Mervyn. I'm not afraid of you."

He let out a short, bitter laugh. "Then you bloody should be."

"No, Mervyn. I trust you."

He turned his face to look at her. In his eye there glinted a tear, but also a tiny glimmer of hope.

44

The story that Laurence Hawker's researches unearthed was a grim one, and a tribute to the strength of will of one man, Felix Chadleigh. He it was who had masterminded a cover-up of enormous proportions, who had forced the complicity in the subterfuge of one of his closest friends, Lieutenant Hugo Strider, and of his entire family, stretching down for generations beyond his death.

It was the power of Felix Chadleigh's personality that had turned Belinda Chadleigh into a murderer, and blighted the entire life of his great-grandson, Graham Chadleigh-Bewes.

Graham Chadleigh was at the heart of it, Graham Chadleigh the golden boy — killed, as everyone knew, on October, 26, 1917, at Passchendaele, within days of arriving on the Continent. He was the hero celebrated in "Threnody for the Lost," his brother's most famous poem.

It was the date of that poem's publication which got Laurence Hawker thinking.

Vases of Dead Flowers came out in 1935, and though the "Threnody" might have been written some time before that, it still seemed an odd time for war poetry.

And it was only a year or so before that Hugo Strider had been writing letters of impassioned guilt to his Catholic confidant, Father Gerard Hidebourne. In one of them he'd referred to a "vow he'd made to F," and in another he wrote,

> *I had a big argument with F last night, or my equivalent of an argument, which involves writing down a lot of points and waiting for F to shout them down. I asked him to release me from the oath I swore to him. I do not feel I will last much longer, and I would like to face my Maker with at least some sense of absolution for my sins. F, as I might have anticipated, refused to listen to me. He's getting very anxious, frightened others are going to find out our secret, and I believe he has been putting pressure on Esmond to do something about it.*

Do something about what, Laurence Hawker wondered. What could Esmond do? Well, he was a writer. He could write something. If there was some cloud over the memory of his brother, what better way to dissipate it than by writing a celebration with the power of "Threnody for the Lost"?

But what was the cloud over Graham Chadleigh? Hugo Strider had spoken of his guilt over his "involvement" in the boy's death. Miss Hidebourne had even hinted that the lieutenant might have been responsible for the death, murdering his junior in the hell of Passchendaele.

But that didn't fit. Whatever Lieutenant Strider had done, it was something Felix Chadleigh had known about, possibly even forced him into. And what kind of man would offer a home for life to someone he knew to be the murderer of his precious son?

Laurence Hawker then wondered whether the cloud hung over the boy himself, whether Graham Chadleigh had committed murder. The only candidate as victim was Pat Heggarty, the boy who had apparently run away to avoid conscription. If it could be proved that the body unearthed in the Bracketts kitchen garden had belonged to Pat Heggarty. . . . But it hadn't been proved, and the police were, as ever, reticent in spreading the results of their forensic investigations.

Still, Laurence now had a thread to follow, and follow it he did, through the piles of dusty papers (which didn't do his cough any good at all). And eventually he found what he was looking for.

The first clue appeared in the document that Carole had looked at in the secret cell beneath the priest's hole. It was definitely in Esmond's handwriting, and it began:

I'm writing to you at the request of my commanding officer who had a request from Lieutenant Strider for anyone who witnessed what happened to his men. . . .

Laurence knew he'd read those words before, and it didn't take long to uncover the photocopies that Graham Chadleigh-Bewes had prepared for Marla Teischbaum. There was exactly the same text, though now written in the uneducated hand of a common soldier, J. T. Hodges (Private).

Yet Esmond Chadleigh's version was full of changes and crossings-out. In fact, his had been written before the soldier's letter. In other words, he had faked an eyewitness account of his brother's death.

With this doubt sown in his mind, Laurence cast a sceptical eye over some of the other documentation of Graham Chadleigh's time at the front. And, though some of the accounts from fellow soldiers had no rough drafts by Esmond, a sufficient number did, to cast doubt on his brother's ever having been at Passchendaele.

Supposing Lieutenant Strider had supported that subterfuge, had lied about the boy's presence by his side in battle . . . then that surely would have justified his later paroxysms of guilt.

So if Graham Chadleigh wasn't on the Ypres Salient in October 1917, where was he?

Laurence found the truth in two devastating documents.

The first was a letter written to Esmond by his mother in 1921. He was then an undergraduate at Oxford and apparently worrying about work pressures.

I know how hard it is for you, my dear boy, and for all of your generation, for whom life is opening up and yet remains shadowed by the knowledge of the many men not much older than you for whom life has closed forever. I know how particularly hard it is for you, Esmond, after what happened to Graham. But do not give in to de-

spair. Do not believe that there is "bad blood" in the Chadleigh family. (I dare not imagine what your father would say if he knew I was writing to you in these terms!)

You must not think that because you are Graham's brother, the same fate awaits you. He was under terrible pressure at the time, and was not thinking sensibly. By 1917 the glory had gone out of the War. Young men knew the likely fate that awaited them, and it was not a comforting one. Graham had not enjoyed his training, and the knowledge that he had to leave for the Front on the Monday caused him great anxiety that last weekend he was with us.

I wish I had been aware of how serious a state he was in, but it is always easy to be wise in retrospect. I was busy with the family and guests, and did not realise how much the talk of your father and Hugo Strider was upsetting him. Mrs. Heggarty's boy had just run off to escape his duty, and your father had much to say on the subject of cowardice. I think it was that which troubled Graham most. He doubted his own bravery; he feared that, in the heat of battle, he might turn out to be a coward.

And some would say he took the coward's way out. Afraid he wouldn't live up to the expectations everyone — especially *his father — had for him, Graham evaded the challenge of proving himself in battle. And yet, although I can never condone what he did, it, too, must have taken a kind of courage. To put a revolver in your mouth and . . . I am sorry. I should not write such things, but, Esmond, I know you are old enough for me to share my weaknesses with you, as you share yours with me.*

You speak of doubts about your father's course of action after Graham's death. I cannot comment on that, only say that your father is an honourable man and did what he thought right, according to his lights.

But, please, dear boy, do not brood on Graham's fate. It will not be yours. As children, you were always different, he a nervy, sickly boy, you always a cheerful little soul. Please, do not even speak of such thoughts. To have lost one of my darling boys is sometimes more than I can bear. Even the idea of losing another is sufficient to freeze the blood in my veins. . . .

So, thought Laurence, *that* was it. Someone should have realised, from the fact that Graham Chadleigh's service revolver stayed at Bracketts. If he had been so thoroughly blown up at Passchendaele that no trace of his body was found, then what were the chances of his gun turning up?

Everything else fitted, though. There was no place for cowards in any household run by Felix Chadleigh. No son of his could be known to have ducked out of his duty to King and Country in such a shabby way.

There was the religious dimension, too. For a Catholic, suicide is the ultimate sin. The boy's body must have been secretly buried, without benefit of any funeral rite, in the kitchen garden, there to stay for more than eighty years, until accidentally uncovered by the spade of Jonny Tyson.

For his father, the reality of what Graham Chadleigh had done was too appalling ever to be made public. An alternative, more pleasing, truth would have to be invented.

So Felix Chadleigh had invented it. And by God only knew what amount of bullying and persuasion, he had forced his family and friend to endorse that new truth.

There was one document Laurence found more chilling than all the others. It was written in 1919 to his wife by Felix Chadleigh, when he was away from

Bracketts, shooting in Scotland. The part that shocked Laurence read as follows:

Do not lose heart, my dearest. We have much to be thankful for. We have each other, we have Bracketts, we still have three children. God has given us reverses, but He has also looked after us. God is on our side. Even at Passchendaele, He was on our side. He saw to it that none of the men with Hugo survived the shelling, and thus made our lives so much the easier.

45

Sheila Cartwright's funeral duly took place, and was duly attended by all the Great and the Good of West Sussex. Lord Beniston recycled the bland appreciation that he had wheeled out for many similar occasions. Sheila's close friend, the chief constable, also spoke. Tributes were paid to her enormous energy and achievements.

And Gina Locke was introduced to some very useful potential sponsors.

An overlooked figure, Sheila's husband was, needless to say, present at the ceremony and the reception that followed. He was so ineffectual a figure, however, that the other guests kept forgetting he was there.

But the one or two who did look at him by mistake, noticed on his face an expression that looked not unlike relief.

Laurence Hawker delivered his report well in time for the next meeting of the Bracketts trustees. In the interim Gina had organised replacements to fill the vacant seats on the board. (Josie Freeman had tendered her resignation. This had nothing to do with recent events at Bracketts; it had been motivated solely by her masterplan for the social advancement of her husband. She had been offered a position on the board of the Royal Opera House, where her presence would be much more valuable to his profile. A few more moves of that kind, continuing carefully targeted — and carefully leaked — philanthropy to the right charities, donations to the right political party, and Josie Freeman felt quietly confident of upgrading her husband's O.B.E. to a knighthood within a couple of years. The only other important thing she had to do was somehow stop him talking about car parts all the time.)

Of course Gina could not appoint new trustees herself. But she could suggest suitable names to Lord Beniston, and he could invite them to join the board. With little knowledge of anyone in West Sussex outside his own circle, and always liking to have his work done for him, the noble lord had accepted all of Gina's suggestions without argument. As a result, the new board had a much lower average age than its predecessor, and contained more members who saw the leisure industry exactly as Gina saw it. None of her apprenticeship under Sheila Cartwright had been wasted.

(In fact, approving the new trustees was Lord Beniston's last action for Bracketts. Confident that he had done his bit during the two years of his involvement, he resigned quickly, to join the board of another, rather more prestigious, heritage property. For him the change had three advantages: first, the patron of the new organisation was a minor member of the Royal Family, so he was mixing with his own sort of people; second, it had been agreed that so long as his name appeared on the letterhead, he wouldn't have to attend any meetings; and third, he got free membership in the adjacent golf club.)

The reconstituted board approved Laurence Hawker's report and accepted Gina's proposal that the research material should be handed over to Marla Teischbaum, who was to be given all cooperation in the future with her biography of Esmond Chadleigh. (There was only one dissenting voice; unsurprisingly, it belonged to George Ferris.) The hope was that the book would be ready for publication to coincide with the centenary of Esmond's birth in 2004.

As it turned out, that objective was

achieved. The book made a great stir when it came out, was serialised in a Sunday newspaper, and sold in large quantities. Marla became a media celebrity, and on her frequent visits to England she dished up her vigorous opinions on every available arts programme and chat show.

And the evidence of his complicity in a major deception revived interest in Esmond Chadleigh.

Gina's pet project, the Bracketts museum, funded by one exclusive donor, was completed in time for the centenary. Though at first a shrine to Esmond Chadleigh, within two years it had been made over and reopened. In homage to the writer's new notoriety, it was then called The Bracketts Museum of Fakes and Fraudsters, and contained the largest collection of confidence tricks and scams this side of the Atlantic. (Graham Chadleigh-Bewes might have been obscurely gratified, had he known that there was a whole display devoted to the Tichborne Claimant.)

In its new incarnation the museum did much better than it ever had before. At the beginning of the twenty-first century, deviousness and cynicism were much more marketable commodities than faith and honesty.

Having turned around the fortunes of Bracketts, Gina was head-hunted for a senior job at the Arts Council, and settled down to a career of dispensing public money to the wrong causes.

Almost all of Esmond Chadleigh's books went out of print. One exception was *Vases of Dead Flowers*. "Threnody for the Lost" remained one of the nation's favourite poems, though the notes that accompanied it in anthologies changed considerably.

The other surprising survivor of the Chadleigh oeuvre was *The Demesnes of Eregonne*. The book had become a minor cult in California amongst the members of an even more minor cult, who tried to live their lives according to its rather flaky principles. They self-published an edition of two hundred.

Jonny Tyson continued to work at Bracketts, and to keep the Weldisham garden just as his father had always kept it. His father died, but Jonny felt sure the same thing would never happen to his mother.

Mervyn Hunter served his sentence in a secure prison. Jude continued to visit him and tried to give him confidence, tried to tell him he was no danger to anyone; and sometimes, briefly, Mervyn believed her. When he was released, he hoped to find work as a gardener. But he was also tempted to reoffend. He still felt safer in prison.

And Jude continued her intermittent sessions at Austen Prison. She worked harmoniously with Sandy Fairbarns, and neither of them ever knew anything about one another's private life. Which suited both very well.

George Ferris started work on a new book. Its working title was *What the County Records Office Can Do for You*.

And, of course, Laurence Hawker died. Working on the Bracketts report had given him only a brief remission from the inevitable. He lived less than three weeks after completing it.

Carole was shocked. Only very near the end had she realised how ill he was; and with that knowledge came the realisation that Jude must have been aware of his condition for a much longer time. Carole was confused between sympathy for Jude and resentment of her neighbour's secretiveness. She didn't like the feeling that she

457

had been the victim of a conspiracy of silence, a subject of clandestine discussion at Woodside Cottage.

Though inwardly anguished, the reaction to Laurence's death that Jude presented to the world was one of serenity. Which confused Carole even more. They had been lovers, hadn't they? Yet Jude didn't behave as if she'd just lost the love of her life. Jude was very odd about relationships; and a lot of other things, come to that; around Jude nothing was ever cut and dried.

Secretly, Carole felt relieved that Laurence was no longer a fixture in Woodside Cottage. And guilty for feeling relieved.

To everyone's surprise, Laurence Hawker turned out to have made elaborate plans for his own memorial service, which was to be a very traditional, religious one. Jude organised the event, in the London church he had specified, and there was rather an impressive turnout. Amongst a lot of spiky, combative-looking academics was a large number of women, many with beautiful Slavic cheekbones. Carole thought this was odd, but Jude didn't mind at all.

And as a final irony, a typical post-modernist joke, Laurence Hawker included in the order of service a reading of Esmond Chadleigh's "Threnody for the Lost."

> *No grave, no lichened tombstone,*
> *graven plaque,*
> *No yew-treed cross beneath its cloak*
> *of moss,*
> *No sense but absence, unforgiving dark,*
> *The stretching void that is eternal loss.*

And almost everyone in the congregation mouthed the words and, yet to know any better, thought of the poet's elder brother Graham, so tragically lost at Passchendaele.